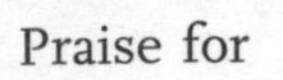

Praise for

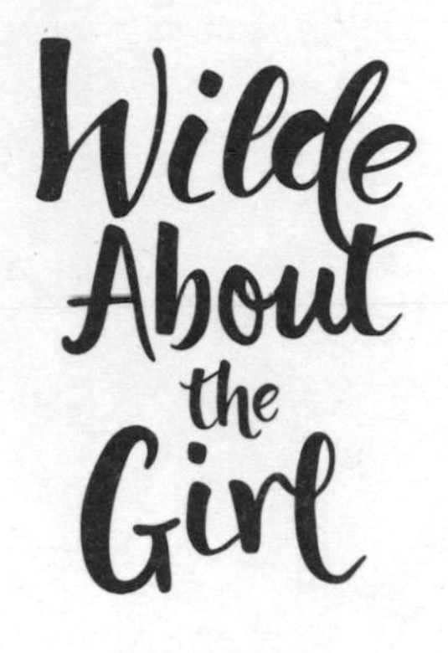

'**Utterly self-assured**, so, so, so **honest** and downright **brave**. *Wilde About the Girl* is **funny**, **sweet**, honest and full of love. Every page is packed with hard-earned **wisdom**, **joy and truth**, I loved – **truly loved** – it. Louise's characters are so real, I felt as though I was sat at the kitchen table, enjoying a mug of (spiked) hot chocolate with Robin, Lacey and Auntie Kath, laughing and crying along with them'

LINDSEY KELK

'A **gorgeous** read. **Beautifully poignant** and **touching**. **I loved it!**'

PAIGE TOON

Praise for

'A **warm and engaging** debut . . . [Robin Wilde is a] chatty, winning, yet **poignant**, heroine'
SOPHIE KINSELLA

'**I'm smitten** with this **sweet and special** story about love, life and motherhood. Reading *Wilde Like Me* feels just like sitting down for a (boozy) hot chocolate with your best friend and **I love Robin Wilde**'
LINDSEY KELK

'I'd love Robin Wilde to be my new best friend. In fact, I feel like she's become it through these pages. **Wonderfully written** and **full of humour** that had me laughing along from start to finish. As a mum, as a woman, you can find yourself wondering whether it's only you that feels a certain way or does questionable things, but this book stilled my pondering mind. **Funny, heartfelt, tender and empowering!** I can't believe this is Louise's first book. I'm thoroughly excited to read more!'
GIOVANNA FLETCHER

'*Wilde Like Me* is **hilarious, moving** and **extremely well written.** I can highly recommend Louise's book'
SUNDAY TIMES STYLE

'I **adore** this book. Louise Pentland writes with so much **warmth, heart and honesty** – *Wilde Like Me* is a **gorgeous, witty, reassuring** comfort read. I fell in love with Robin and her family before the end of the first page. If you're having a bad day, I think this book would instantly make it better. Pentland's exploration of mental health issues is **refreshingly honest**. If you've ever felt like the only person in the world who isn't perfect . . . this is what you need to read. A fabulous mix of escapism and relatability, this is a **hug of a book**'
DAISY BUCHANAN

'This book is a **winner**'
OK MAGAZINE

'If it's **great big belly laugh**s you're after, then meet Robin Wilde'
FABULOUS MAGAZINE

'*Wilde Like Me* is a **fun**, light-hearted read'
SNAZZY BOOKS

'Everyone needs a bit of Robin Wilde in them'
THE BOOKBAG

'This is a **fantastic read** full of **wit** and **warmth** . . . when I finished I felt **empowered**'
CHARLENE JESS

'There's a lot of **girl power** in this novel, and although there's romance too, the love between mother and daughter and the love for oneself come out on top. Full of **humour**, **warmth** and **conviction**, this is a **sparkling debut**'
CHICK LIT CLUB

'The story [is] simply **perfect**'
KATIE SNYDER

Wilde
About
the
Girl

ABOUT THE AUTHOR

LOUISE PENTLAND's debut novel *Wilde Like Me* was an instant *Sunday Times* number one smash hit in the summer of 2017. She is the award-winning and number one YouTube 'mummy blogger', a fashion designer, an author and a UN Global Ambassador for Gender Equality.

Wilde About The Girl is her second novel.

@LouisePentland
@LouisePentland
YouTube SprinkleofGlitter
www.LouisePentlandNovel.com
#WildeAboutTheGirl
#WildeLikeMe

ZAFFRE

First published in Great Britain in 2018 by
ZAFFRE PUBLISHING
80–81 Wimpole St, London W1G 9RE
www.zaffrebooks.co.uk

A CIP catalogue record for this book is available from the British Library.

HB ISBN: 978-1-78576-462-2
TPB ISBN: 978-1-78576-463-9

Also available as an ebook

1 3 5 7 9 10 8 6 4 2

Typeset by Palimpsest Book Production Limited, Falkirk, Stirlingshire
Printed and bound by Clays Ltd, Elcograf S.p.A.

Zaffre Publishing is an imprint of Bonnier Zaffre,
a Bonnier Publishing company
www.bonnierzaffre.co.uk
www.bonnierpublishing.co.uk

For Eli, who is smart, witty, kind and creative,
just like Robin

Part One

FAKE IT TILL YOU MAKE IT . . .

ONE

MARCH

'I'M TOTALLY ACING LIFE,' I think with a smile as I slam my car door shut with one hand and pick my Starbucks order off the roof of the car with the other, all while balancing a hefty stack of paperwork and some samples in one arm and hanging my old slouchy brown handbag (soft leather with a brand-new YSL lipstick inside and space for a bento box, thank you very much) over my shoulder. What is this amazing skill you develop once you have children? One minute you're drinking cheap snakebites out of plastic cups with your student friends, and the next, you're a sober working mother to one small human and you can competently carry 846 items with just your left arm. I tell you, there's always something new to discover.

After crossing the road without dropping a thing and pushing open the door of MADE IT, I feel a rush of warm air hit me and silently wish the girls didn't always blast the heating so high. It's not a hot yoga class, it's an office, for goodness' sake. My office, to be exact. Well, it is while Natalie isn't here.

MADE IT was and is the brainchild of Natalie Wood, the most together, savvy, inspirational businesswoman I know, and my friend now too, I guess. Natalie set up her make-up artistry and modelling agency here in Cambridge just before her first son was born. Now he's at university, she's taking some well-earned time out and travelling the world with her wonderfully supportive husband Martin, while her two other perfect sons are excelling in their school programmes. And here I am – once her assistant but now second-in-command – running the place while she's away.

It took a lot to get here, and I want so much to do well at this. Last year was one of the worst and best of my life. But after tackling some major drama in New York City (seriously, don't ask) where I showed Natalie that I could step up to the plate, she asked me to take over while she took her first proper break in years. At first, I was apprehensive but if life – and Natalie – have taught me anything lately, it's that you have to put your best foot forward and believe in yourself. This year, that's how it's going to be. And, while I'm at it, I'm going to show my little girl that's the way to do it too.

I've been holding the fort since January, and Natalie will be back at the start of April. If anyone asks, I'm loving every second, everything's under control and I don't lie in bed at night ticking off a mental list of things I need to work through the next day. I'm absolutely *not* sometimes desperate for Natalie to come back, I don't *ever* have a five-minute stealth panic in the toilets and I never have to search the 'LadyBoss' tag on Instagram for motivation before meetings (even though I detest the term – we don't ever say 'GentBoss', do we? It's not that incredible that a lady can be a boss, is it? But I digress). OK, so maybe I do freak out about it all from time to time, but if I think back to where my life was twelve months ago, I'm bloody glad to be here and wouldn't change it for the world. Unless by 'world' you mean a billion pounds, calorie-free carbs and a child who listens to me when I ask her to get dressed for school.

So here I am – Robin Wilde, Badass Boss Single Mum Extraordinaire – acing it. Well, maybe I'm hiding in my office with my caramel mocha, hoping to limit any interactions with Skye Bristly, the office darling, who intimidates the shit out of me, while also appearing cool and boss-like enough to earn the adoration of the other girls who pop in to file their reports and portfolios and pick up new briefs.

All I really want to do is keep my head down, work out the budgets, chair the creative meeting, handle the booking rotas and plan next month's shoots without being embroiled in conversations about reality shows or the latest vegan yoghurt. I can't keep up with all these things. I'm more of a Netflix-and-chill sort of a woman. As in, watch actual Netflix, eat my seven-year-old daughter's leftover fish fingers and slump on the sofa in a position where I don't have to use a single muscle in my body.

Like I said, I'm totally acing life.

I sit down at my desk and take a deep breath. Today is definitely the day I blitz all the piles of paper in front of me. The expenses to sign off, budgets to input, ideas to arrange on mood boards, invoices to chase, rotas to finalise and old jobs to file. I might even tackle the stacks of paperwork I have in 'organised piles' on the window-sill behind me, too.

I love having my own office. There's something very satisfying about having your own walls and your own desk and your own drawers to fill. I wouldn't say it's exactly 'Manhattan corner office' glamorous but there's a window on to the street below, my own radiator to warm my bum on in winter and two huge noticeboards to fill with inspiration and, of course, pictures of my daughter Lyla. I've got almost a whole gallery wall of her (her as a baby lying on a crocheted blanket from Auntie Kath, us at a local petting farm feeding a goat, her, aged five, sitting on my best friend Lacey's knee, her paddling in the sea during a rare visit down to Cornwall to see Mum and Dad). Add to that a couple of (fake) succulents and a secret drawer of Curly Wurlys, and you have all the essentials for a busy day at the office. Also, since nobody can see my laptop screen, I can fill one hundred per cent of my time with Very Important Work and never, ever get distracted by pointless videos on Facebook, like that one where the swans are reunited after the lady swan had surgery. Or the one where the panda in the Chinese zoo keeps climbing out of the basket. Or the one . . . it doesn't matter, I don't watch them. I very, very rarely watch them anyway. I'm a professional.

The door opens and I look up. Skye is standing in the doorway flicking her extensions over her shoulder. 'Oh, you're in,' she says in surprise, as if I'm never in the office. The office that I run now. I'm going to show her who's boss. I'm going to be so badass.

'Yep, here I am. Just grabbed a mocha on my way,' I say with an apologetic laugh, lifting my cup off a stack of expense forms. Why do I sound apologetic? I'm supposed to be badass! Natalie wouldn't do this. Natalie wouldn't have to do this.

'Didn't Natalie send a memo round last year saying we should all use BPA-free keep-cups for drinks and steel bento boxes for food?' she asks condescendingly, eyeing my take-away coffee cup and continuing to loiter by my door. She has a point, I reluctantly admit to myself. I don't *often* succumb to the lure of the coffee shop but this morning I had such a hankering. And I do own a couple of bento boxes since all the Posh Mums at school started getting competitively creative and regular lunch-boxes of sandwiches and Penguin bars fell out of vogue. The boxes I have are plastic, though . . . I don't know if they have BPA in, whatever BPA is.

'Thank you, Skye. I'll bear that in mind,' I say with a smile that hopefully says, *Back off, lady, I'm armed with a hot sweet drink here* or at least *I'm sorry, please stop pointing out that I'm wrecking the planet and move on to the next thing*. 'Is there anything I can help you with?' I finally say out loud.

'Yes, what's the rota? Neil, my boyfriend, wants to take me away for a long weekend. Natalie was always really prompt with letting everyone know a fortnight in advance, so we could plan our lives. She used the noticeboard in the kitchen especially. Maybe you could get up to speed with that?'

Of course Neil wants to take her away. I bet Neil's favourite thing to do is parade his Gisele-like girlfriend on weekends away. A year ago I'd have been jealous, but now I can't think of anything I'd like to do less than spend time watching Neil scoop out his protein shake powder or cut the sleeves off his T-shirt to make bicep viewing easier for us all. What I want to do at the weekend is hang out with Lyla and take it easy – this being a boss thing is tiring.

'Right, well, I've just got here and I'm about to finalise the bookings so as soon as I know, you will too,' I say, very professionally, taking a sip of my warm coffee nectar and feeling soothed.

'OK, well don't forget to print it and put it on the noticeboard as well,' Skye responds bossily, placing a well-manicured hand on a jeans-clad hip with more attitude than I think possible for 9.15 in the morning. Skye's wearing the most perfectly tailored black jeans I've ever seen. I bet even Piper would lust after them. Piper, by the way, is my best friend Lacey's little sister. We all grew up together and now she lives and works in New York on the art scene. (If you tell me you've seen a more stylish, confident, swish young woman, I'll tell you you're wrong.)

I don't think I've ever found a pair of skinny jeans that don't make my soft bits squish out over the top or cling tightly enough round my ankles, but Skye has. Her ankles are showcased by the dark denim and there's not a jot of squish anywhere. Maybe that says more about our body shapes than the jeans, though . . . Along with the jeans of perfection, she's wearing a snug khaki long-sleeved cotton crop top with a lot of criss-crossing fabric over the bust, a Gucci-style belt (*is it real?* I wonder) and chunky black heeled sandals. Basically, her idea of casual March workwear is my idea of full glam summer Going-Out wear. She's tanned all over (I suppose you can't do my 'just bits you see' method if you wear stringy crop tops) and seems to have no trouble standing in her stilt-like shoes. I, on the other hand, am in blue skinny-ish jeans that have a good amount of stretch in them so they're super comfy, an oversized cream cable knit jumper from ASOS in the sales last year and pale pink Converse. My conker brown hair is up in a high pony and I've only gone for a light layer of BB cream because my skin, thankfully, is having a good week. It's not that I don't have nice clothes or don't look OK in my outfits, it's just that when you're only just managing to juggle your work and mum life like I am, you don't prioritise contouring and fake-tanning your stomach! Plus, call me old, but that crop top looks cold! Chunky knitwear and easy flats for me, please. I'm still acing it. I'm just warm, comfy and acing it.

'Yes. I will. Just like I said.' Oh, she will not have the last bloody word here. I am the boss. Like a gorilla in the jungle, I must assert my power.

'Ok, great.' More hip, more attitude, no moving away from my door, though. 'Also, you know those coffee companies don't pay tax, right? Something to look into next time you want a little "treat".'

Urrgghh. I know her game. She wants to knock me off my perch, dammit. She will not win. Not today, missy.

I employ my best Mum-isn't-taking-this-shit look, the one I reserve for Lyla when she refuses to get out of the ball pool at soft play and shows I mean business. Eventually, after I almost tear up from not blinking, Skye slinks off, no doubt to make herself some organic black chai in a sustainable keep-cup.

This is the thing about being the boss. You think it's going to be cool to have a higher-level job, but then you find you have to deal with the likes of Skye and her cronies. The rest of the team are sweet, but whispering that stops as soon as I enter a room has not been unknown. They all seem to absolutely adore Skye and treat her like she's their queen, which doesn't help the ego she seems to be carting around on her tanned, slender shoulders.

But, no – think leaderly thoughts, Robin.

I know why Natalie hired her. She's a good make-up artist. Really, really good, in fact. She has an amazing creative edge which clients love, is fully trained in special effects, is astounding at general beauty, has enough in common with the models to make them love her (if there's ever a woman who has mastered the Insta-pose, it's Skye. How she even gets some of the angles I will never know) and, frustratingly, she works harder and longer than anyone else. Is it any wonder I'm so intimidated by her?

And suddenly it's time for our creative meeting. I love this part of my job the most. Anyone who has bookings for the week ahead comes in, we run through the jobs, discuss ideas and talk through any concerns. When I joined MADE IT, I would sit in these meetings in awe of Natalie. She'd listen carefully to each idea and smoothly guide the conversations so that everyone had a say, encouraging those (usually me) who were a bit shy. These meetings feel like the heart of the agency, and show how far we've come – once it was all local jobs, little photo shoots and wedding make-up. Now we still do all those things, but MADE IT has grown so much that we're getting jobs from far and wide. Every meeting there are more bookings, more opportunities – and I *so* want to show Natalie I can handle it. Once she's back from her sabbatical she'll chair them again, but for now I'm head of the table, along with my non-eco-friendly cup that I make a mental note to change.

There are eight of us this week, but as we list the upcoming jobs and offer each other advice, it's clear that Skye is dominating the meeting. Try as I might to interject, she has the room hanging off her every word and frankly, she has the best ideas and tips.

'OK, so,' I chirp as confidently as I can, 'we have a job for a group of children with special needs next week. They are transforming their centre into a fairy garden for the day and have asked us to send two juniors out to apply delicate eyeshadows, fluttering false lashes and, I'm sure, a whole lot of glitter.' Skye jumps in to suggest adding little special-effect latex tips to the tops of their ears to give them the pixie effect. And since neither of our junior MUAs are fully trained in special effects yet, Skye agrees to take one of their places for a lower fee than normal. I am astounded, but of course the rest of the office just accept that Skye the Wonderful would be so gracious. Kareem, one of our part-time MUAs, actually puts his hand on Skye's shoulder and says, 'You're such an inspiration.' Skye coolly looks down at her lap and smiles with a nod. Have I turned into a massive cynic?

We reach the last section of the agenda. I open the floor to anyone with 'any other business' and, of course, Skye has some.

'Yes, Skye, please do share,' I say in the encouraging tone I learnt from Natalie.

'Have you sorted the rotas yet?'

What? We spoke about this an hour ago. Is she deliberately baiting me in front of an audience?

'We spoke about this, Skye,' I say calmly. I'm like a swan. Cool and collected up top but paddling like billy-o under the surface.

'We did, but, as you might remember from a couple of months ago when you were a part-time make-up assistant, Natalie always made sure to have the jobs out a fortnight in advance and printed on the kitchen board. She was always so efficient, you know?' Skye says smoothly.

Wow. Just wow.

One of Skye's fangirls, Nix (it's short for Nicola. Apparently you can just put an 'x' in your name and make it cool. Call me Robix from now on), jumps on the bandwagon. 'I don't want to sound harsh, but Skye's right. Natalie was, like, really organised with the rotas and a lot of us have lives outside this place. We need to work around that and like, yeah . . .'

'Thank you, Nix, I know exactly what you mean, I have a hectic life too and will be as prompt as I can with your rotas,' I offer with a smile akin to one of the nuns in *Call the Midwife*. I chant to myself; *Kill them with kindness.*

'No, I mean lots of us like going out or going places, that sort of thing,' Nix says. She might be a brilliant make-up artist but I'm not sure she's a brilliant mind.

'Yes, Nix, I know what "having a life" means,' I snap, cross with myself for letting it get to me.

'I don't think Nix meant to upset you, Robin, I just think we all need a bit more organisation on your part,' Skye says in the most patronising tone I've ever heard, while Kareem nods sagely and some of the others start to shift in their seats, clearly picking up on the tension. Like the mature leader I am, I put a stop to this.

'Right. Lovely. All good points then. The only adjustment being Skye on the fairy job. Everyone else knows what they are doing. Rotas will be up by lunchtime. Let's all crack on.'

And with that, I stand up, gather my rather yummy rose-gold and pink stationery, plus the sodding rotas, and leave for my office, my sanctuary, with my heart in my Converse but my head held high.

Now, rota done, meeting managed, budget document . . . opened. No emergencies. Skye only sent one round-robin email, this time demanding that 'the person who insists on changing the sound system to Radio 2 must consult the group'. Sorry, no can do, Skye. After all, who doesn't like Radio 2? It's cool now, OK?

All in all, a grand day. As I'm saying goodbye to Stuart and Alice, the admin team, Skye appears. 'Robin, don't forget I won't be in next Monday. My boyfriend Neil is taking me away, remember?'

'Mmmm, you mentioned that this morning,' I say probably a bit less enthusiastically than I meant to. I just really want to get out of the office, I'm hungry, ready for dinner and Monday is a full week away.

Taking my lack of passion to heart, Skye fluffs her metaphorical feathers. 'No need to be salty about me having a boyfriend, Robin. I'm sure you'll find one someday.' Stuart and Alice almost gasp at the audacity of this, probably enjoying the drama. What's got into her? Maybe this is because I didn't sagely nod when Kareem told her she was an inspiration.

What does 'salty' even mean? Why do these young people have so many new meanings for words I don't understand? I take a wild guess, stand up an inch taller than usual and formulate my cutting response.

'Skye, thanks for once again highlighting your relationship status. I'm very pleased for you. My self-validation doesn't depend on a romantic attachment, nor does my well-being. Perhaps one day you'll feel secure enough in yourself to not seek a man's approval but until then, I'm off home.' Satisfyingly, Skye looks momentarily shocked, then like thunder and, with that, I turn on my heel (not before noticing Stuart's gobsmacked face and Alice's eyes alight), strut out and cross the road to my car.

One–nil, Badass Boss Single Mum Extraordinaire.

What would I have done differently if I'd known that, in less than four weeks' time, I'd be on the verge of losing *everything* I'd worked so hard for . . .

TWO

Home! After blasting the best eighties power ballads Spotify has to offer in the car, normality resumes. I say 'normality', but in truth I'm hit with what looks like an explosion in an apothecary. Lotions, potions and dozens of bunches of little dried purple sprigs are strewn all over the lounge floor. Of course I pretend I'm not worried about any of them staining the brand-new cream carpet I had laid when we moved in at the end of last year. (My old house had a hard-wearing oatmeal sort of affair, so as a treat, to match the beautiful oak furnishings and battered brown leather sofa I brought with me, I bought the carpet. It comes to something when a carpet is a treat, doesn't it? Will scouring the internet for a better fixed-term mortgage be a treat next? Or buying myself summer season passes to stately homes and gardens? What about finding the best deals in bargain supermarkets? I have recently become obsessed with Mum vloggers doing pound shop hauls on YouTube. Perhaps I'll watch a few more once Lyla's in bed.)

We're starting to feel more settled in our lovely new place. I bought lots of wooden Moroccan-style frames and finally printed off a load of photos from my phone and made a gallery wall in the hallway, we have colourful tiny flowers in little glazed pots dotted around window-sills and – just like all the best interiors Instagrammers – I've invested in the fluffiest, most tasselled rug imaginable for the front room. Here's hoping I can keep it clean for more than three weeks.

I realise I've let my mind wander and I need to focus on being in the moment. Lyla and our beloved Auntie Kath look up to greet me with happy smiles on happy faces.

'Auntie Kath brought her crafts over, Mummy! We're making lavender bath bombs. We've been doing them for hours because you've been at work so long. I thought you might be sleeping there tonight. Why are you *always* at work, Mummy?' my energetic seven-year-old demands before I can even say hello.

'Nice to see you too, Bluebird!' I say as I pick my way over plastic moulds, spoons and measuring cups to go in for a big cuddle. Ah, the best part of my day.

'Hey, Kath!' I add to my auntie, who beams back. She is a godsend for picking Lyla up from school and babysitting until I can get home. Lyla squeezes me so hard around my tummy I almost squeak.

'Hello, lovey. She's right, we're making lavender toiletries. It's very relaxing. It does wonders for the night sweats now I'm going through The Change! When I don't use them I wake up wetter than a lady of the night, but if I do, I'm fresh as a daisy,' Kath responds cheerily.

I try to keep a straight face.

'So I'm utterly obsessed with lavender, lovey. I've been reading about its healing properties on the web and we've been talking about it all week at Cupcakes and Crochet. Sue said the lavender oils completely cleared up her problem skin from The Change, and you remember what a pizza-face she was!' Kath titters. But I'm busy picking bits up and looking at the little spots of purple staining my aforementioned very sophisticated new carpet.

'Are they for you or a gift?' I ask, almost nervous to hear the answer. I'm not sure I want lavender soap infused with carpet fluff, biscuit crumbs and an, er, intimate drying effect.

'For *you*! You can have all of these because I've been working on them non-stop at home. I've got hundreds already,' Kath says, busying herself with opening the moulds and popping out little purple spheres. They look pretty good, actually.

'Oh, lovely, erm . . . thanks!' I say, picking my way back over to the door to dump my bag on the little hall table I picked up at a boutique shop in town. I've always wanted to be one of those women who has a big entrance hall and a small table with a 'catch all' tray and an elegant bunch of flowers. Our flowers are fake from Poundland but you wouldn't know from far away, and only Lacey raises her eyebrows at them (she's a John Lewis girl herself). 'Fresher are better,' she'd say, but she'd add kindly: 'I'll get you some'. It's probably quite easy to keep fresh flowers in the house when you own a bloody florist's, I often point out.

'I've done them for all my friends,' Kath continues, gaining momentum. 'Moira swears by them. She said after she had a soak with the bath-ballistic I did, she felt so sensual she took the moisturiser into her boudoir and asked her Allan to apply it for her! Well, you can guess what happened next . . .'

I am literally horrified by the thought of Kath's neighbour Allan slathering her latest creation all over his wife's naked torso but I manage to keep it in and nod enthusiastically, trying to shake the idea out of my head. Even the lady of the night image was more appealing than Moira and a frisky Allan. I hope Kath's OK. Is it normal to spend all your time making hundreds and hundreds of senior-sex-inducing bath bombs in your spare time?

'What's a boudoir?' Lyla pipes up, her glacier-blue eyes and pixie nose the picture of innocence.

'A bedroom! Another word for bedroom, sweetie, that's all,' I jump in with quickly, trying to think of something else to say before she asks what 'sensual' means too.

'Shall I put some jacket potatoes in?' I say, heading into the kitchen and away from the madness.

'No need, lovey. There's a lasagne I made this morning, I've got garlic bread in the fridge and Lyla helped me make a salad when we got in from school. I've done crumble for afters.'

'Oh, Kath,' I say, going back in and navigating my way back across the lounge to give her a hug. 'What would I do without you?'

THREE

It's my day off and I've been looking forward to this day for ages. I'm off to see Lacey. The joys of working flexible hours and the odd weekend: a day off in the week. Instead of heading home after the school run for a cheeky Twix (you just can't indulge in early-morning chocolate with a seven-year-old in the vicinity, they're like sniffer dogs for any kind of confectionery – unless you want a hyped-up crazy on your hands, you have to hide anything worth eating till later in the day), I drive over to Dovington's.

Since accepting Natalie's offer to run MADE IT, I've seen less of Lacey and it's a shame. I really miss our weekly natters around the giant oak table in the back room of the florist's she inherited from her grandmother. Lacey is my oldest and best friend and my favourite person to put the world to rights with.

Before I go in, I glance up. There's a flat above the shop belonging to a nice old lady who we suspect is a bit lonely. She keeps herself to herself but Lacey will often do an essentials shop for her, and at the end of the day, she'll often leave a selection of the flowers they've not sold by her front door. As usual I can see this week's proudly displayed in a vase on the upstairs front windowsill.

Pushing open the door and hearing the familiar bell tinkle makes me smile straight away. Dovington's is such a welcoming place, beautifully scented with a mix of delicate florals and warm incense dotted around by Terri, Lacey's right-hand woman. You can't help but feel at ease here. The front half of the shop, with its huge floor-to-ceiling window, is laden with every kind of flower, all displayed in big white vases and buckets in the centre of the room. It's organised so you can either go in and pick up a ready-made bouquet or, my favourite option, you can take a flat wicker basket and choose each individual stem and make your own arrangement, a floral pick and mix. On one wall, big metal shelving units show off trendy planters, watering cans, succulents, little plants already in bloom, tempting ornaments and gifty trinkets and beautiful vases and pots. At the back there are a couple of big high desks with piles of paper and cellophane for wrapping and an old bashed-up till that's seen better days.

Beyond the till is my favourite part: the big back room. Lacey uses this for crafty projects, hosting workshops ('How to Make a Fresh Floral Crown' is always fully booked out during festival season) and, most importantly, gossiping with me over big cups of hot tea.

'Only me!' I say, popping my head round the door of Lacey's 'office' (the least office-like place you can imagine). It is like stepping into a warm hug from a friend. Though it's spring, it's still nippy outside. The radio is playing some happy playlist and Lacey's table is covered edge to edge in scraps of pastel crêpe paper, wire, string and the odd pair of scissors.

'Ah, hello! Just the person I need! How would you like to spend the next hour of your life helping me finish these bloody pastel pompoms?' Lacey asks with a despairing look.

'I've never wanted to do anything more,' I say, taking a seat and fluffing about with tiny bits of tissue paper. 'What exactly are they? What are they even for?'

As Lacey gamely explains how to make a paper

pompom (good old Pinterest, a fountain of craft inspiration) and why we were making forty-five of them (to hang from the shop ceiling for her upcoming Mother's Day display, one of her busiest times of year), I can tell her mood is low.

'What's on your mind?' I ask, wondering how much I'll have to push to get it out of her.

'Oh, I'm just getting sorted for Mother's Day. It's a busy, busy time,' she says, trying to brush me off.

'No, I mean what's actually up? I can tell there's something.' I'm not easily fobbed off, and she knows it.

'Honestly, everything's great. Karl's just got his promotion, Piper's still loving New York, I'm happy here, everything's great.'

Good try, Lacey.

'Lacey Hunter, you can lie convincingly to a lot of people but never to me. Come on, talk to me.' I surprise myself at how sternly the words come out.

'Wow, you've really taken that managerial position to heart, haven't you?' she replies.

'Yes. I have. I am a very badass firm lady boss and I demand you tell me.' I think it's best to add a spoonful of humour to help the stern tone go down. It seems to do the trick until Lacey stops smiling and twiddles a piece of wire round her thumb.

'I love you, Lacey, I want to help, even if it's just to listen,' I say, taking a much softer approach.

'I know, I just hate going on about it,' she says, looking down at her hands sadly.

Straight away I know.

'It's this Mother's Day stuff. I thought I'd be a mother by now or at least be blooming in pregnancy, but *again* I have to watch everyone else being celebrated, while I carry on "trying" and getting nowhere. Karl and I are really struggling. There's no fun to be had in a scheduled optimal ovulation shag and we bicker constantly. It's hard, Robin.' Big fat tears drop down her cheeks and soak the little scraps of lilac crêpe in her lap.

'Oh, Lace.' I reach out to put a hand on hers but she moves hers away. 'It's going to happen, it really is going to happen.'

'You say that but it still hasn't. It's been so long. We're seeing the consultant, but it's horrible. I've lost hope. Karl tries to put on a brave face but I know he's starting to worry too and it's showing in his snappy mood. It's shit, Robin, I feel like a massive fucking failure.'

I can see Lacey spiralling into a familiar hole and know her well enough to know I can't pull her out with platitudes and reassurances.

'You are absolutely not a failure – nowhere near – but

that pompom will be if you don't stop crying all over it,' I offer, trying to distract her.

Lacey lets out a wet, teary half-laugh and looks up at me, needing more.

'I know it must be so shit, Lacey, shitty-shitty-shit-shit, but you're on the right track. You're seeing the right people and I just know you'll find a way in the end. If there's anyone in this whole world who would be the most amazing mum, it's you. It's going to happen. BUT, until then, let's keep going, let's make these bloody puff things, let's decorate the shop to perfection and let's have a good day of it!' I say with as much gusto as I can muster. I can't promise she will get pregnant, but what I do know is that somehow – somehow – she'll find a way to be a mum. But *somehow* isn't an easy word to hear. I don't think I would hold it together if I were her, either. The only thing that seems to work these days is distraction.

'It's not fair. We've been on "the right track" for so long. Karl's mum said when we moved into the house after we got married, "New house, new baby", and now every time she comes over I think of that. It's not a new house anymore.' Her voice wavers.

'Well it's not the house that's going to get you bloody pregnant, is it?' I say.

'That'd sting!' Lacey can't help but let out a weak laugh and I take this opportunity to laugh with her. She wipes her face, takes a deep breath to reset herself and starts to quiz me.

'So,' she says, changing the subject entirely. 'How's it going with secret lover-boy?'

'I've no idea who you are talking about,' I reply breezily.

'Your mystery man from far-off shores,' she nudges further.

'Nope, still not with you.' Ha! I won't bend.

'Mr Lover who takes you out for wine and pasta and you end up shagging by 10.30 p.m.' Now I wish I hadn't told Lacey about the post-pasta sex last time I'd seen him.

'Sorry, still not sure who you mean, there's no "Mr Lover" in my life.' I'm making a point now, to myself as much as to Lacey. Love has nothing to do with it.

'Oh, fine. *Edward*! The guy from New York you see *every* time he's over here!' Lacey throws her hands in the air in exasperation, sending bits of paper puff scattering all over the table.

'Oh, *that* guy! Yeah, Edward's fine – probably. It's not like we talk much, he just looks me up when he's back in England,' I bluster as I think of that dreamy date-that-turned-into-a-full-weekend in January. 'I saw him a couple of weeks ago. I popped down to London when he was working there, we saw a gig, had some lovely pasta—'

'Had some lovely sex—'

'Ha! But yes, I suppose it was lovely.' I laugh at the thought of describing sex that way. It is, though. It's not 'loving' but it is lovely. My ex, Theo, was all thrusts and grunts, and Lyla's dad Simon was fumbles in the dark, but Edward and I just seem to fit together well.

'So you're falling for him, then?' Lacey probes, with a smile and a sparkle in her eye.

'God, no! I'm not falling for anyone, Lace. I'm just happy doing my work thing, doing my mum thing, doing my pompom thing,' I say, flipping a pompom about. 'I'm honestly not looking for anything serious – I don't want another Theo on my hands.' I mean it. Things are fine just as they are.

'But Edward isn't Theo,' Lacey says matter-of-factly.

'But Edward is a man, Lacey, and I don't need one of those. I like him. That's it. And that's enough,' I respond in kind.

'Don't tar every man with the same brush, Robin. This one seems quite nice, that's all I'm saying.' Ugh, why is she being so reasonable? She has a point but I'm not going to accept it. Things are fine. I don't need anything or anyone to mess them up.

'Yes, he's nice, yes, I like hanging out with him but no, I'm not "seeing him", I'm just sometimes seeing him.' I give her a hard stare which means I'm done.

'OK,' she says, thankfully sensing the tone. 'I'm proud of you for standing strong, Robin, for not being swept up and for loving the life you already have.'

We spend a few minutes tying thin wire round the middle of the pompoms with the help of a YouTube tutorial. Then we pile the completed puffs on the table. It actually looks quite cool and I'm impressed I've been a part of making them.

'Are things still going well with your Other Friends?' Lacey asks in what she probably thinks is a casual tone but I sense the slight panic in her voice. She's always been this way, ever since primary school when I sometimes played with another little girl called Sarah (I wonder where she is now? I'll have to Facebook-stalk her when I get home) and Lacey was worried she'd be my new best friend. I had to give Lacey three Pogs (remember those?) and a friendship bracelet to fully convince her she would be my best friend forever. So far, so good!

'Do you mean Finola and Gillian? All good. I think we're having a get-together next week at Finola's stables with all the children, which will either be amazing or, most likely, utter chaos,' I laugh, noticing the look on

Lacey's face. I'm not sure if it's 'you have new friends' or 'you have children to socialise with' that caused the flash of sadness, but I don't want to see her spiral down again so I quickly change the subject.

'I'll tell you what though, Lace, Skye is a total pain in the arse. I can't handle it.'

Lacey instantly perks up at the prospect of a bit of mild gossip or slaggery-offery. Good.

'The really pretty, really young, really talented one that you hate?' she says a bit too eagerly.

'Yes! No, well, I don't *hate* her and if I did, it wouldn't be because she's young and pretty and talented, which she totally bloody is. It's that she's patronising with it. The other day she saw me reading a Sidebar of Shame article about feminism and told me that *she*'s not a feminist, she's equalitarian. Good for her, I said, but when I told her I'm a feminist, loud and proud, she said, "Oh, it's not cool to use labels". It's the fact that she thinks she is always in the right, as though everyone needs to be bloody perfect, like her,' I say.

'You're perfect, too, though.' Lacey supports me without a second of hesitation.

'But everyone loves her, she's amazing at her job, she looks great, she saves the planet, everything! The other day we both went on an editorial job and it went really well. We each had our own areas and set-ups so although we were there together, we weren't really working as a team like me and Natalie used to, even though she was meant to be assisting me. She did the base work and I would do more of the artistry – I don't get much chance to do it now I'm in the office so much. Anyway, the photographer came over at the end of the day and gushed about how much she loved what I did with the models and how beautiful their eyes were. Without skipping a beat, Skye thanked her for her kind words. Skye didn't do any of the eye work. I was so flummoxed, I just stood there. As if that's not enough, on our work Facebook page the photographer has left a positive review thanking Skye Bristly for "the best eye make-up in town and her wonderful attention to detail". That should have been me but now, as usual, she's the queen of everything and I'm just plain, boring Robin hasn't-done-the-rota-on-time Wilde,' I say, flumping down my latest half-made pompom.

'Now it's my turn to give you a pep talk. Robin Wilde, you are ace. Look at everything you've achieved in your life. You run your beautiful new home like a dream, you are the big boss of a major office, you're a single mum with no support at all, you're juggling a long-distance relationship AND you have time to help your friends make crazy paper decorations. You are the bee's knees, the cat's pyjamas, the wildest Wilde in the West! Don't let anyone take that away from you!' Lacey says with a sudden burst of passion that makes my heart sing.

Everything she's said is hugely over-exaggerated, but Skye makes me feel a bit crap so I'll take it. Yes, I have a cleaner now, and I'm only the boss temporarily; I have childcare support from Simon and his girlfriend, Storie, as well as Kath, and I'm not in a relationship with Edward. But sometimes, you just have to smile and say thank you. God bless Lacey, the best of eggs. It feels so cruel. My poor Laceyloo. God, I hope she and Karl make up. I don't know how many more of these crushing monthly disappointments their marriage can take.

There's nothing I wouldn't do to give her what she wants so badly.

FOUR

Saturday at last! It's been a long week and I'm glad to be spending some much-needed time with my little girl. We're headed out to Finola's stables, we've finally managed to co-ordinate a date (with kids' clubs, work commitments and various husbands getting in the way it was surprisingly difficult to make today happen) and I'm actually quite excited. How far I've come from anxious hours spent at soft play at weekends and parties, searching for the 'right' thing to say to the intimidating 'good mums'. It's funny what a year can do.

Lyla and I aren't exactly outdoorsy people. We're more at one with John Lewis's beauty and toy departments than the great outdoors but lovely Gillian, who's been here before, assures me there's a kettle, power points to charge my phone and the sweetest ponies, horses, dogs and chickens that Lyla will fall in love with (oh God, I hope she will!). I'm really taken by the idea of us letting nature into our lives and bonding with animals. We've tried ponies before but Lyla wasn't having any of it. Still, I've high hopes that now she's older she'll feel differently. Desperate as I am to make sure she has a well-rounded childhood that isn't all screens and soft play, I don't even mind if there isn't Wi-Fi and I can't check my work emails for a few hours.

I tried to dress Lyla in stable-appropriate wear – leggings, T-shirt, sweatshirt and wellies – but she's seven and has other ideas. I quickly realised it wasn't a fight worth having and stashed the sensible attire in my bag to bring with me, so we're travelling over in a sequinned two-piece, a raincoat and a tiara. My princess knows how to do things.

I've gone for super-old boyfriend-style jeans, with worn frayed bits on the inner thighs (I know, so sexy, but no one's going to see), and a slouchy sweater that when I bought it I thought made me look cute, but in actual fact makes me look like a marshmallow. What can you do?

We drive into the huge parking area, littered with trailers and horseboxes, and I can see Gillian has arrived but hasn't got out of her car yet. We pull up beside her sensible silver Qashqai and wave like over-enthused loons, only to see Clara looking tearful and Gillian looking vexed. It's so unlike her not to be serene and relaxed.

'Ooo-oooo,' I chorus as I step out of my car and tentatively wave with raised eyebrows and a little smile. Lyla plods behind me, tiara catching the weak sunshine and glinting.

Gillian gets out of the car, red-faced and flustered. 'Hello! Sorry, God, it's one of those bloody days!' she says, opening Clara's door and grappling with the seat belt. I'm too stunned to respond because Gillian has *sworn*. It's only 'bloody' but this is a Big Deal.

'Clara is refusing to get out of the car,' Gillian continues, half talking to me, half talking to the stubborn seven-year-old who has turned herself rigid on her booster seat. Looking at her, you'd think Clara was an absolute angel. Long, straight, ash-blonde hair down to the middle of her back with a perfectly cut fringe that I could only dream of (I had a fringe once – I'd end up bent over the sink washing *just* the fringe because I didn't want to have a full hair-wash day and really, nobody should have to live like that!) and big blue eyes with lashes – again – that I could only dream of. Clara is basically a doll. A perfect little creature you'd think could do no wrong unless you were witnessing what I was right now. 'Clara seems to think that this is acceptable behaviour, that Mummy is going to stand for it. Well Mummy isn't standing for it and Mummy is getting very, very cross!' Gillian's voice rises in pitch at the end. You know it's bad when you start talking in the third person.

'Let me help. Do you want me to hold your bag while you lift her out?' I offer. I'm not sure that would be a great deal of help but what do you do when a kid is almost planking in defiance? Gillian's usually buttermilk skin is going red and blotchy with stress and I can see the whites of her knuckles as she grips the frame of the car door.

Suddenly I see a shimmer of sequins squeeze past me and Lyla has crawled into the car through the passenger door. The last thing I want or need right now is to anger the Gillian-beast and make things worse. Before I can step in to remove my jewel-encrusted offspring she starts talking.

'Clara, come out of the car my side and we'll go and play,' Lyla says gently with a smile.

Clara immediately softens and replies quietly, almost in a whisper, to Lyla, 'I can't. I hate him.'

Gillian and I look at each other, panic-stricken. Who is 'him'? Is she being groomed? We were warned about this at Mr Ravelle's 'Online Safety for the Modern Child' seminar last term. It was terrifying. The only saving grace was the selection of free pastries the catering staff had left out by the tea and coffee station. No time to think about that, though, as clearly Clara is in terrible danger.

'Hate who? Roo?' Lyla asks innocently. She's obviously not gone down the 'grooming' train of thought and has instead blamed Finola's pudding-faced, bowl-cut-haired little boy for any potential drama. Oh no. Have I instilled that in her? Does she think all boys are bad? Do I need to start singing her dad's praises to balance her view of men?

'Not Roo, Fudge. He's too big and kicks at me,' Clara responds, welling up. Her huge blue eyes squeeze shut as the tears plop down her cheeks.

'Well, then we won't go near his stable. You can hold my hand. I'll look after you,' Lyla says, reaching out her hand.

My baby has saved the day. It's a miracle. I look at Gillian, thinking she'll be as relieved as me, practically ready to fist-pump or even do like the kids and 'dab' in celebration. She just stares wearily at Clara as she climbs out of the booster, hops down to Lyla and scuttles off. Just as she's out of earshot Gillian lets out the biggest sigh.

'Sorry about that,' she says, locking the car and putting the keys in her Mulberry. 'She's been hard work all morning. I don't know where I'm going wrong.'

'Fudging Fudge!' I say with a smile and a wink and notice her facial expression loosen and a wry smile appear. 'Don't worry about it, Gillian. Honestly, I spend half my life wondering where I'm going wrong. If I was as chilled as you, as often as you, I'd be happy! You're doing a great job, and we'll just avoid this Fudge guy. Avoiding guys is my thing anyway, so we'll be fine.'

I walk beside her up to the stables where I can see Lyla and Clara playing with Honor and Roo, who have been riding since they were able to hold their own heads up. Honor and Roo are Finola's children. Honor, a handsome little girl of ten, is just like her mother, doesn't mince her words and walks with a slight march. She has sensible brown bobbed hair that is often pushed back with a thick Alice band and loves nothing more than to take charge of her friends (as she's doing now by stamping her foot and yelling at Roo, Clara and Lyla, 'No, you stay there, wait for my command and then run to the stable doors for the treasure!'). Roo, Finola and Edgar's seven-year-old son, is Lyla's partner in crime, yin to her yang, Schofield to her Willoughby. Roo is an adorable little boy. Ruddy cheeks and thick brown hair, soft green eyes and a strong jaw, you just know he's going to be breaking hearts (potentially even Lyla's, poor thing) in ten years' time. How weird to think of Lyla as a seventeen-year-old. God, I'll be thirty-nine! Stop it, brain. Thankfully Finola breaks my thought spiral.

'Ah! Hello, you two. Ready to hack?' calls Finola as she strides towards us in jodhpurs, riding boots and a padded gilet. Finola is possibly the most horsey woman that ever walked this earth. Married to the oh-so-affluent Edgar, Finola's life revolves around her two children and the stables. Finola lives and breathes horses, dogs and everything surrounding them. Cut her in half and she'd bleed *Horse & Hound* magazines.

'Oh, what a shame! If I'd have known we were going to hack I'd have worn proper boots,' I say, scrambling for a get-out. Obviously I don't have riding boots, but I think Finola assumes everyone in the universe has the full equestrian kit in their possession, so doesn't question my flimsy excuse.

'Plus we can't leave the children alone. Clara's already a bit on edge about Fudge,' adds Gillian understatedly.

'Fair point. I don't want any of them upsetting him. He's racing this weekend and doesn't need any nonsense,' concedes Finola as she takes off her helmet, missing the point entirely with the horses-versus-children argument. I won't correct her on it, anything to not have to 'hack'.

'How are you both, anyway? So glad to have you out in the sticks!' Finola enthuses. 'This is where you can really breathe and let go. Really let it all out, darlings!' She demonstrates, taking a big breath in. We both obediently do the same. All I can smell is manure and wet dog but I'd imagine to Finola, that's her idea of an oasis.

'Mmmmm, so fresh,' I say, with Gillian nodding earnestly next to me. 'Did you say there was a kettle in the, er, staffroom, Finola?'

We move into a huge wooden building filled with ladders, buckets, brushes, spades and riding helmets hooked on the walls, and sit down.

While Gillian natters on about what she'll be planting this year (yes, she will have a bag of manure, thank you very much), I sit and look out of the doorway, smiling at the children playing with Finola's plethora of dogs, without a care in the world. How wonderful to be a seven-year-old.

Finola passes the tea round. 'Well, my dears, I heard from Rose last night, Mrs Barnstorm has had the results back.'

We take a sharp breath. Mrs Barnstorm is Head of Pastoral Care at Hesgrove Pre-Prep School and a bit of a battle-axe; Rose is her companion. She knows Finola well and is our ear to the ground. Last November, Mrs Barnstorm started looking pale and missing school. Mr Ravelle, the school head teacher, wrote in the first newsletter of the year that she was battling breast cancer and would be taking time off for treatment.

'The tumour hasn't gone. It's smaller but not without threat and so another round of treatment will be needed,' Finola says gravely.

We all look out to the children, trying to think of something to say. She has never been my favourite woman, and has often berated me for my lack of motherly organisation and poor timekeeping, but towards the end of last year I'd felt a thawing.

'Well, let's not mope. It is what it is and us being forlorn won't help.' Good old Finola, pragmatic as ever.

'I'm sure there's something we could all do to help, all of the mums I mean,' offers Gillian in a brighter tone.

'Perhaps not *all* the mums,' I say, taking a sip of my very welcome sweet tea. 'I can't see Val being overcome with charitable spirit and goodwill.' Only last week I heard Valerie Pickering, one of the not-so-friendly mums at the school gates, laugh at one of the reception mums for having an iPhone 5. 'Oh, I haven't seen one of those in ages! It's practically a relic now, sweetie.' I think the reception mum might have been new and went bright red. I remember being *that* mum. I don't know why Val even cares. Best avoided, that one.

'Ooh yes, but you know why,' interjects Gillian with a

rare glint of mischief in her eye. She's on fire today. First a swear word and now a hint of gossip. Before we know it, she'll have gone off the rails, got a tattoo and be dealing 'meow meow' in the school playground.

'Her husband has left her! Apparently he was sick to the back teeth of her constant spending, her belittling him and the subsequent arguments. He's fallen in love with his twenty-three-year-old PA, moved into her terrace in town and left Val with Corinthia, the house and three of the cars,' Gillian says in hushed tones, as if the children can hear us above all the racket they're making with the dogs.

'Oh my God!' I say in shock.

'Men are like dogs. Patient and loving until you cross them, then they'll snap and you'll be sorry,' says Finola matter-of-factly.

'He's certainly snapped all right. Snapped up his PA!' I laugh. 'She'll be even worse than usual then, when we go back after Easter. I wonder if they know on the PaGS?' In January, with a new lease of life in me, I'd decided to sign up to the PaGS (Parents and Guardians Society), which advertises itself as a committee to help fundraise, run extra-curricular events and be a support for other parents at the school. Much better than that, it's turned out to be a fortnightly gossip group of bored mothers who live and breathe everyone else's business. I know I shouldn't love this but I do. A girl's gotta get her kicks somewhere, eh? How else would I know that we have a new mum's twin daughters joining Year Two after Easter? Apparently *Gloria* is a single self-made millionaire who has just sold her business and is, as Helen Wilson, head of the PaGS put it, 'very colourful'. I suddenly feel a twinge of worry. As much as I love catching up on all the news, I'm struggling with it now. Between more hours at MADE IT and the fortnightly PaGS meetings, I'm having to really lean on Kath for childcare. Lyla's dad, Simon, is happy to do his days but he works full-time too so it's been a bit tricky, especially with the Easter holidays looming. I feel like I'm constantly giving chunks of myself to different things and all Lyla wants is her whole mummy. Once again, guilt knocks at my door.

We share our theories on what Valerie Pickering will do next and I share the news about Gloria.

'That'll put the cat amongst the pigeons,' says Finola with raised eyebrows as Gillian sips her tea and nods. How exciting!

Then we herd the children into the stables and watch Finola give Lyla and Clara a lesson on mounting and dismounting the ponies, while Honor and Roo take two of the bigger horses out for a trot around the adjacent field.

'Mummy, look!' Lyla shouts over to me as she and her pony walk in slow circles round the yard. She looks so proud of herself sitting up on him with her little feet in the stirrups. 'Mummy, look! Are you looking, Mummy?'

'Lyla, I'm looking!' I say slightly exasperatedly as I haven't taken my eyes off her for a second. 'You're doing really well!'

'Look properly then! Take a photo!' she calls. God, what have I instilled in her? That it's not looking unless you have your phone up and are snapping away? Maybe we need to have a chat about technology.

Just as I'm googling 'digital detox' on my phone, Roo canters past on a steed as big as a Land Rover and calls out, 'Mummy, Julien isn't cantering at full speed but I've given him a good run.'

'Well done, poppet,' Finola says back nonchalantly as she continues to lead Lyla and Clara's ponies round the yard.

Maybe this is it – we are becoming outdoorsy people. Storie (Lyla's dad's hippy but well-meaning girlfriend) would love it and I could be secretly smug that it was me who encouraged Lyla's love of the natural world to blossom. Ha! What a role reversal that would be.

Either way, this has been a gorgeous day for my daughter and I haven't stressed about work once.

FIVE

LYLA IS SPENDING EASTER weekend with her dad and Storie. Lyla and I had a fake Easter the day before with eggs, little bunny toys in a wicker basket Kath had customised with lilac gingham lining, violet pompom trim and a little spring of lavender tied to the handle (this lavender phase is really in full swing). With an empty house, it is the perfect opportunity for some Me Time. I decide to drop Edward a message and allow myself to daydream a little bit.

Hey Edward! How's it going over there? We are just starting the Easter hols, which is a great excuse for me to eat chocolate guilt-free, ha! Are you back in the UK any time soon? Let's hang out x

Send.

Actually I wish I'd spent a tiny bit longer on that. Is 'hang out' still a 'cool' thing to say? Lyla said 'in a bizzle, bae' the other day when I asked her to fetch her reading folder and I almost had to reach for a dictionary. Well, I've sent it now, I'm not going to torture myself. He won't care anyway, it's Edward. That's what's so great about him. There's no stress.

He's a Brit living and working in New York – maybe it's the distance that makes it so simple. We both know what to expect of each other. I met him last year in a bar while I was working on a movie set in Manhattan (yes, I know how glamorous that sounds – I'm fully owning it). We ended up going back to his, having an incredibly liberating one-night stand (or so I thought it would be) and every time he's back in London for work, we meet up, have some drinks and a fantastic repeat. I'm not looking to marry him or even date him but he's fun, we get on and the sex is good. He knows the score. After Theo, I want no strings, no fuss – a man's dream, surely? And he's in exactly the same place. *Robin Wilde, you have really lucked out,* I think, as I unscrew a bottle of cold, crisp white wine.

Our first proper date when Edward was over in January was lovely. Hanging out again in February felt like we understood each other. He was over for a week that time, thanks to a new project for the interior design firm he works for. I don't know exactly what he does – I don't need to ask the 'whys' and 'what fors' – but I do know that he scouts new designers for his American firm to collaborate with. The company also has a smaller branch in London, which means he travels back and forth a lot, which is nice for me, but I know he loves where he works in Manhattan.

It felt like fate when he dropped me a message on one of my rare February Fridays off from MADE IT and asked if I was free. Lyla was at her dad's – she was booked on a Wild Flora and Fauna Identification course with Storie on Saturday morning (lucky kid) – and so I hopped on a train. When we'd seen each other the month before we'd had a good time, so there were no nerves or sweaty-under-tits moments this time.

On the train down I thought back to those anxious journeys on the way to see my Turned-Out-to-be-a-Total-Bastard ex, Theo. How I'd almost pulled muscles in my fingers trying to open his texts as fast as possible, how

I'd felt butterflies so strongly in my stomach that I'd almost thrown up into my empty Starbucks sandwich bag. I remembered anxiously waiting for his replies, texts that he only ever really sent when it suited him. I was never anything other than a distraction for Theo – someone to play with when he had nothing better to do, or couldn't have the woman he really wanted. I'm not proud of how I let him walk all over me. I'd thought it exciting and magical, but now I can see how exhausting it all was. And wrong for me. Seeing Edward is so simple. I don't have to worry about anything – least of all introducing him to Lyla. I just get dressed, rock up, we have fun, we go home.

ARRIVING AT LONDON LIVERPOOL Street station back on that freezing February day, I took my phone out to check for messages.

Hey! Running a bit late so won't make it to the station to greet you! Are you OK to meet at Seven Dials in 30 mins? x, Edward texted just as I unlocked my phone.

Yep, no worries, gives me 30 minutes to say goodbye to my other fancyman x I tapped out in reply.

What do you think I'm doing at the office?? Ushering out all the strippers before I can leave x he fired back.

Perfect – extra time! I popped into the station loos

(worth every penny of the 30p charge), zhooshed my hair, topped up my concealer and set off for the tube. I might not be in love with the guy, but it's nice to look nice, eh?

Half an hour later and I was perched outside the Mercer Street Hotel. I always think there's something lovely about that place. The Mercer Street Hotel is my favourite smell in London. Yep, that sounds slightly unhinged, but every time I'm in Covent Garden I pop into the lobby just to smell the incredible candles they have lit. If you step outside there is a bustling crossroads with a huge monument in the middle that has little stone ledges you can sit on and watch people come and go. People-watching is one of my favourite pastimes (after bingeing on Netflix and online beauty tutorials) so I was surprised when Edward walked up with a smile and a 'fancy seeing you here!'

'Of all the men in all the world, you had to walk into my . . . Seven Dials,' I said, trailing off from my confident start.

'That didn't go as smoothly as you'd planned, did it?' He smiled, his greeny-brown eyes creasing rather attractively at the corners.

'No. But I tried. Do I get marks for that?' I smiled back.

'Yes, forty points to the lady with the fabulous dress!' Edward said, throwing one arm in the air as if to announce my winnings to half of Covent Garden.

'This old thing? I wear it for all my jaunts,' I said deliberately casually. I don't. It's new, but he needn't know that.

'Well, let's make the most of it then! Are you hungry? I've booked a table at Balthazar round the corner, but I'm happy to go somewhere else if you'd prefer.'

'Balthazar sounds great, I've been wanting to try it for ages.' Oh, yay! I really had.

'Don't your other "fancy men" treat you as well as I do then?' he asked with a wicked look in his eye.

'No, I'm lucky if I get a Pret sandwich with them. You're by far my favourite!'

'You'll have to keep me then,' he said with a grin.

I hesitated.

'Ha, I will keep you until dinner's finished!' I said with a smile and a laugh.

'Deal!' he replied, not sensing my unease, and took my hand as we headed off towards the centre of Covent Garden.

Balthazar was just as beautiful as I'd heard. I'd have been happy with arancini and a pizza at Zizzi, so this was a real bonus. *Theo would have liked it here,* I couldn't help but think. *It's grand and showy and very him* . . . I quickly banished him from my mind and focused on the task at hand, walking to our table behind a very smart and slightly intimidating waiter.

Although our conversation is always easy and light-hearted, I have to admit, Edward really is a gentleman. It was lovely to have my chair pulled out by a nice man, and the restaurant was just right. It wasn't a personal hiring of the Oxo Tower à la Theo Salazan, but I wouldn't have wanted it to be. I liked being lost in the crowd with this man. My heart wasn't racing and I was in no danger of suffering third-degree wax burns up the backs of my legs . . . But that's a story for another time.

We perused the menus.

'Is it a bit sad to have macaroni cheese in such a lovely place?' I asked, suddenly wondering if I should go for something more refined.

'No! You have what you like,' Edward responded without a second thought.

'I think you might be my soulmate with carb reasoning like that.'

'I might be,' he said, looking a little bit serious.

'I'm just going to nip to the loo,' I garbled, fumbling for my new black-patent clutch bag and moving my chair. I headed to the ladies', red-faced and managing not to make eye contact with him. *He's going to think I'm such an idiot, getting flustered by what was clearly a joke,* I thought. *Why did I do that? Chill out, Robin.*

I walked up the opulent stairs to the ladies' bathroom, feeling stupid for being so nuts. I needed to relax. He wasn't asking me to sign my house over and take his surname, it was banter. Healthy 'bants'. *I love the 'bants'. I can 'bant' all day,* I told myself. *I'm going to have a nervous tinkle, wash my hands, take a deep breath and carry on enjoying a nice, normal evening with a nice, normal guy. I'm not wearing this lacy thong for nothing.*

'Tada!' Edward said as I arrived back to the table much more serene than when I left five minutes before. I looked down at my place and there was a tall glass of pink fizz. 'I ordered you a glass of pink champagne,' he said proudly, 'to go with the mac and cheese.'

'Thank goodness!' I replied. 'I never eat cheesy pasta at home without a bottle of Moët Rosé. I like to keep things classy, you know.'

I took a sip of my champagne and decided to delve a little deeper.

'So, Edward, I know all the basics. You live and work in Manhattan, you were raised in Hampshire, you like good design, good food –' I gesture to our plates with my fork – 'and good . . . erm . . . nights –' good sex sounds a bit presumptuous – 'but I want to know more.'

'Oh, really?' he said with a grin. 'What do you want to know?'

'Well, let's start at the beginning. What are your family like?' I asked.

Edward took a big breath as if he was about to really exert himself.

'OK, well, I'd say we're a pretty normal bunch. Mum and Dad, or Amanda and Dominic to you, run a residential care home for adults with severe learning difficulties. They're lovely. A lot of the residents have been there since they opened the home when I was a teenager, so I always pop in for a visit when I'm home and say hello. They're honestly the sweetest people you'll meet.'

My heart went squishy at how compassionate Edward sounded. 'Wow, that sounds like a real vocation for them.'

'Yeah. They've worked in the mental health sector since it wasn't the done thing to talk about it and it was all kept a bit hush-hush. They've done such a lot to change attitudes. If anyone should be caring for the types of residents they have, it's them. They love it. Dad's almost seventy now and Mum's not far behind him, so they have managers to do the day-to-day running, but Dad still goes in every day and to oversee things. Mum doesn't as much, she spends a lot of time helping my sister now.'

'Oh yes?' I prompted.

'Annabelle, she's five years older than me, although you'd think she was at least ten, she's so bossy. She got divorced recently and is having a bit of a rough time. They have four children together – ten, eight, six and four – so she's up-the-wall busy. Mum goes over most days when the children are home from school and just helps Annabelle keep on top of things, you know?'

'Your mum sounds like my Auntie Kath. Is she obsessed with lavender and crafts?' I asked, with a smile as I carried on eating the most delicious mac and cheese I'd ever tasted. Or maybe it was the champagne making everything taste better.

'Aha, no, not quite as eccentric as the infamous Auntie Kath, but just as lovely I'm sure,' Edward said.

'So, a care home, two children and four grandchildren – your parents have a lot on then,' I summarised.

'Well, a care home and three children, actually.' Edward paused. 'My brother Thomas was killed in Afghanistan in 2002. A roadside bomb.'

I stopped eating because I didn't know how to react. 'Edward,' I said, instinctively reaching for his hand, 'I'm sorry. You don't have to say more if it's too hard.'

'It's OK. I like to talk about Thomas because I don't want him to be forgotten. He lived, he died and he is still my big brother. He was twenty when he was killed and I thought he was a legend. He was braver than any of us could ever be.' Edward seemed very calm and collected as he talked. I'd be a mess, I'm sure.

'I'm sure he was. I'm glad you talk about him, and with love rather than sadness.'

'We all do. Annabelle's eldest is named after him, and Mum and Dad planted a tree in his honour at the home that the residents decorate with little trinkets they make, it's very special to them.' Edward smiled a sad smile and caught himself suddenly. 'Now, let's not bring a good evening down with all this.'

'It's not bringing it down. Honestly, I'm so touched you shared. He should be remembered, he's your brother.' I lifted my champagne flute. 'To Thomas, your lovely brother,' I said, and Edward picked up his glass too and clinked mine with a much happier smile.

I spent the next little while talking about my family. I told him about all of Kath's recent phases (the lace, the pompoms, the shells and now the lavender), Lyla's penchant for music and dance, the hippy ways of Simon and Storie and glossed over Mum and Dad a bit. After his parents seeming so lovely and so involved, I didn't want to dwell on how little my own parents seem to care about anything beyond the Rotary Club and the demands of retiree life in Cornwall.

Conversation flowed easily and, before I knew it, we'd finished our food, the restaurant was clearing out and it was time to leave.

I offered to pick up the bill, or at least go halves, but Edward waved it off and said he'd got it. Not in a dickbag 'I'm so much better than you' way, but just in an easy 'it's just friends getting dinner' way. Who was I to argue with a man who insisted on buying me comfort food and bubbles? I would insist it's my turn next time. I won't be a kept woman.

'Well,' I said, more than slightly tipsy, 'I ought to get back to the station.'

'You don't have to. My Airbnb is lovely, it's very "mac and cheese with Moët", very you.'

'What are you suggesting, Mr Edward from New York?' *Maybe I am a bit more than tipsy*, I thought, as I pawed at his tie in what I could only hope was a seductive move, rather than a wasted woman half swinging from a vine.

'I think you know what I'm suggesting, Ms Robin from Cambridge,' he said, taking my hands off his tie and kissing me on the mouth. I closed my eyes briefly; champagne kisses are nice.

We headed into the night air and I stood under the spinning ballerina outside the theatre opposite, kissing Edward back, running my hands up into his hair, pushing myself into his body and ignoring the middle-aged woman in a fur-trimmed coat tutting and the 'geezers' falling out of the nearby pub shouting, 'Oi, oi!' as they stumbled past.

'Sacking the train off?' Edward asked, pulling away.

'How far to your place?' I said, going back in for a kiss.

'Two minutes,' he mumbled with his mouth still on mine.

We walked back to his, hand in hand, stopping occasionally for more streetlamp-lit kisses and what felt like a lot longer than two minutes later, fell through his door. My nice little dress was pulled over my head, he fumbled with the clasp on my bra and I almost ripped at his tie. For about four seconds it was sexy, and then we both stopped and smiled at each other because we realised it would be much quicker if I dealt with my own rather tricky clasp and he dealt with his own tie.

He walked backwards, leading me to the bed on the far side of the trendy exposed-brick studio flat and pulled me onto him, tumbling into the mattress. I was so glad

I'd semi-prepared and had smooth legs, matching underwear (well, both black and lacy at least) and a cheeky bikini line shave. I felt good. He felt good under me. Everything felt good. Everything felt good over and over for about two hours until we were both sticky and breathy and exhausted. Good.

When I left him with a kiss after breakfast the next morning, I felt light and bright and breezy, and excited to get home for a cosy weekend with my girls.

SIX

APRIL

NATALIE IS BACK! SHE and Martin had an incredible travel sabbatical but now she is throwing herself back into MADE IT with more gusto than ever.

I loved trying my hand at running the place, but her return is welcome. I've held the place together – yes. I've learnt a lot about management and how a business runs, but it's been hard, really hard. I won't admit it to anyone, not even Natalie, but I've felt like a bit of a fraud, or as though I'm playing dress-up. I come in every day with my head held high and my manicured hand clutching my keep-cup (I couldn't handle another 'helpful chat' from Skye about sustainability), and I like to think I do my job with an air of dignity and confidence, but on a daily basis I've felt little wobbles. Nothing major, not like the wobbles of The Emptiness last year – when I was at my lowest – but still I feel a little worried that someone might see through me and say, 'You're scared of messing this up, aren't you?' or, 'You might not be as good as other people think you are.' Obviously nobody has actually said this, but after a few months of really challenging myself, I'm ready to be comfortable again for a bit. I'm ready to feed into the weekly creative meetings, not chair them, and not feel undermined by a bunch of trendy twenty-somethings who think I'm an old granny just because I once asked how you get the filters on Insta stories. I'm still going to be managing a lot of things – including, it turns out, the rotas – and having my role in the office, but just knowing Natalie is steering the ship again is a relief. I'm proud of myself but I'm ready to get hands-on again with make-up. I love designing a look, finding what makes a client feel great or what makes a model come to life in front of a lens. I love doing something I know I'm good at.

'I have news,' Natalie announces in our first team meeting, with a radiant smile. She seems so energetic, and her deep brown skin is glowing with health. Her trip with Martin has clearly given her a new lease of life and a bit of extra pep in her well-heeled step. 'Something has come in that I've been exploring while I was away . . .'

God, she never actually stops. If I were travelling round the Serengeti with my wonderful husband, I don't think I'd be checking my emails. Natalie is a machine. A machine that can find Wi-Fi in the most unlikely of locations, I might add.

This is exciting. And a welcome change of subject after Skye made sure to highlight to the meeting that she has excelled in Natalie's absence and had excellent feedback from *all* her clients. Natalie was impressed. I should talk to Natalie about this. I've missed being on jobs. My make-up kit is gathering dust and I feel a pang of jealousy for Skye, who is getting to spread her creative wings so wide. I need to get back out there. I hope the younger, bouncier Skye doesn't usurp me. You know you're getting older when you worry about the younger ones. I was a younger one two minutes ago. Where did time go?

Back from my mind-wandering, I can feel there is a frisson of anticipation around the table, and Natalie takes a breath to continue.

'London Fashion Week showcasing Spring '19 is in five months. It is the biggest fashion event of the year and it would be a big deal if we were part of it. Mara Isso has asked us to pitch for the hair and beauty for her new collection.'

There's a collective gasp around the room.

Mara Isso brings out stunning collections every year and constantly sets the bar for creativity.

'We have less than a month to pull together a groundbreaking pitch!'

Everyone looks at each other wide-eyed with excitement.

'This year,' Natalie continues, a glimmer of excitement in her own eyes, 'Mara is smashing the norms again and changing things up. Noting the dire lack of body confidence in the average British woman, Mara has decided to drive a change in perceptions of beauty in the creative industries and is using only plus-size models from a variety of ethnic backgrounds on her runway.'

This is big.

Kareem lets out a quiet, 'Bloody hell,' and I offer, 'Hurrah!' This is what we've been waiting for. A chink of hope for women everywhere flicking through magazines with masses upon masses of bodies that bear no resemblance to their own. And since NYC last year, this is the kind of creative opportunity *I've* been waiting for.

'This is a big move. We've seen plus-size models before

but never have we had such a top-end designer fill the entire runway with models everything *other* than alabaster-white, tall, impossibly thin and, let's be honest, ill-looking,' Natalie says. 'As always, Mara is going to be going all out for the collection and so we need to match this. She's sent me some samples, and they're . . . breathtaking!'

She pauses and looks at each of us.

'It'll be a whole team effort, all hands on deck, but I think we have the skill, finesse and creative dynamic to pull it off!' I can hear the determination in her voice as she speaks.

'Remember, we'll be up against some of the best. Time is tight. We have two weeks to research, draft and design, a week to refine and practise the pitch and then I'll go down to her offices and present. I have every faith in us. Are you with me?' she finishes with a smile.

I open my mouth, but Skye jumps in before all of us.

'YES! This is absolutely amazing, Natalie! We'll smash this out of the park, won't we, guys?' she says to the rest of the team. They all nod and agree happily like she is their supreme leader. 'And we're the right team for the job – after all, we're the perfect mix of young and fashion- forward . . .' she pauses and gestures at herself 'alongside the kind of non-conventional bodies and faces that we don't usually see on the runway.' She looks pointedly at me. I seethe – but am determined to rise above it.

'I'm really excited,' I add. 'How fantastic to have a more accurate representation of women on the catwalk. Clothes we can all genuinely aspire to wearing.'

'Exactly, you've nailed it, Robin. This is a big deal for fashion, for beauty perceptions, for women. It'd be an honour to win this job, let alone a lucrative business opportunity,' Natalie responds.

Ha! In your flawless face, Skye!

'Skye,' Natalie continues, 'I'd like you to head up the initial stage. Alice, please dig out every proposal we've ever offered for any other runway job. Stuart, provisionally block out everyone's calendars for that week in September.'

Fuck. She wants *Skye* to head it up? She hasn't even mentioned a role for me. What? Haven't I done a good enough job while she was away? *Team effort,* I remind myself, and try to muster a convincing smile.

'And Robin, I want you overseeing the whole pitch. You absolutely nailed it in New York last year, and these last few months. I need your level of expertise on this, and I know you and Skye together will make something incredible.'

Skye looks as thrilled as me, i.e. about as thrilled as a

woman who's just accidentally 'liked' one of her ex's photos by mistake.

'No problem, Nat, it'll be lit,' Skye says, quickly composing herself.

Nat? *Lit*?

'Yes . . . marvellous, we'll get right on it,' I say in more understandable language as I make a note to find out just what 'lit' means and maybe start using it to increase my 'street cred'. Is 'street cred' even a phrase these days?

FOUR HOURS LATER, THE buzz of the meeting has worn off, my other admin is done and I'm starting to think about how we're going to pitch. We need to be vibrant. We need to stand out. This will be a celebration. Women with plus-size bodies strutting their stuff down the runways of London Fashion Week is surely something to be jubilant about. I'm not thrilled that I have to work hand in hand with the diva that is Skye, but I am thrilled to be working on this job and being part of a bigger picture. I thought working on a Manhattan movie set last year was *the* career highlight but if we won this job, if my – OK, *our* – pitch won, that would take my work life to a whole new level!

I fire off an email to Skye, who has gone home for the

afternoon to find the right 'vibe' for the proposal. The email:

Hey! So excited to be working on this proposal, I'm sure it's going to be super-lit, I begin.

I've googled 'lit'. It means 'good'. Easy. I can do this.

> Why don't we get together tomorrow, or perhaps make an evening thing of it and throw some ideas around? Time is tight but I know we can put together something amazing by Friday for Natalie to polish.
>
> Robin

There. No point stressing about having to work with her. She's the most creative artist on the books, I know she's going to have some amazing ideas. In the meantime, I'm going to do some research of my own. And I need to do more than scroll Pinterest and peruse the fashion and beauty bloggers to show Natalie her faith is justified. Skye will come up with some killer looks but it's my job to think big – to tell the story behind those looks. I think of all those years spent telling bedtime stories to Lyla. This is it – it's story time. It's showtime.

PICKING LYLA UP FROM Homework Club at 5 p.m., my brain is still whirring. I've spent the whole afternoon ignoring my inbox and trawling through our back catalogue of *Vogue*, searching for inspiration. This is going to be so much harder than I thought. It's hard to come up with a really refreshing *new* beauty idea. I want our models to stand out. Mara's samples are all gorgeous. Lots of vivid colours – buttercup yellow, lime green, pops of neon pink, but all blending seamlessly into each other and flowing on the fabric like watercolours. I'd considered some bold ideas like vibrant-coloured false lashes or even adding some colour to the brows, and had noted them down ready to discuss with Skye. With only days to go until we need to submit to Natalie, the heat is on . . .

'Mummy!' Lyla says with joy as I turn up to collect her.

'Lyla!' I chime back in the same voice. I take her hand, leading her out of the huge iron gates and toward the car, carrying her book bag for her.

'We had the best day! Mr Ravelle did an assembly on fire safety and a fireman came in and we went outside and a firewoman let us go in the fire engine and Roo turned the sirens on even though he was told not to and Mr Ravelle went all red and blotchy,' Lyla says, almost jumping as she walks. Scandal at seven years old is pretty endearing.

'Wow! That sounds like the craziest day ever,' I say,

smiling. I wish I'd spent the day with hot firemen. 'Guess what I've done?' I ask as we climb into the car.

'Watched TV?' she says, shrugging.

Is that what she thinks I do all day?

'Erm, no,' I say, furrowing my brow and feeling a bit concerned that that was her first answer.

'Done make-up on people?' she says just as flippantly.

'Still no, but I did go into the office,' I say, encouraging her to have another guess.

'Don't know,' she says, throwing her hands in the air dramatically.

'OK, I'll tell you. It's exciting! A top fashion designer is going to let us pitch for her show!' I say with more gusto than I had anticipated.

'Huh?' I glance at Lyla in the mirror now I've got into my seat too, and she looks totally lost. Of course she would be. I need to mum this up a bit.

'OK, there's a lady called Mara Isso and she makes beautiful clothes. She's going to have a show, to let everyone see the clothes. She'll have models wearing them at the show and she's asked me and Natalie if we will do the make-up.' Not strictly true but, like I said, I've 'mummed' this up.

'Oh, a make-up shoot! Can I come?' Lyla says, understanding it at last and sensing excitement.

'I'm not sure.' Oh bugger, I don't want to rain on her parade at the first moment. I keep going. 'Do you know what the most exciting thing is?'

'What?' She sounds only slightly interested.

'The models are going to look like very normal, happy ladies, like Mummy and Finola and Gillian!' I say, slightly high-pitched with glee.

'So? They always look like that.'

I love the fact that to my seven-year-old, there is no difference between me and a model.

'Well, yes, but usually they choose very, very slim, extra-extra-pretty models. And this time, they're going to choose lots of people – white and black and brown-skinned, and some might not be very slim but will just be very lovely normal people,' I offer, smiling at her in the rear-view mirror. I feel like I'm nailing this beautiful self-love life lesson moment.

'Will they be fat?' Lyla enquires without hesitation.

What? 'They'll be all different shapes and sizes, Lyla. Plus size means you are a little bit bigger and very beautiful. And that's what's so great about this – we shouldn't all want to look the same,' I say as tactfully as I can. This isn't going quite how I thought it would.

'Fat is disgusting! They need to do a DASH diet!' Lyla says passionately.

I nearly slam on my brakes in shock. Why is my lovely girl saying this? Where on earth has this come from?

'Lyla! Who told you that? What's the "DASH diet"?' I say, horrified.

I see her drop her head a bit. She's seven, she knows what 'fat' means. 'Corinthia told me. She said her mum is so fat it's disgusting, and so she has to have her lunches and dinners made in little boxes in the fridge.' Lyla says this as matter-of-factly as if she were telling me it might rain later. 'Corinthia said her mum is having a job on her boobies and is going to look fabulous by autumn.' She says the last three words in a voice suggesting she's mimicking Val, which I suspect is what Corinthia did.

I stay quiet, dumbstruck for a few minutes as we complete our short journey.

We pull up into the drive, loving the fact that our new house is so close to school (I really should walk the journey when the weather is nicer). I take a deep breath. I need to address this immediately. I take my seat belt off and turn round to face Lyla. Eye contact is key.

'Listen, this is really important.' I try to stress the point in as calm a tone as I can manage. 'Everyone looks different, and that's OK. If someone is "fat", it means their body is a bit bigger than some people's bodies. That's nothing to do with you and it's not for you to say it's "disgusting". We only use kind words when we talk about other people, and "disgusting" isn't a kind word when you're saying it about someone. You would be very upset if someone called you disgusting, and so would I. Corinthia's mummy is beautiful.' Ugh, that pained me. I really can't stand the woman. 'If Corinthia's mummy was big or little or tall or short, she would still be beautiful because everyone has something special about them.'

'Then why is she on a diet with all her food in boxes?' She sounds confused.

'What Corinthia's mummy does with her food is none of our business. It's up to her, OK?'

'Then why is she having a job on her boobies to make them bigger?'

'Well, that's her own choice. If she wants to do that, she can, it's her body and her choice,' I say, making note to tell Gillian and Finola immediately about this titbit (no pun intended). I was right about the Botox and surgery, ha!

'But *she* said she was fat and disgusting. Corinthia told me it was her mum that said it, it's not *me* saying it!' I can see Lyla getting frustrated at the injustice of this forced chat.

'But you're repeating it. You should say to Corinthia,

"No. Your mummy is beautiful." Then get on and do something else. Us girls have got to stick together. We don't need to say nasty things and make each other feel bad, do we?' I raise my eyebrows as I ask the last question.

'No.' Lyla fiddles with the hem of her skirt, looks up at me with big eyes and says, 'Mummy, I think you're beautiful, the most beautiful mummy out of all of them.'

My heart. It melts. What a sweet-talker.

'Baby, I think you're the most perfect Lyla the world has ever had. Shall we go inside and have some fish fingers?'

We climb out of the car, walk up the beautiful drive, take our beautiful selves inside and have a beautiful dinner of fish fingers, mash and beans. Crisis, hopefully, averted.

SEVEN

On the drive to school the next morning, I play 'I Am Woman' by Helen Reddy to really drive home the message of female empowerment. Hopefully the subliminal message that everyone is a winner will set in and she won't call anyone fat and disgusting again. Although honestly, I can't wait to tell the girls about this supposed boob job! Then I remind myself that Val might be mean, but I should listen to my own advice.

'Morning!' Skye chimes the second I sit down in my office. Skye, as always, is looking 'on trend'. Today she's sporting loose boyfriend-style jeans (I'd wager they're not actually her boyfriend's jeans since his thighs are so bulging with protein shakes he'd need extra-large ones just to accommodate his girth) with a faded Gucci T-shirt tucked in. She's wearing one of those little black plastic choker things round her neck and has her hair in two identical topknots on her head. Basically, if the Spice Girls re-formed, she'd fit right in. She could be Beauty Spice. Or Sassy Spice. Or A Little Bit Arrogant Spice.

I secretly wish Skye might give me a brief window to do my 'essentials', like checking what the deal of the day on Amazon is and having just one obligatory Facebook scroll (even the most Professional of Professionals do this, I believe). But alas, here she is, with a worn-looking, yet uber trendy, tote over her shoulder and make-up clearly inspired by Kylie Jenner, except, frustratingly, Skye looks better. She looks gorgeous.

She comes in, carrying her eco-cup of something earthy and sits at my desk.

'So, I've been thinking, this Mara Isso job, it's a big deal,' she says to me as if I'm new to this industry.

'Erm, yes, very big,' I say in a breezy tone so she doesn't sense my annoyance or low-level fear of her.

'So we need big make-up,' she says firmly and launches into her ideas. 'I'm thinking some special effects with holo, lash extensions, maybe some clever strobing. What do you think to body art? Maybe we could add on-trend tattoo work or body gems. Nothing cray, but pops of intrigue here and there, really make the models stand out.'

Skye sits back in her chair and sips the earth juice (I bet Storie would know what it was instantly – charcoal-matcha-turmeric-something, no doubt) and looks smug.

Taking a long breath in to stall before answering, I try to envisage her proposals. Holographic work is hard but can look gorgeous done properly, Skye is incredible at special effects so I'm sure she'd make something striking. Lashes? Yeah, lashes are always nice, and I could share my idea of colouring them to match or contrast with each outfit and the models' skin tones. Body art, tattoos and gems all sound like the models would certainly 'stand out'.

'I love all the ideas individually, but are they the right fit? Should the clothes be doing most of the talking?' I ask, still mulling over her suggestions and imagining my acid-green lashes alongside holographic shimmer, gems, airbrushing, body art and glitter. Is it all a bit much?

'I want the models to stand out, though. I want them to look so savage that you won't even care about the clothes,' she says assertively.

'But that's the point of London Fashion Week. The fashion. The clothes. The actual outfits,' I reply gently.

'I know, but this is our chance to shine,' Skye responds

without skipping a beat, staring at me as though she thinks I don't get it.

I don't think *she's* getting it. I think she might be seeing this as a chance to fully showcase her work, which of course it partly is, but she's missing the wider point. I don't want to squash her ideas or crush her creativity because, as much as she drives me berserk, she's amazing at what she does, and I don't want to hurt her feelings, so know I need to be tactical.

'I see what you're saying,' I begin. 'I love how you've taken the brief of making something special and brought the Skye flair to it – that's why Natalie picked you to lead the creative, because you're amazing. I just think you can have too much of a good thing, you know? Perhaps we should take your ideas, which are all individually amazing, and assess which ones would work the absolute best. Right?'

Skye shrugs, then nods. Flattery will get you everywhere.

'Why don't you leave your ideas with me, and we'll chat again this afternoon. Perhaps I just need them to percolate and then we'll find the sweet spot,' I say in my most maternal voice without being patronising. A fine balance.

Skye blinks. 'If that's what you want, yeah. I've found

the sweet spot already but if you wanna think about it for a while, then I'm chill.' Clearly she did not appreciate the effort it took to find my fine balance. 'I guess I just work fast and some people . . . well, I guess you just need to take your time.'

My God, she's good at pushing my buttons. I smile tightly as she gets up to leave my office and the second she's through the door frame, open Facebook to find that video of the swans again. *It's not procrastination,* I tell myself, *it's therapy*.

HOURS LATER, AFTER SEVERAL attempts to map out potential looks with holo effects or body art or lashes or all of the above, I'm stumped. I can't see this being the way forward; something about it isn't gelling. And time is running out.

I ping Skye a message to see if she's free to pop back into the office. She lives locally but is often out on shoots or planning and prepping from home, like I was last year, but she agrees to come in. You can fault her for a lot of things (well, I can), but her dedication is on point.

Forty-five minutes later and she's back in my office, still pristine and glowing. Can she really look this good at home? Surely she appreciates the joy of a braless oversized T-shirt and pyjama bottoms?

'So, I've been thinking about your suggestions,' I begin. I need to not make this sound like I'm completely shooting her down but, ultimately, I'm completely shooting her down.

'Yep,' Skye says, casually flipping her PopSocket on her phone with one well-manicured hand.

'I love the concepts,' I start, keeping things positive, 'and I'd love to see them in the flesh at some point . . . but I just don't think they're right for this.'

'You're wrong,' Skye says with so much understated confidence I envy her. 'These girls will need to stand out, need to be special, and my idea is special.'

'That's the thing, though, Skye, they already are special and will stand out because a) they're in Mara Isso's new collection, and b) they are the first fully plus-size models Mara has ever used. No other designer is going to fill their catwalk with models like this. Perhaps we don't need to go all out with every trick in the book.'

'So what then? Just let them go on barefaced and say, "Look at these models, aren't they so special"?' Skye says with a slight hint of venom in her voice.

'Yes! Exactly . . . Oh my God, Skye, you might have nailed it there!' I say, jumping up at the brainwave. 'Why don't we do the most beautiful, silky, natural looks, with flowing, natural hair, nude nails, soft lips, gentle eyes, glowing skin? The whole point of this show is that all women are beautiful. Let's take that and weave it through the hair and make-up as well, and, as cheesy as it sounds, let their inner beauty shine.' I feel almost light-headed I love the idea so much.

Skye narrows her eyes and frowns at me for a moment. 'No body art then?' she says in a last-ditch attempt to have her way. I'm going to have to placate her.

'Look, I don't want you to feel like I don't like your first idea because I do. I've seen your work and I know how skilled you are. Body art and holo effects from you would be insanely good. I just don't think they're right for this particular shoot. Another shoot, though, maybe even another Mara Isso shoot, yes – get your brushes because you're the woman for the job!' I say, smiling and nodding in the most uplifting way I can. The way I do when I'm trying to convince Lyla that something is a really good idea.

'Fine. Although I think my ideas would have looked crazy-hot on the models, plus size or not.' She's grudging but still taking this more graciously than I expected. 'I can see this is a big moment for the industry, I'm not stupid, I know women will live for this. I know it will be lit. Natural beauty, then,' she says, clapping both hands on her knees. 'Sure.'

'Huzzah!' I say jubilantly, but Skye just looks at me side on, like I've said something crazy. 'I think we've got it. Soon nobody will leave a shop feeling crap about themselves! I love that someone is shaking things up, and with ideas like this, we might get to be a part of it. Hurrah, huzzah again!'

'You have such weird little words,' she says quietly, shaking her head and getting up from her chair.

'Yeah, I know, and you're so lit,' I say sarcastically, but from her blank expression I can see it's lost on her. 'Are you all right to put a rough draft proposal together? Just some face maps, product suggestions, a few pictures demonstrating what we're going for, and I'll send over the written blurb to accompany?' I'm excited about telling the story behind the great visuals I know Skye can come up with.

'I'll have it done by the end of the week,' she says efficiently.

'Great! Then Natalie can perfect it with plenty of time before the official submission of the proposal,' I say. I love having this new role, being creative from this angle. I'm feeling that buzz again. I was missing the thrill of doing an amazing job, like last year when things went so well in Manhattan, but now I feel like that thrill is returning. The joy is seeping back in and I'm so pumped to be working on creative jobs again, especially on such a groundbreaking one as this. If Skye wasn't still in my office, I'd fist-pump the air.

'Sure,' Skye says calmly, perhaps a modicum less buzzy than me.

Meh. Life is so sweet right now I've enough buzz for the both of us.

EIGHT

I FEEL LIKE MY FEET don't touch the ground all week. After getting the basics of the pitch sketched out, I was called out to two shoots (a commercial catalogue and a wedding trial), ferried Lyla about to three separate play dates (this child has a significantly busier social life than I do) and took several upset phone calls from Lacey, who had come on her period, despite being so sure that this was the month. I don't know what to say to her anymore except how sorry I am. I can feel her pain through the phone and want to just reach out and fix it all but know I can't.

Sitting down on Friday night on the old sofa (it might be a big, new house but these comfy, brown, slightly battered leather sofas are never leaving me, even if they do have crumbs down the sides and the odd stray Ferrero Rocher wrapper under the cushions), I suddenly realise how exhausted I am. The pitch document has gone to Natalie, Simon picked Lyla up from school tonight and is having her till Monday and I've got a whole weekend stretching ahead. With the busyness of the week, I didn't even think to plan anything in. What I should really do is put on some speed-cleaning vlogs, blitz the house, organise the junk drawers, clean out my work make-up kit and catch up on the ironing.

Little birdy tells me you're in town this weekend, I text to Edward.

Is that little birdy a thorough Facebook stalker? he replies straight away.

Shit.

It wasn't that thorough. You 'check in' at Heathrow, then at the Ace Hotel. You'd be a terrible prison escapee.

Good job I'm not on the run then! Wanna hang?

'Wanna hang' sounds so breezy and casual. Theo would never have said such a thing. He'd be too busy booking cars and museum tours or, actually more likely, finding ways to avoid me and make me feel like shit. Good old straightforward, sexy Edward. And each time we see each other the sex gets better and better . . .

I think about my options. Hoovering and ironing alone all weekend with nobody but YouTube for company, or hot sex and easy chat with lovely Edward, who is only here for a week and is probably very lonely. Really, I'd be doing him a favour. It would be the noble and right thing to do.

Borough Market, noon tomorrow?

See you then, sweet cheeks, he replies immediately.

Who needs ironed clothes anyway?

NEXT MORNING, I LUXURIATE in the bath for over an hour, pampering, primping and, most importantly, shaving. We all know where tonight is going and as every good fling-friend knows, preparation is key. I don't want him to think he's a booty call but, at the same time, I don't want to feel caught out.

Thinking back to our Balthazar night last time, I feel a little uneasy. I was a bit more tipsy than I'd thought. That pink Moët flowed very easily and before I knew it I'd gone from upright in a swanky restaurant to very much less than upright in a man's bed. I don't even fully remember all of it – it's a bit hazy. I'd thought I was quite sober until I had to go and have a very quiet, very demure tactical sick-up in the bathroom. I turned both taps on to avoid detection and brushed my teeth after. I got away with it, but still. This time I'll rein it in a bit, not rely on bubbles for confidence and grab the bull by the horns, so to speak.

WE MEET AT BOROUGH Market and before any nerves can set in, we're swept up by the throngs of tourists and local hipsters wanting to sample a million different cheeses, steaming-hot street food and freshly squeezed orange juice. The sights and smells are intoxicating: everywhere you look there's a stall or table laden with amazing artisan foods, local delicacies, fresh flowers, handmade crafts, bespoke artwork, and each table is surrounded by people straining to get a look.

We stop off at a stall near the door and Edward buys us each an overpriced (in my humble-but-won't-say-anything-out-loud opinion) fresh orange juice. But then I sip this nectar from the gods.

'Oh my, I don't think I've ever tasted anything so incredible in all my life,' I say, bending my knees and shutting my eyes in a swoon-like fashion.

'What about this, then?' Edward says, and leans in to kiss me on the lips, in the middle of the market. OK. Brazen. I like it.

Smiling back at him as he pulls away, my swoony thoughts are interrupted by a market vendor's heckle.

'Love's young dream, is it?' and a hearty cackle from his stall-mate.

'Something like that,' Edward calls back as I turn beetroot with horror. I want to run back, slam my drink down and shout, 'No, we're not in love! We're not in a dream! I nearly had all that and it fell to shit. This is different. I'm in control, I can't get hurt here. This is just fun, no strings, easy fun. Shut your mouth, Mr Market Man!' But instead, I force a smile, look at the floor, sip my drink and say, 'Oh, they've got a lavender stand! Kath would kill me if I didn't take a look,' and steer Edward away.

The stall would be Kath's absolute heaven, with big, long, fresh stems, cellophane bags of dried lavender and an array of products infused with tiny flecks of blue and purple. I grab a couple, pay the lady and put them in my rucksack. Or at least, I try to.

I had decided there was no point beating about the bush and pretending I wasn't going to be staying over, so opted for my black leather Whistles backpack that I could stuff a few overnight essentials in, rather than carrying on a charade with a tiny cross-body number. I'm all for spontaneity but I at least want deodorant, toothbrush, fresh clothes and my favourite make-up.

Edward studies me, trying to fit the bags in. 'Did you pack the kitchen sink as well?'

'Ha ha, no, I just brought . . .' I pause and try to shove the bags in '. . . a couple of . . .' more vigorous shoving '. . . essentials. For the day, I mean.'

'Oh, just for the day?' he says, a wry smile forming on his frustratingly kissable lips.

'Yes, Edward, the day. This is a day trip, is it not?' I stand on tiptoes and let my face sway very close to his.

'Hmmm, not to my understanding,' he says quietly, his lips so close to mine I can feel the warmth from them.

'Oh, well, in that case it's a good job I was in the Girl Guides and always come prepared with overnight attire, a ball of twine and a small tent,' I say, grinning now.

'Why are we still at the market?' he says, putting his hands on my waist.

'I have no idea.' I kiss him hard on the mouth and give zero shits when Mr Market Man heckles again. 'Get a room, you two lovebirds! This is Borough Market, not the Moulin Rouge!'

Forty-five minutes, one very heated black cab ride of my life later and we're in Edward's hotel room and he's in me.

THE NEXT MORNING, AFTER hours and hours of sex, chat, hair-stroking (oh, the hair-stroking: I love this about

Edward. Not *love* love, just, you know, really-quite-like) and copious amounts of room service (thank you, posh hotel on his work expenses), I roll over to look at my phone and see there are four missed calls from Lyla's drippy dad, Simon.

The last thing I want to do right now is ring my ex-fiancé while I'm naked, smelling of sex and in bed with another man, but I remind myself this isn't a video chat.

'Hi, Simon, I had some missed calls. Everything all right?' I say with a firm, businesslike tone.

'Well, yes. Ha. No, actually no. Lyla's a bit, um, sick.'

'Sick? As in she's been sick, or American "sick" when they mean "ill"?' I ask, frustrated that he's not being clear, and fearing something terrible.

'Erm, both, I suppose,' he stutters.

'What's happened?' I butt in before he dithers some more.

'Well, ah, Storie and I enrolled on a, er, wild mushroom course. We are thinking about setting up an organic herb and vegetable business from Storie's mother's garden, so we were researching the new venture . . .' He seems to think I should know what that means. That's just a fact, not an explanation. What is wrong with my little girl?

'And?' I query, growing more frustrated.

'And yesterday we were encouraged, erm, to let Mother Nature blend with us during our mushroom, er, exploration.' He stops.

'Blend with you? What do you mean, Simon? What's actually happened?'

'We think Lyla, possibly, has let Mother Nature blend with her, and—'

'What are you talking about, Simon? Just speak normally without all this Mother Nature bullshit!' I snap, frantic to know what's happened to Lyla.

'Lyla's eaten some wild foliage she found near the mushrooms, we don't know what it was exactly but we do know she didn't have . . . er . . . have an . . . erm . . . actual mushroom, just some wild herbs. She's been up all night being sick and Storie's remedies aren't working,' Simon gabbles, panicked.

'For fuck's sake, Simon! Why didn't you call me straight away? What the hell kind of remedies has Storie given her?' I feel like I'm about to explode. I've completely forgotten that Edward is sitting naked and concerned next to me and all I feel is guilt that my sweet baby girl is in pain and I'm not there, but sprawled out in a luxury hotel room with a man, instead. I'm disgusted at myself.

'We were dealing with it. We thought she'd be OK,'

Simon says with a hint of irritation in his usually pitiful tone.

'Well, call the doctor. I'm coming home right now and I'll pick her up in a couple of hours, OK? She needs to be with her mum. I'm in London at the moment. On a job. In the meantime, give her plenty of water, take her temperature, administer Calpol and don't give her any more of Storie's Mother Nature crap!'

I stab my finger at the screen and hang up, furious.

Edward reaches out a hand to stroke my bare back and I pull my knees up to my chest and let out a couple of huge sobs. I don't even care that he's seeing me like this. I couldn't be more vulnerable right now, crying and naked, but I feel so wretched on the inside, it doesn't compare.

'Oh, Robin. Are you all right? Can I do anything to help?' he says softly.

'I need to go, Edward. My daughter's not very well and her father seems to be utterly incompetent,' I say, wiping my eyes hard and smearing even more make-up about than I did half an hour ago when my head was face down on the 1,000-thread-count sheets.

'I heard . . .' he carries on stroking my back '. . .I heard.' He plants a little kiss on the top of my head. 'He sounds a bit flustered.'

'Sorry to ruin the fun,' I say, turning to him.

'Don't worry at all. You're her mum, you've got to go. This can wait till next time,' he says gently and not wincing at all at the sight of my messed-up face.

Wow, he's nice. Calm in a crisis.

I smile weakly, nuzzle into his shoulder briefly, climb out of bed, shower quickly, throw my crumpled things into my bag and leave with a kiss on the lips that was perhaps more lingering than I meant it to be.

STORIE WAS A MESS when I arrived at theirs, having lucked out with a fast train. Lyla looked pale and tired, Simon looked the same as ever (smudged glasses and unkempt hair) but Storie had clearly been crying. Her maxi-dress looked even more crumpled than usual and her kohl was smudged all over her eyes. I found it hard to summon sympathy. The woman had let my precious baby nearly poison herself and didn't seem able to explain to me what the doctor had advised.

'Mother Earth does not want to harm her, Robin,' she blithered as I wrapped Lyla's coat around her frail, little body, cradling my phone under my ear with my shoulder as I called NHS 111.

'I'm sure she doesn't, Storie, but you don't let bloody seven-year-olds eat God knows what from the forest floor!'

I huffed, far too angry to handle Storie and her hippy ways or even to mind my language round Lyla.

After a temperature check I drove my little girl home to a fluffy nest of pillows, blankets and dressing gowns on the sofa.

We're just going to take it easy for the rest of the day. The lady on the phone told me to keep an eye on her, keep her fluids up and call back if her temperature changes, so that's the plan. Why this was such a hard plan for Simon and Storie to handle I will never know, but I'm happier at home with my girl than leaving them to it.

I'm starting to feel a bit sick myself in sympathy. What we both need now is a good night's sleep. Tomorrow is a brand-new day . . .

THANKFULLY, LYLA'S TEMPERATURE STAYED normal and there was no more sickness, so school on Monday is a go-ahead. I feel like I'm coming down with something – when you're so hyper-focused on your child's well-being, it rubs off and manifests itself in weird ways.

Since I'm not feeling tip-top, I can't say I've made a huge amount of effort for the school run. It's April but one of those bitterly cold days still, so it's skinny jeans, fake Uggs, a sweater and a giant puffer jacket. This, I feel, is still a distinct step up from the PJs-under-my-coat look of last year and so is to be commended.

As we walk in I spot a familiar weasel-like figure: Valerie Pickering, my least-favourite school mum and all-round misery guts. Naturally, Val is oblivious to the weather and is wearing jeans so skinny they could have been sprayed on, a black silk cami and a tiny three-quarter-sleeve blazer emblazoned with some designer logo I don't recognise. Her hair is slicked back into such a tight ponytail I can't tell if she's got a Botox top-up or just a really good hair bobble, and her make-up is equally severe.

I'm not in the mood for the 'Val Experience' today – Skye handed in our proposal to Natalie on Friday and we're having her feedback this morning, and the sooner I get to the office the better – so I walk purposefully by with a small smile and a 'Morning, Val,' as I go.

'Charming!' calls Val as I walk through the door, holding Lyla's hand. She literally cannot help herself.

'Pardon?' I say, turning around unenthusiastically.

'Well, I thought you'd have more to say than that,' Val says with a wry smirk, but I see the hint of vulnerability in her eyes. Against my own better judgement, I feel sorry for her. She never seems to have any friends, these dieting issues obviously come from her deep-seated unhappiness, her husband has left her and all her conversation seems to be sniping at people she sees as less than her.

Well, I'm not biting. Not today.

'Sorry, I don't follow,' I say.

'I heard you'd taken the minutes for the latest PaGS meeting a couple of weeks back, and you still haven't sent them out to us parents,' she says.

Why does she care so much about the minutes? They are basically the same every month – we never do anything that thrilling. It's organising a raffle here and there, coordinating parent volunteers for the children's disco . . .

I look back at her, lost for words.

'I thought now you're an *ambassador* for the parents, you'd make more of an effort with the other mothers, but I can see you're barely even making an effort with yourself. Are you styling yourself on the Michelin man now, or is it just the newest way to disguise a bit of weight gain?' She gives a small tinkly laugh and saunters off in her heels.

I stand there, stunned. What a bitch. I take a deep breath and try to be zen. She has a shit life right now and can't help but let her nastiness seep out. I should pity her; I do pity her. If I had more energy, I'd obviously say something witty and dignified back but right now I just need to drop Lyla off at her Early Risers Club and get to work.

'What did she mean, Mummy? Why would you wear a disguise?' Lyla asks, looking up at me, still holding my hand and not fully grasping Val's dig.

'Is it bad to gain weight? Do you need to eat your dinners from little boxes and do the DASH diet?'

I can't face trying to give her another enriching life lesson today, but I don't want to hear about this bloody diet again. 'Do you know what, my love? Valerie doesn't feel nice on the inside and so she is struggling to be nice on the outside. She feels rotten, so she's saying nasty things to try and make other people feel sad too. We can choose not to listen to her. We can choose to be beautifully happy on the inside and let that shine through to other people. Plus, I think she must have fallen out of bed on the wrong side this morning and is just being a massive grumpy-guts!' I laugh. Hopefully that was enriching enough.

Lyla finds this a suitable answer, laughs with me (I force out another little chuckle) and we walk down to the Early Risers room and say bye-bye for the day.

NINE

PARKED UP OUTSIDE MADE IT, I take a deep breath, check myself in the rear-view mirror (I'd put a little bit of emergency make-up on in the school car park; you can't turn up to a key meeting at a modelling and make-up agency looking like shit on a stick, after all), pinch my cheeks a bit to add some more colour, flick my hair and step out into the chilly air.

I feel sick with nerves knowing today's the day Natalie feeds back on all of mine and Skye's efforts. Should I have gone with the holographic body art extravaganza?

'Natalie's waiting in your office with Skye,' Alice says as I walk past the front desk.

What? Why are they already in? It's only 8.50. I'm not

late. What if they open my office drawers and see all my half-eaten snacks and notepads of doodles that I do when I can't get my thoughts flowing?

I walk briskly down the short corridor as if getting there a nanosecond earlier will make any difference, and reason with myself that they are probably waiting with big smiles at how incredible the proposal is. I know it is. I went through every page last week and all Skye had to do was add in the example photos, product links and references. It's a good, strong piece of work. I am a good, strong woman.

Fuck, I want to throw up.

I open the door and step in.

NATALIE'S FACE LOOKS LIKE thunder and if Skye had it in her to show a full range of emotions, I think she'd be crying.

Natalie sits on my side of the desk and gestures me to sit down. I don't even take my coat off.

'I founded the agency on integrity, equality and hard work,' Natalie says, looking at me directly before she even says hello.

'Er, yes.' This is ridiculous. I glance at Skye and she's staring straight ahead, avoiding my gaze. 'I'm sorry, I don't know what's—'

'Is the Mara Isso job a joke to you?' Natalie interrupts, every muscle in her face tense.

'What? No. Why would it be?' I'm getting a bit annoyed now. I feel like I'm being assaulted and I don't know why.

'What's this?' Natalie spits, holding out the proposal documents so tightly I can see the bones of her knuckles straining against her skin.

I take them off her, look at the cover page, look back at her, squint and reply, 'The proposal. Are you unhappy with it?'

'Unhappy with it? I'm horrified by it! If that had gone out our entire reputation would have been in jeopardy. MADE IT would be ruined!' Natalie is almost hysterical. She's usually unflappable but today something has definitely flapped her. 'It would get round the whole industry, we'd lose everything from wedding bookings all the way up to the film franchise job!'

'Natalie, this is unfair. I have worked very hard on this and so has Skye. We do think that natural beauty is the way forward, and I do think those plus-size models are more than enough to light up that runway without all the extra frills and thrills. If you don't like the idea then we can change it, but I don't think it's agency-ruining.' I look at her blankly. I've said my bit. She's clearly going mad. I'm a bit scared but I'm not going to let that show right now. The world's gone topsy-turvy.

'Then why on earth have you called them "*fatties*"?' she says, breathing heavily.

'*What*?' I'm entirely lost.

Skye finally moves, takes the papers out of my hand and flips to page four. *It all looks fine,* I think as I scan through the blurb about natural beauty, see a good stock picture of a stunning plus-size lady on the catwalk and below, a list of cosmetics.

'I'm sorry, I'm still—'

Skye jabs a finger at the slightly smaller, italic font under the photo of the model. '*Insert fatty pic here.*' What the actual fuck?

I turn more pages and in tiny type under every picture Skye's inserted, it says, '*Insert fatty pic here*', '*Fatty pic here*'. The more I turn, the more I see and I feel like my heart is in my throat.

I'd asked Skye to do the references and stock imagery and she'd obviously made that awful little note for herself to break up where each shot would go and then not removed it. What a cock-up, what a horrendous cock-up.

'Natalie, I'm so sorry, we—' I begin, and glance at Skye, who's looking at the floor.

'I put you in charge of this, Robin,' Natalie says, cutting

me off again. 'I put my faith and trust in you. I was relying on you. You've been my right-hand woman all these months and I thought you'd do a good job.'

'Yes, you did. Skye and I worked on this idea and feel it's the right fit for the job,' I begin, not really knowing where I'm going with this. 'I think it's a good thing that we have found this error and have time to rectify it, and then we can send this strong proposal off and focus on the next steps.' Wow, I've surprised even myself with that.

'Who did this?' Natalie says without a jot of recognition for what I've just said.

Skye is now staring blankly ahead, perhaps in shock, and I look at Natalie. She must know I didn't do it but I can't throw Skye under the bus. This isn't the headmaster's office that time Ruth Ogalvie spat in Ms Simpson's paintbrush water. This is real life. Adult life. And what Skye has done *is* horrifying.

'I want an explanation. A justification for this sloppy, offensive error,' Natalie says, a tad calmer but not much.

I wish Skye would own up to it, but she's turned mute and is apparently paralysed. Cool, thanks Skye.

'I managed this part of the proposal and I must take responsibility for it, Natalie,' I say with clenched jaw. I wish I'd read it through before it was sent over to Natalie.

I wish I'd managed this better; I wish I'd insisted I double-checked it all. It's too late now, though. I'm going to have to take this very painfully on the chin.

I turn my head a fraction to look at Skye. One of the bones in her jaw moves the tiniest amount in recognition of me giving her the perfect opening to own up, to take her mistake into her own hands. The pause feels like a lifetime, but she's as frozen as one of those street performers who paint themselves silver and pretend to be statues. She does not own up. I can feel my chest, neck and face reddening. I'm having to take this. Natalie is going to think I make stupid mistakes but, worst of all, that I would label anyone 'fatty,'. That I would be so derogatory. Fucking Skye. Fucking me. *Why* didn't I do one last read-through?

Natalie stares at me for a moment, looks over to Skye, who makes zero eye contact, and then looks back at me. I can't work out what she's thinking. Bloody hell, she'd be good at poker. Then her face seems to soften.

'OK. Robin, you're off the job.' She says this with such disappointment in her voice I want to cry. It's worse than her fury. She takes a breath. 'I'll have to fix this up and send it off. I'll let you know how we get on with it.' She gets up to leave.

'But it was my idea. I love this concept!' I say in alarm.

'Robin, this is unacceptable. Take the day off. Skye, get back to work. I'm going home to fix this and think about what, if anything, I can trust either of you with. I'm utterly let down,' Natalie says as she gathers all her papers together and picks up her phone and Chloé bag.

As she leaves, I feel tears welling up. I didn't deserve that. I worked hard on that proposal, and Skye's obnoxious views have shot it down in flames. But I'm an idiot, too, I tell myself. I was working too hard, too tired to stop mistakes like this getting through. Maybe Natalie *was* wrong to trust me. I look up at Skye, still silent, and I feel my rage bubble up again. I shouldn't have taken the blame for her. Now, because I tried to do the honourable thing, I'm probably going to get sacked. If I lose my job how will I afford the house? How will I look after Lyla? What will I say to Kath? Skye leaves silently behind Natalie. She doesn't even look at me on the way out.

THE REST OF THE day is miserable. I decide not to go home, despite Natalie telling me I should. If I go, I'll just wallow, so instead I stay and sort through all my usual admin, ensure the rotas are in good order, make a few calls about upcoming jobs and book myself onto all the straightforward ones for next week because I want to keep busy.

The morning's events have left me utterly exhausted and the sick feeling hasn't dissipated. But it's no bug making me feel ill – I'm sick to the core with the humiliation of it all. It's like that feeling you had when you were at school and your dad says he expected so much more of you when you got a D in your Physics mock-GCSE. It's that same horrible physical shame all over again.

Lyla is back with Simon tonight (now fully recovered from wild-herb-vom-gate and a bottle of Calpol packed in her rucksack to live at Daddy's amongst the St John's Warts or whatever it's called) to make up for his lost day yesterday, and the thought of an evening of soup for one doesn't seem all that appealing.

On the drive home I give Lacey a call to see if she wants to pop over. I could do with a bit of girl time. Maybe a makeover night like the olden days, or a few glasses of wine to drown my sorrows. I worked so hard on the proposal, and I desperately want Natalie to know it wasn't me. I would never call someone a 'fatty'. I'm not Valerie Pickering, for God's sake! I think of all my efforts to teach Lyla about body positivity, all wasted. I consider telling Natalie the truth but I'm scarred by the time in junior school I 'grassed up' Gary Boldman and he threw gravel at my face during lunch break and yelled,

'Snitches get stitches!' I didn't need stitches but I have always steered clear of telling on anyone ever again. I'm mortified by it all. I'm mortified by what Natalie must think of me now. I need a friend.

The phone rings and a chirpy voice answers. 'Hi!'

'You sound very chirpy for five on a Monday evening,' I say, smiling for the first time since the morning. It's nice to hear cheer. Maybe it'll seep into me and I'll feel it too.

'Karl's coming home early and we're having a bit of an evening,' she says with emphasis on 'evening'.

'Oh, very nice. I don't suppose my offer of wine and chit-chat is any competition for an *evening* with Karl, then, is it?' I say, half hoping that actually it is.

'Ah, I'd have loved to but I'm ovulating,' Lacey says as though that's a perfectly normal thing to say.

'Um, OK . . .'

'I've bought these kits. They tell you when you're at peak fertility and today's the day. If we don't do it today, we have less chance of fertilisation this month. We didn't do it yesterday to strengthen his sperm so they're in maximum condition tonight,' she says perkily.

'Oh wow, that sounds super sexy,' I joke.

'Needs must! I'm determined to do everything I can before we turn to IVF, and if the stick says I'm fertile, I'm going in!'

'More like he is!' I say, and we both laugh.

Good for her, I think as we hang up. I'm glad she's happy and I'm glad she's going to have an *evening* with Karl. I hope he's as up for it as she is.

By the time I get home, dump my bag and coat in the hallway and pour myself a glass of wine, I feel a bit calmer.

I sit down at the breakfast bar, flicking aimlessly through my Insta, and think about Lacey and how rubbish it must be to constantly test for ovulation, map out every date and diarise every period. Thinking of periods, I remember to flick to my nifty little app that tells you the exact date your next one is due, as I'm sure mine's this week. A big old dose of cramps and mood swings is just what I need when I'm feeling this drained and crap.

I tap open the app and the home screen telling me how many days long my cycle is flashes up.

What the fuck? Why has my cycle been thirty-nine days? That's not right. I'm a twenty-eight-day-er, every month since I was about fourteen, apart from when I had Lyla. The app must be faulty. I flick to my iCal to see when I last had my period and my heart stops. It *was* that long ago. And there was the pink champagne and macaroni cheese night. I was so drunk. I know we used the condoms I bought, but it was such a long night with so many goes. Did we properly use one for every go? We can't have. I can't actually remember . . .

Fuck my life.

Am I *pregnant*?

THE PERILS OF PINK CHAMPAGNE

TEN

THE NEXT TWENTY-FOUR HOURS are a blur.

I spend the night alternating between total denial, sipping my wine and flicking through trash on TV (particularly the ones where young people are cooped up in giant warehouses and only let out to get wasted and shag each other – none of them get knocked up, do they?), staring at the dates, googling symptoms like sickness and fatigue, starting to accept the inevitable, feeling guilty for sipping the wine and trying to build up the courage to go out and buy a pregnancy test.

I think about doing a test at least a hundred times, but know once I've done it and the little blue lines flash up, it will be real. But even without one, I think I already know it's real. This isn't my first rodeo and I know what being pregnant feels like. Still, if I don't take the test I can simply pretend it's not happening. I can drink this glass of wine and not feel bad, I can carry on with my happy, single life and tell myself nothing is changing.

But my head is spinning.

Oh, God.

Lyla doesn't need a sibling right now. For the first time in a long time, everything is going well. Lyla's thriving at the school she's lucky enough to go to because of Granny Wilde's money, we have our network of Posh School Mums, or PSMs, for play dates and birthday parties and Kath loves to babysit. Asking her to look after Lyla – a potty-trained, communicative child – is one thing, but asking her to deal with a baby, too, so I can work? My job (until the shit-show today, I remember with a lurch) has been going well enough to fund our lifestyle. Basically, after so long doubting myself, I've finally stopped feeling like a totally shit mum. I can't manage going through all that early stuff again.

I try to imagine telling Lyla that I am going to have another baby. How would I even begin to explain it to her? How would I explain this to *anybody*? I think about work. Natalie already hates me, thanks to Skye and her 'fatty pics'. I can't imagine that she'd be thrilled to hear 'I'm pregnant', after investing so much faith in me and giving me the huge bonus and promotion last year. Of course Natalie's not the type to make it hard for women – but it's still not an easy conversation to have with your boss. And would I have to let go of all I've achieved? How on earth would maternity leave work? I've only just gone from freelance to fully employed, so I don't even know what I'm entitled to. I think about my hefty new mortgage. It was different last time. Simon was a financial help (if useless in all other ways). I'd have to go from badass single mum to broke-ass single mum.

And how would I tell my mother? She's never been the same, since the 'biggest mistake of my life', which was leaving nice, safe, dependable Simon, even though I've explained time and time again that he was the one who cheated on and left me. 'He was going through a midlife crisis, dear. It happens to a lot of men!' she'd say from her house in Cornwall that she helpfully moved to shortly after Lyla was born. He was in his mid-twenties – it was not a midlife crisis, despite what Mum or any of the ladies from the Rotary Club think. Kath, I think, would handle it well – after the initial shock – so at least there's the chance of some emotional support there.

And then there's the biggest question. How would I tell Edward? 'Oh, hi, Edward, I'm so casual, so breezy, it's cool you live across a whacking great ocean and we're not in a relationship because now I'm having your baby and we are bound together for the rest of our lives . . . do you want to talk about shared custody now, or once you've thrown up with the shock?'

This is a mess!

The next morning, I wake up after tossing and turning all night, and for a split second, I've forgotten. Everything is beautifully normal and all I have to do is get up and go to work. The nausea hits me first, the moment my bare feet land on the carpet, and then the sinking realisation that I am probably pregnant.

I can't face going into MADE IT, so I text Natalie (I can't even face ringing her) to say I'll be working from home but that I am available if she needs me at all. She has read receipts turned on so I know she's read it, but she doesn't reply. Her biggest issue with me right now is the botched proposal. I wish that was my biggest issue, too.

After a twenty-minute stint on the bathroom floor with some delightful waves of sickness and a small, self-pitying weep, I reluctantly scoop myself up, throw on a white T-shirt and some navy velour tracksuit bottoms (if there's ever a time for velour, this is it), head downstairs and force myself to nibble at a slice of toast and drink a cup of tea with extra sugar. Everyone makes tea in a crisis. Tea solves everything . . . Except it doesn't.

How has this happened? People try for months and years to get pregnant but can't, and here I am, pregnant after one boozy night of pink champagne and mac 'n' cheese.

Oh my Jesus in heaven. *Lacey*. Of all the people I know, how on earth will I break this to her? How can I be so awful as to show any hint of this pregnancy being unplanned and unwanted when there is literally nothing in the world she wants more right now than to be pregnant herself? Oh, what have I done?

OK. Thinking about Lacey helps me take stock of the situation and come out of my own head. If I'm pregnant then I'm pregnant. I need to know. I need a test.

I decide to drive to a supermarket forty-five minutes away to avoid any chance of seeing someone I know while buying the test. It feels like a huge neon beacon in my basket, so I walk round the shop and add in all sorts of crap I definitely don't need, just to dilute the presence of the little box. I threw it in hastily after spending as little time as possible perusing the different versions. How ironic that they stack the pregnancy tests next to the condoms. *Bit late for that now*, I think. Or maybe they're there as a warning. 'Don't use a condom and just look what happens,' I imagine a judgy middle-aged woman saying to me. Possibly my mother, although

I can't envisage her actually using the word 'condom', she'd mouth 'protection' instead.

Sitting at home, after using the self-service till to mitigate any chance of conversation re the box of potential doom then driving back feeling sick and panicked, I look at the white and blue stick on the kitchen worktop. *It's not a big deal,* I tell myself. *Women handle this every day. I can handle anything. It might be negative. Maybe I have a bug and my period is just weirdly late. It's still an option.*

A cup of tea later, half to soothe, half to help with the peeing-on-demand situation, I take the test into the downstairs loo and contort my arm into an undignified position to wee on the stick that will decide my fate.

There. Done. Test taken.

I put it on a square of tissue (I have just peed on it, after all), wash my hands as slowly as possible to put off the inevitable and finally take a look.

Pregnant. Fully and totally with child, pregnant.

Dealing with this in the most pragmatic and mature way I know how, I throw the stick in the bin, grab a selection of healthy items from the kitchen (a chocolate orange, two packets of Skips, a child's smoothie carton and a banana) and head upstairs to spend the rest of the day in bed.

By 3 p.m. I've managed to sleep and brainlessly gazed

at daytime TV for long enough to numb the shock and so the outing to collect Lyla from school is significantly less stressful than the outing to the shops this morning. I summon all my Magic Mum energy (this is very similar to the mum powers of holding 850 items in one arm, and I got a lot of practice during those grim days when I was trying to hide The Emptiness), swoop her up and switch into full autopilot as we head home. We talk about her time with her dad, go through spellings and homework, I sympathise when she tells me Corinthia deliberately danced right in front of her in ballet (that's such a twatty Val-type thing to do), cook the dinner (tonight I actually enjoy spending time in the kitchen, baking a fish pie from scratch), wash her hair, blow-dry it and tuck her into bed. It comforts me to go through each step of our evening methodically and diligently, as if the more I channel myself into each task, the less I will channel my thoughts into the new life growing inside me and what I'm going to do about it.

As I settle onto Lyla's tiny single bed adorned with one duvet in a fancy frilly white cover (a John Lewis Christmas present from Mum, who clearly has no idea what little girls want from Father Christmas despite having been one and had one herself) and about six crocheted blankets from Kath that Lyla can't choose between and so has them all, propping myself up on cushions and cuddly toys to read her a bedtime story, the world feels very calm. I love this time of day.

The room is lit only by fairy lights and a small bedside lamp, Lyla smells delicious thanks to her strawberry shampoo and we are lost in a story about mice who live in hedgerows and adventure through the seasons, worrying only about collecting berries and taking care of each other. I relate to those little mice. All I really want to do in the world is collect what I need, take care of my sweet daughter and hole up in our cosy nest, blocking out the rest of the big, wide world. Lyla listens to the story carefully, gently stroking my arm without really realising as I read each page.

Once we've finished, I feel myself welling up. I've taken stock of how precious my life with her is, how much I love her and how I can't bear for things to change when I've only just got things as good as they are.

'Are you sad about the mice, Mummy?' Lyla asks quietly.

'No, silly Mummy's got something in her eye,' I whisper back, forcing a smile and nuzzling into a big cuddle with her.

'Silly old Mummy, I love you,' she says, cuddling back.

My heart feels like it might burst. Maybe another one like her wouldn't be so bad?

ELEVEN

THE BRIEF GLIMMER OF hope I had last night at story time dissipated this morning as I threw up while trying to make a ham sandwich for Lyla's lunchbox. It seems you can go from general queasiness to full-on routine vomming pretty quickly. Morning sickness is here to stay, then.

Great.

What was I thinking last night? I can't do this! I can barely manage our morning routine, let alone do the whole single motherhood shebang all over again from the start.

No.

I drop Lyla at school and flat-out ignore every other

human I walk past. People might have been speaking to me, I don't know, but I just keep my head down, hoping they can't tell I am secretly harbouring a new life in my womb. Am I emitting the 'glow' already? When I was aged sixteen and four-and-a-half days, I lost what I would describe as *half* my virginity to a boy called Oliver Mansell, despite secretly fancying Simon and wishing he'd get his act together to properly ask me out. As I walked the ten minutes home from his house, I remember wondering if passers-by could tell I was a 'woman' now that I'd had three shambolic pokes from a scrawny boy from the music college. I wanted to shout, 'Hi, yes, I am Robin Wilde and I am SEXUALLY ACTIVE,' with naive teenage pride. I feel a bit like that now, minus the wanting to shout about it. Can people tell? They might be able to see a bump or a sign. I really might be emitting that glow. Though probably not, given that I threw up forty-five minutes prior to getting in the car.

Lyla, thankfully, seems not to notice my inward panic and skips off to the cloakroom to hang up her coat and book bag without even a backwards look. Normally I'd feel a stab of pain that she can be so nonchalant, but today I'm just grateful that she exists in LylaLand and isn't worried about everything going on around her.

I can't face work today. I can't face anything.

Hi Natalie, I'm really sorry but I'm not feeling well today. I'm going to take the day off. If there are any emergencies I'll be here, but I think best not to pass anything on to anyone in the office. Ever so sorry, Robin xxx

I know I've gabbled on but I can't help it. I hope she doesn't read between the lines and see it for what it is: 'I am pregnant and freaking the fuck out.' *Of course she won't,* I tell myself, *that's totally paranoid.* But it's not working. I take some deep breaths. I've not said anything unusual; she won't suspect a thing.

Thank you for letting me know, comes Natalie's swift and sharp reply with no pleasantries. I should have rung but I feel too sick and tired to even care right now.

At home I dump my bag on the hall table and head up to bed to wallow in self-pity. No sooner am I in bed and having a habitual scroll through Facebook, than a message from Lacey pings up.

You're online! Aren't you at work?

Shit, I forgot to cunningly switch myself to 'appear offline'. Rookie error.

Oopsie! Meant to switch to invisible! Having a sick day! I reply, trying to sound normal.

Oh no! Are you poorly? Lacey replies straight away with a sickie emoji.

What do I say? I'm not poorly, I'm not OK, but for the

first time in our friendship, she's the last person I can chat to about this.

No, I'm OK, just worn out and fancied a home day to chill out, I lie.

Say no more! she replies with a wink face, OK hand sign and a shooting star. God, she loves those emojis. I go to reply but she's offline and I'm ready to pull the duvet up, take off my bra and hoodie, switch on the TV and gaze mindlessly again. I know I need to face all this eventually but one more day of hiding my head in the sand won't hurt. Tomorrow I'll book an appointment with the GP to discuss options, maybe even speak to Edward, tackle it head-on. But not today.

Forty-five minutes later, the doorbell rings. I haven't ordered any parcels and Kath's in town on a half-day pressed-flower course (I love that she takes herself off to do these things by herself, and always seems to have a ball), so I pull a crumpled T-shirt over my bare torso, schlep downstairs and go to see who it is. I'm assuming it's a delivery for one of the neighbours or a cold-caller, but see to my horror as I look through the peephole that it's Lacey.

'Yoohoo, I can see you through the glass! It's only me!' she sing-songs merrily.

I freeze.

'Hang on, just struggling with the lock,' I lie, as I deliberately make a big deal of wiggling the key about and opening the door.

'For someone who says they're not ill, you look like shit!' Lacey laughs, walking past me down the hall and into the kitchen.

'I've brought supplies,' she trills, plonking a Starbucks bag on the breakfast bar, diving in and pulling out fruit toast, butter, jam and setting down a tray with two large coffees in. The smell of it all wafting about makes me sway with nausea.

'Oh . . . great,' I say weakly, not managing to sound at all convincing.

'What's the matter?' she asks, sensing my lack of enthusiasm.

'Nothing, I'm just a bit tired,' I respond unconvincingly.

'Oh my God,' she whispers excitedly, 'he's here, isn't he? Upstairs! You've got a man in your bed!' You'd think we were fifteen again and she'd just caught me snogging in the school toilets. To be fair, that really was an exciting lunch break.

'What? No! Jesus! Definitely not. I'm just not feeling too well,' I say, trying to force out a little cough as if that's going to prove my point.

'I thought you said you were skiving,' she says,

narrowing her eyes and smiling as if I'm about to reveal some exciting gossip.

'I am, I suppose, but I'm also a bit under the weather,' I say as quickly as I can.

'So you're not skiving?' She's enjoying this cat-and-mouse game.

'Oh God, I don't know, Lacey! I'm just feeling a bit shit, OK?' I snap.

She instantly looks injured.

'Wow. Sorry. I'll just have a wee and then I'll leave you to it,' she says, half hurt, half annoyed.

Guilty and relieved at the same time, I sit down on one of the breakfast bar stools and watch her slink down the hallway, wondering if, when she goes, she'll take the Starbucks with her. Since when did everything smell so strong? Pregnancy is a strange beast. I feel terrible for stinging Lacey like that but it's better than telling her the truth. I'll have to apologise and make up something later about being on my period and feeling hormonal. If only.

I sit at the breakfast bar folding, unfolding and refolding the Starbucks napkins into little squares. Why is she taking so long? The mum in me almost shouts, 'Are you having a poo? Do you need the wet wipes?' but I'm not sure she'll appreciate that, especially after I've just rebuffed her.

Time ticks on. I look at the little digital clock on my shiny, chrome, built-in microwave (urgh, I love this new house so much) and it shows she's been in there over five minutes.

'Everything OK?' I shout.

She doesn't reply. Bloody hell, I hope she hasn't passed out or something.

'Lacey? You all right?' She's always been the more dramatic one but I can't imagine she'd be in that much of a huff with me that she'd lock herself in the loo and ignore me.

'Lacey? I'm getting a bit worried about you . . . If you don't answer, I'm going to get a coin and unlock the door,' I gently threaten.

At that, I hear the door unlock and Lacey's very slow footsteps come down the hallway. What's she playing at?

Oh my God.

Lacey is standing in the doorway of the kitchen, pale as a ghost, holding my positive pregnancy test in her hand. I'd thrown it in the bin yesterday intending to empty everything today for the big bins, but hadn't expected visitors.

Fuck. Fuck, fuck, actual fuck.

'Lacey, I . . .' I start and then trail off.

'Whose is this?' she says quietly and eerily calmly.

I just look at her, head tilted, mouth closed, desperately wishing she could read my mind and know how sorry I am that it's not hers.

'Is it yours?' she says, still calm.

'Lacey, I didn't mean for this, I never—'

'IS THIS YOURS?' she erupts, angry tears starting to fall down her cheeks. I've never seen such furious, hurt emotion. I don't know how to handle this at all.

'Yes. It is. It wasn't planned. It just happened.' As soon as the words tumble out of my mouth in a bid to soothe her, I know I've made it worse.

'What I'd give for it to "just happen" to me,' she says, leaning into the door frame for support, letting her hand, and the test, drop despairingly to her side and sobbing. 'I'm happy for you, but . . .'

'Lacey,' I say so gently I can feel my own tears starting to well, 'you don't have to be happy for me. I know this is so shit and so unfair and I am so sorry to hurt you in this way. You know I didn't do this deliberately.'

'I know that!' she says, anger bubbling again. 'I'm not stupid, I'm just fucking barren!' She cascades into a shout, throwing the pregnancy test halfway across the kitchen floor. Neither of us move to go and pick it up, we just stand and stare at it for a few moments.

This is getting intense. They don't give you instructions

on how to tell your desperate-for-a-baby friend on the side of the bloody pregnancy test, do they? Maybe they should include a helpful pamphlet covering some of the basics.

'You're not barren, it just hasn't happened yet,' I offer weakly.

'In the meantime, though, it's happening to every single other fucking person I fucking well fucking know.'

Wow, three 'fuckings' in one sentence.

'Lacey, I don't know what to say to make this better. I'm in an impossible position. If I say it wasn't planned, I hurt you. If I say it was planned, I hurt you. If I say I want it, I hurt you. If I say I don't want it, again, I hurt you. I know how much you want *this*, but I don't know how to make it right. I'm sorry. I'm sorry this happened to me and not to you, and I'm sorry you found out like this and I'm sorry we're even having this conversation! If I could offer you a magic wand to make everything better, you know I would!'

'You're in an impossible situation? Are you kidding me? You have everything right now! You already have one perfect, healthy child and now you're having another, but you stand there with the audacity to suggest you might not want it!'

'That's not what I'm saying,' I say, panicked.

'So you're keeping it?'

'I . . . I don't know. Yes, I think so.' As I finally say the words aloud, part of me panics, part of me wants to celebrate. But right now, I need to push all that to one side. For the moment, I need to concentrate on Lacey and the pain you can almost feel coming off her in waves.

'You *think* so? But you don't know so? You've been given the greatest thing anyone could ever be given, and you don't fucking know?' This is so hard.

'Lacey, you're being unfair. I'm not in your shoes. I don't have a Karl or stability or anything like that. I'm a single mum who just about has her shit together. You know how long it's taken me to get this far. To be even semi-stable.'

'So you're going to *abort* it?' Lacey practically spits.

'It's not that simple, Lacey! "Abort it" sounds so harsh.'

'Well, it is. It's wrong. You're wrong.' Wow. I know we all have different opinions, but I don't think she has the right to say it's flat out 'wrong'. This is my body. My life. My mess.

'I think this has gone too far. I know you're angry and I know this hurts, but you can't judge other people – judge me – based on your own circumstances. Try as we both might, we can't put ourselves in each other's shoes. I'm your best friend and I love you, always and forever, but at this moment, actually, I need that in return, Lacey.'

'I can't. I can't be that person right now. Not while you have everything I could ever want and I have nothing,' she says, almost in a whisper.

Her eyes drop to the floor but I can still see every bit of pain she's in.

'I'm sorry, Lace, I'm sorry,' I say, as big, fresh tears plop down onto my origami-folded napkin.

She walks over to the breakfast bar, stepping deliberately over the pregnancy test lying on the slate floor, and I think she's going to go in for a warm gesture like a hug or hand-hold but no, she silently picks up her bag, gives me a look so full of sadness and walks out of the house.

Lacey and I have been through all sorts together over the years. But I think of the look on her face as she left and this feels like the worst thing that could have happened to us. I take in a deep, slow breath to try to centre myself and, as I do, I catch the scent of the cooling coffee and throw up in my own hands.

Two hours go by and I feel no better. I spend what's left of the morning cleaning the house. I'm not normally one of those women who gets a kick out of new cleaning products or actually puts into practice any of the tips and tricks I watch on those speed-cleaning videos on YouTube, but today, it's cathartic. The more I tidy and wipe and wash and polish, the less I think about the future, the pregnancy test, Lacey, Lyla or me. I'm lost in the rhythm of making my house shiny.

One by one, I do every single room. I start in the kitchen by taking all the rubbish out, including the Starbucks that I would usually have enjoyed, emptying the fridge of anything gone off, wiping all the surfaces and mopping the floor. I get down on my hands and knees to wipe down the cupboard doors (and the little bit of sick splatter I made earlier). I take a wire brush to the stove and scrub it for much longer than I need to. I put all the dishes away, pair all of Lyla's snack boxes with snack box lids and disinfect the big old dining table. Arms already aching, I move into the hall, the lounge and then the downstairs loo, hoovering, mopping, polishing and wiping. I look at the wicker bathroom bin and feel a pang of pain for what's just happened but push it out of my mind.

I do this for hours. While I'm working, my brain is quiet. Then 3 p.m. chimes and, like a reverse Cinderella, I must change out of my rags into something more presentable, get into my carriage (well, my car) and drive to collect Lyla.

The usual gang – Gillian, Finola and someone I don't recognise, perhaps a new mum – are there but I rush past. 'Can't stop! I've left a chicken in the oven,' I say in a fake cheery voice, taking Lyla by the hand and bustling back to the car. There's no chicken in the oven. Unless the chicken is a bun and the oven is my womb.

I can't face going back home. The space between now and bedtime feels like an eternity and in that eternity I might think about the baby, think about Lacey, think about the decision I have to make – and right now, that's far too much.

I know exactly where I need to be.

I drive to Auntie Kath's. If there's anywhere you want to be in a crisis, it's there.

TWELVE

Stepping into Kath's house is like stepping into a cuddle. A teddy bear cuddle with sweet perfume. Sweet lavender perfume.

At first glance, Kath's house is an assault on the senses. Every surface you look at has a colour, pattern or texture. Swirly 1960s technicolor carpets, textured wallpaper in the hallway, flock wallpaper in the front room, orange and yellow floral murals hand-painted (by Kath and her late husband Derek in the 1980s) in the kitchen. In every alcove or corner there's shelving or a display case cluttered with frames and ornaments and mementos of Kath and Derek's adventurous lives together, trinkets they collected on their travels. Kath's taste in art is unique to say the least. She has no qualms about mixing classic oil paintings with modern prints, and no issues with putting ornate gold frames alongside white IKEA ones.

On the surface it sounds hideous, but once your eyes have adjusted to the myriad colours, it all works. The chintzy floral sofas with lace doilies and pompom cushions fit right in, and even Mollie the dog has a bed covered in rainbow crochet.

Today it seems a little more chaotic than usual with every available coffee table, worktop or shelf space covered in lavender crafting paraphernalia. She's really taking this phase further than all the others (including the time she hot-glued strips of lace to literally everything. Even my duvet was Kathed).

'Hello, love. I was just bottling up my latest batch of creams for the WI. I'm giving them samples for their Spring Family Fun Day,' Kath says as we mooch through to the kitchen and plonk ourselves down at the table overflowing with bottles, jugs and labels.

'You're doing really well with all this,' I say, absent-mindedly picking bits up and putting them down again.

Kath notices my lacklustre attitude and sends Lyla through to the front room to watch videos. Kath is the only person I know who still has a VHS machine. She buys children's videos at car boot sales and in charity shops and Lyla absolutely loves them.

Once Lyla's scampered off with a plate of peeled and chopped-up apple (Kath is the kind of loving person who washes, peels and chops fruit. She's a better woman than I), I take a deep breath.

'Kath, I'm not having a good day,' I say, looking studiously at the table in case by making eye contact she reads my mind and works it all out.

'Are you not, lovey? Do you want some of my lavender essential oils? Moira's been putting some in her bath at night and says Allan's never been more attentive. Even more so than with the cream I made her. She said it's been years since he took it upon himself to go—'

'No!' I interrupt urgently. 'I don't need any oils.' I really don't think I can face the rest of Moira and Allan's re-invigorated love story. 'Thank you, though, really lovely of you. But I think I'm going to need more than oils for the trouble I'm in.'

'Is it the bank? I know you're working hard but that big mortgage is a lot on your shoulders, petal,' Kath says, sitting down at the table too.

'No, it's not that, it's . . .'

'It's man trouble, then, isn't it? Has that wrong'un Theo been sniffing around again? I tell you, if I ever get my hands on him he'll certainly know about it!'

Bless Kath for constantly being in my corner.

'Man trouble of a sort, I suppose. It's all because of a man – well, because of me and a man and a stupid bottle of pink Moët. And I think it's going to lead to more man trouble, anyway.'

I look at Kath and I can tell from her face that she's worked it out. Kath's not stupid, and she's certainly read enough romance novels to know what man plus woman plus champagne plus trouble equals.

She reaches across the table and takes hold of my hand, with a questioning expression on her lovely face.

I nod slowly and my eyes start to well up. Without meaning to, my other hand moves to rest on my stomach. I flinch.

'Robin, you're not alone. I love you and I love Lyla and between you, me and her, we'll have enough love for this baby,' she says, squeezing my hands extra hard.

With that, I let myself cry more big, fat tears. This time, though, they're not tears of sadness or pain, they're tears of relief. I'm not alone, there is someone to stand by me and love me and not judge me. Any last thoughts I had of not keeping this baby leave me and I know that whatever happens, I'm going to have to make the most of it. Kath continues to hold my hand very tightly.

'I know, lovey, I know. It's a lot but you are so much stronger than you think. I'm constantly amazed by you and how much you can do. Look at all you've achieved: Lyla is a treasure, your new job, your beautiful home, all your gallivanting about!'

'It's all that gallivanting that's got me in this mess!' I say, and try to smile through my tears.

'This is not a mess, my love. This is a blessing wrapped up in a mess. All we have to do is have a think, sort out a plan and look at all the positives.'

'But I'll have to raise it by myself, I don't think I can do it.' The idea of having a newborn again is overwhelming, especially on my own. Simon wasn't good at a lot of things but he was good at helping me in the night, making tea, taking Lyla out in the pram so I could sleep. I won't have any of that this time. Edward's on the other side of the sodding planet.

'Don't think you can do it? Look at Lyla! You're already doing it, and you're doing a blooming marvellous job of it! Has he said he's not interested, then? This chap with the pink Moët?' She's let go of my hand now and is fiddling with a bottle top while she tries to piece it all together.

'The chap is Edward, the one from New York who comes over.' Kath nods in understanding, having heard about our brief encounter last year and knowing we've messaged a bit since then. 'And he hasn't said anything yet because he doesn't know. I only found out a couple of days ago and all I've done since is cry, be sick and clean my house to distract myself.'

'Well, there we are, some positives already, your house is clean! That'll save me a job when I next come over,' she says, smiling and rubbing my arm enthusiastically until I relent and let out a weak laugh.

'I suppose so.'

'Now, we don't know that this Edward isn't interested until you speak to him. You're going to have to tell him at some point and the sooner you do, the better. Derek always used to tell me, "Half the job is in starting", so why don't we start now?'

'Start how?' I feel horrified that she might just grab the landline and ring him up. 'Hello, this is Auntie Kath and Robin has something she wants to tell you' isn't going to go down well. Of course she isn't, though. It's not 1998, and even Kath has a mobile. I eye it on the table and hope she's not going to proffer it to me.

'You could write him a letter. That way he has time to digest and come back to you. I've got some lovely stationery upstairs, shall I fetch it?' OK, so it's 1948 now and we're corresponding by snail mail.

'As much as I'd love to use the lovely stationery' – God bless Kath – 'I think I'll go for an email instead. It'll reach him quicker,' I add to spare her from feeling like I've spurned her ink and quill.

'Righty-ho. Remember, though, whatever happens, this will be all right. I'm here, you've got all those nice new friends at the school, Lyla will be more help than you think and Lacey, I'm sure, will be thrilled that you're expecting. She loves babies, doesn't she?'

Then I tell Kath about earlier with Lacey. Kath fully understands. She and lovely Derek, a wonderful, kind man who we truly miss, never had children. I've never really questioned this, I don't know how I would even try to ask for more details, but I've always assumed it was a similar set-up to Lacey and that that's why she's always so sympathetic. She really is the best, my auntie Kath.

Less than an hour later, my tears are dried, I've had several more pep talks from Kath about how this is a blessing in disguise and Mollie the dog has offered me her soggy favourite toy several times. Now the table is laden with buttered new potatoes, green beans, perfectly cooked carrots and tender chicken breasts. Lyla comes in just as it's being dished up, bleary-eyed from zoning out in front of the TV.

'Is this the chicken in the oven?' she asks.

'Pardon?' I say, confused.

'You told the other mums we had a chicken in the oven.'

'Oh, yes, I suppose it is,' I laugh, thinking how everything turns out OK when Kath's around. Maybe this lovely family moment with my girls is a sign of things to come. Maybe it will all be OK.

THIRTEEN

THE NEXT DAY I'M back in work. I already feel like I've let Natalie down completely, and I know she's still deciding what to do about my part in that horrible pitch document fuck-up. I need to fix things. I know from the calendars that she's not in today, she's on a shoot, so I figured I'd go in, work hard and keep my head down.

I've been sick twice already by 10 a.m. (once before I woke Lyla up for school and once just after I'd dropped her off, darting quickly back into the house before I spewed in the car), but thanks to heavy-duty concealer and super-absorbent translucent powder, we're all good. Thank God for a good mask of make-up.

I've gone for skinny jeans (hooray for New Look adding elastane to their denim) and a loose shirt. I know there's no bump there – other than the usual squashy tummy – but I'm paranoid and don't want to face any conversation or speculation at all. Hair in a high ponytail (a practical necessity when you keep having to lean over a toilet) and diamond stud earrings (I say diamond, I mean whatever it is Accessorize puts in their jewellery) and I think I actually look quite good. Maybe I have got that 'glow' after all!

After a quick chat with Alice and Stuart about the 'mystery bug I must have caught from one of the children at school', I get into a rhythm working through the pile of admin they have put on my desk. Then Skye knocks on the door. She enters before I've even said 'Come in'.

Skye actually looks a bit sheepish. Usually she's such a powerhouse of poise and opinions, so to see her with even slightly slumped shoulders is strange. She's wearing black gym leggings and a baggy hoodie with her hair in a messy topknot. In fact, she looks almost fragile.

'Robin, hey, I . . . er . . . I just wanted to say I'm sorry about last week. I should have said something but I froze,' she fumbles, looking even more fragile than she did a second ago, still hovering by the door.

'Why don't you sit down,' I offer.

'I know I shouldn't have left those . . . bits . . . in there. I should have deleted them before I sent Natalie the proposal, I just forgot. They were just there to remind me to slot in the shots, you know? And I know I should have just said something but I didn't want Natalie to fire me. I need this job, I love it, it's the only thing I'm good at, really. I was going to talk to you sooner but you've had that bug and I thought you'd be really angry so, yeah, sorry. And thanks, I guess.' Skye looks at me. Even though she's just been so open and she doesn't have on her usual armour of tight clothes and fierce brows, she still has an unreadable face. She'd make a good spy.

For a second, I think of all the things I could say to her. I settle on, 'Thank you for coming and saying that, Skye.' I want to go into this some more because she hasn't actually apologised for *what* she wrote, just for not deleting them before Natalie saw, but I'm feeling delicate and right now – not least because my job hangs in the balance because of this – I'll take what I'm given, half-arsed apology or not.

'Yeah. Well . . . I owe you,' she adds, confidence returning a little to her voice now she knows I'm not going to go absolutely crazy at her or demand she tells Natalie the truth.

'OK, that's good to know,' I say, finishing the conversation. Thankfully, Skye senses the tone and leaves. We're never going to be friends, but at least we're on decent terms now. I wish I could feel that way about Natalie, too. I've not heard from her, and there's nothing in my inbox from her either.

I take a deep breath. Only a few days ago I couldn't imagine a bigger mess than my work woes. But the pregnancy makes it pale in comparison. It's time to face it head-on.

Like lovely Derek used to say, 'half the job is in starting', so I open up my email and type in Edward's name. What have I got to lose? We were never an item, we were never a thing. Yes, deep down in my core perhaps I occasionally let myself daydream about more, but I've got to accept it's not going to happen. Right now, I just need to make him aware of the situation. We're not emotionally connected. I just need to be clear and to the point. I can absolutely do this. Kath reminded me of my inner strength last night, so I'm channelling that as I begin to type.

'Dear Edward'. No, that's too weird and formal. 'Hey Edward'. *No*, you can't tell a man you're growing his baby inside you with a 'hey'. Bloody hell, this is even harder than I thought it would be.

I take a swig of full-fat cherry Coke. Oh dear, is that bad for the baby? I ought to do some research on what you can and can't have – it seems I've forgotten everything I knew with Lyla.

After agonising for a while, I realise I just need to be myself. Despite the two of us getting pretty damn intimate, this will be the most open, the most personal moment I've ever actually had to have with this man, and so I think the best thing to do is just say it how it is. Yes. Here we go.

Edward,

It feels weird to be emailing you rather than just dropping you a text but when you read the rest of what I'm about to say, you'll see why this was best.

I wish you lived nearby so we could nip out for lunch and I could tell you face to face, but as much as I'd love a Sarabeth's New York brunch right now, I don't think it's going to happen.

I have really enjoyed spending time with you this last few months. You're fun and easy-going and that's exactly what I was looking for, even though I wasn't really looking at all.

The thing is, I think all of that's going to come to an end when I tell you this next thing.

I'm pregnant.

I found out three days ago and have been in shock until now. I think it was the Balthazar night. I hadn't planned any more children in my future and for a couple of days wondered if I would even go through with this, but I have decided that I will.

I don't know what your thoughts are on all this but I will say, nothing is expected of you. I've thought really hard and I'm prepared to do this alone. I know I can do it, I've already done it with Lyla for all these years. I know you have your busy life and we are not in a relationship, so all I ask is that you take a bit of time to let this email sink in.

I'm sorry to spring this on you, I thought a 'letter' would be best so you didn't feel put on the spot by a phone call.

I don't really know how to finish an email like this, so I'll just leave it here and hope you are OK.

Robin x

I decide to limit it to one kiss after initially typing quite a few.

After reading and rereading it for about twenty minutes, I shut my eyes to gather myself, inhale sharply and press send. There we are then. He knows.

FOURTEEN

Walking into MADE IT a few days later, I feel almost peppy. Only one bout of sickness this morning, after nibbling on ginger biscuits, and I've donned another confidence-boosting stretchy-jeans-and-loose-T-shirt combo. Hair in a messy bun with about 3lbs of kirby grips and 3lbs more of dry shampoo, but nobody needs to know about that.

After Kath's promise of standing by me, I feel like I can do this. I know it'll be hard, there'll be sleepless nights and I might never really get my shit fully together again. But although Lyla was (and sometimes still is) hard, she's the most perfect thing in my life, so a little more of that kind of tiny human perfection will actually be a blessing. Kath was right.

I decide to ring my GP this morning and arrange a midwife booking-in appointment, and also have a trawl of some of the pregnancy bumph online. You know, how big the baby is right now, what I should and shouldn't eat, best maternity jeans on the market, and so on. If I'm going to do it, I'm going to do it right. And as well as me seeming to have forgotten so much of this stuff from when I had Lyla, I guess times change. There'll be new guidelines, no doubt, and – I cheer myself by thinking – new gadgets, new baby must-haves and, hooray, new maternity ranges. So, in between liaising with clients, putting together job ideas and assigning staff to various jobs, I sneakily google things like 'pregnancy massage' (a girl's gotta make the most of things), 'best newborn cribs' and 'will this sickness ever stop'.

By lunchtime I'm feeling surprisingly good, given how the week started, and then I hear a familiar 'ding' from my phone. A notification from my personal emails.

Edward.

He's replied.

Suddenly the room feels like it's closing in on me and all the oxygen has been sucked out of it. I was 'fine' and 'breezy' in my email but whatever he has to say now feels frightening. I want to stay in my happy bubble trawling through ASOS maternity, not confronting whatever the father of my unborn child has to say.

I stand up, walk over to the open window, stick my head out, take in a deep breath of delicious fumes from the street below, come back in, log on to my personal emails on my work laptop (I'd rather be sitting up and looking forward as I read this, not hunched over a phone) and click 'open'. I can do this, I'm a badass single mum either way and I can definitely, absolutely do this.

'Dear Robin . . .' OK, he's gone for the formal approach. I wonder if he toyed with a 'hey' or not as well.

Dear Robin,

Thank you for emailing me and for being so honest, that must have been very hard to write.

I am so sorry to not be living nearer to you too. If I were, I'd want to be there to take care of you, whatever that might mean at this point for us.

Like you, I didn't have children, babies or pregnancy on my agenda right now but I have often found that the best things you ever have are not found on a map or in a plan but in the unexpected surprises life offers you.

I want to be a part of this, Robin. For you and for me and for the baby.

I don't know how that will work at the moment but I want you to know I'm here, I'm present and we will walk through this together. Call me when you feel ready. It'll be OK, I promise.

Love,

Edward xxx

Fuck. Me.

I sit stunned and read through the email at least five times before I realise I'm crying. Not big, heaving sobs like at Kath's and not hot, frustrated tears like with Lacey in my kitchen but slow, relieved tears of joy. I'm not alone. He's here, he's on board, the baby will have a daddy.

Reading it over and over, I can see there are no hard and fast plans for what we're going to do but there isn't a single jot of apprehension in his tone. It's mature and tender and kind. Also, he's signed it with 'love' and three kisses. I know I was trying so hard not to fall for anyone, but when you're carrying a man's child, he tells you 'we will walk through this together' and you're a mess of hormones, it's hard not to.

I think Kath was right: this baby *is* going to be the biggest blessing.

FOR THE REST OF the day I feel like I'm floating. Something that had seemed so dark and despairing at the start of the week has turned out to be the opposite.

I know there's still a long way to go. Work don't know (if, after this pitch disaster, I still even have a job by the time I'll need to tell them), Lacey's heartbroken, Mum and Dad will have to be told at some point (God, Mum will be horrified – I've been impregnated with no sign of wedlock on the horizon. What will she tell the ladies of the Rotary?), the PSMs will be surprised and, of course, Lyla is going to have to wrap her head around the idea of having a baby brother or sister, but I know we can do it. I've got Kath and Edward on my side.

Later in the day I mooch through to the main office to see if Stuart or Alice want anything from Starbucks. I've got that 3 p.m. lull, I haven't been sick since before I arrived and could do with some fresh air and a little walk. Also, Skye's not here to berate me for succumbing to corporate temptation so we can get away with our dirty coffee sins.

'Ooohhh, I'd love a skinny latte. I'm exhausted,' says

Alice, stretching her arms up in the air and groaning elaborately.

'You all right? You sound . . . achy,' I ask awkwardly, not really knowing how to say, 'That was the most dramatic thing I've seen all day and I've had an email from my fuck-buddy in New York to say he's going to stand by me and my unborn baby.'

'I've just been helping Natalie so much with the pitch. They loved her idea of natural beauty, and the first round of presentations starts Monday,' Alice replies. She suddenly looks awkward, realising her faux pas.

'Um . . . I think it's really awesome what you did for Skye,' she says quickly.

'Oh.' I'm struggling to think of where to go with this. Is it a trick? I know Alice thinks Skye is amazing.

'Natalie would have taken Skye off the team if you hadn't stuck up for her,' Alice continues. 'Skye told me everything. You're really cool, Robin.'

I'm completely shocked. I mean, not as shocked as the oh-you're-pregnant situation but still, this is a big moment. I do the very British thing and gloss over it.

'Thank you, Alice, that's kind of you to say so. Just a skinny latte then?' I ask as breezily as I can manage.

Stuart says nothing and doesn't look up from his laptop, though I can tell he's agog at what's just happened. I'm a hundred per cent sure they'll talk about it when I leave.

Walking into town to get the coffees, I feel odd. I didn't know that they loved the idea (my idea, thank you) and that Natalie was going to London next week. Ordinarily I'd feel massively hurt and left out (it's been really stinging since I was taken off it, I've never been canned like that at work before), but today it doesn't seem like anything can penetrate this positive, happy mood. After being so, so low at the start of the week, nothing can feel as bad as that.

Graciously, I contemplate how happy I am that my idea was well received. *It doesn't matter who takes the credit for it,* I tell myself. I know it was mine and that's all that matters. I may not be on the pitch team, but whenever that nagging voice of doom and doubt pipes up in my mind, I'll still be able to tell myself that this is proof I can come up with great ideas. *Best of luck to Natalie,* I think, as I step through the doors to Starbucks, breathe in the smell and have to dash to the loos for a sneaky sick-up.

So much for my zen moment.

FIFTEEN

I'M FEELING ON AN even keel again. The crashing, panicky low of facing pregnancy alone, and the elated high of realising that Kath and Edward have got my back have balanced each other out and I'm left doing a pretty decent impression of a normal person. I responded to Edward's email, suggesting we talk soon, and he's good with that. It's Sunday afternoon, and Lyla is with Simon and Storie (who are under strict instructions to feed her only food they've bought and paid for, and not foraged mushrooms, wild flowers or anything else that 'blends us with Mother Earth'). I've taken the weekend to myself for self-care and to let everything settle in.

I've lit all the good candles, the ones I usually save for

'special occasions' that never happen. There's something decadent about having your best candles lit during the day – and even better, the smell isn't triggering my nausea. I've had two bubble baths, treated myself to some luxury M&S ready meals with pre-prepped veg (this seems like a fair compromise – baby needs nutrients but I need rest), and caught up on all my 'continue watching' programmes on Netflix. More importantly, I have allowed myself to imagine things like taking the baby out in a pram for the first time, or choosing tiny Babygros for him or her to wear. I've thought about some of the things I loved most about Lyla when she was little. Holding her warm little body on my chest and lightly stroking the peach-fuzz hair on her head. I'm going to do it all again. I'm going to have a brand-new warm peach-fuzz bundle to love and nurture and raise.

Kath's coming with me to my first midwife appointment on Friday. On the phone I could hear her voice thicken with tears at being needed like that. God bless Kath. Even though she never had children of her own, I know she sees me as a surrogate daughter, and with my mum not winning any Mother of the Year awards any time soon, I'm grateful. By my rough calculations I should be having my twelve-week scan in late May, so I'm going to ask her to come to that too and see the baby waving about.

Just as I'm starting to think about what I should do with my evening, the doorbell rings.

Heaving myself off the sofa, I pad out into the hallway in my fluffy reindeer slippers ('tis not the season but 'self-care' calls for such things) and look through the peephole, expecting it to be Kath, excitedly bringing round more of her lavender creations.

It's Lacey.

I can't handle this right now but I know she's seen me through the glass, so I open the door and stand awkwardly in the longest pause two women have ever endured together. My God, she's as stubborn as me.

'Can I come in?' she asks tentatively.

I move back out of the way and gesture for her to enter, still not saying much. I don't know what to say to my closest friend. I still don't know what's best to say, what's best to leave unsaid. Quite frankly, I'm terrified of making things worse if I open my mouth.

We walk through to the lounge and she assesses my multitude of candles and dirty plates.

'Good weekend, then?' she asks, settling herself in the armchair.

'It's been a bit of a week,' I say quietly.

'I'm sorry,' Lacey says, bluntly and quickly. 'I shouldn't have flown off the handle like that. Things just . . . I don't know, it was like the final straw. I was so sure I was pregnant, I was two weeks late, but I've been down that road before and I know where it leads,' she says, turning her face away from me and towards the window.

'Oh God, Lacey, I'm so sorry. Another false alarm, but it will happen. I know I say this all the time but I just know it will.'

'I know it will, too,' Lacey says, still looking out the window.

What? She's never this positive. She's really taking this well. Maybe Karl's had a calming chat with her, or something. 'It's good you're being positive. And, just so you know, I'm not going to make a big deal out of my situation. I'll just get on with it myself and nothing will change, OK?'

'So we can't go Babygro-shopping together?' she says, turning to me with the biggest smile I've ever seen in my life.

Maybe she actually has lost her mind.

'Um, well, yes, we can, if that's what you'd like,' I stutter, completely shocked at this transformation.

'It's just that I'm probably due about six weeks after you and it'd be fun to buy our babies' things at the same time,' she says, almost squealing at the last bit of the sentence.

'What?' I scream, jumping up from the sofa.

Lacey jumps up too. 'I'm pregnant! I'm actually pregnant! I was late and thought it was the same-old, same-old, and didn't do a test because I couldn't bear the idea of a negative, but oh my God, Robin, I'm pregnant too!'

'I can't believe it. This is the best news ever!' I say, jumping slightly, like a giddy child after jelly and ice cream.

'I know. We found out yesterday. I know they say not to tell people before twelve weeks but I couldn't not tell you. It's a miracle. My miracle baby. I'm having a baby!'

'And we get to do it all together. We'll have best friend babies!' I scream, feeling so full of joy I could throw up. Again.

'I know! Robin, I'm truly sorry for how I was last week. It's not an excuse, I know, but I felt like I was going crazy. I've felt horrible for ages. But you know, I can't think of anyone I'd want to share this pregnancy with more than you. We'll have matching bumps and matching babies. This is amazing!'

After five more minutes of shrill exclamations about how incredible this is, we sit down to work out unofficial due dates. Lacey seems to know more about this than I do, even though this isn't my first. She's mapped her ovulation and when that means she's due, and she's already calculated that if you get pregnant when I did, you're due at Christmas.

'Christmas baby for you, February baby for me,' she says with more enthusiasm than I've ever seen from anyone about anything. To be fair, I don't think there's a single day of the year that she wouldn't have been thrilled to have as her due date, such is her joy just to be pregnant.

'Yay!' I say, thinking anxiously for a second about all the people I know who hate having a late-December birthday, and immediately start picturing a child's tantrums at having shared birthday and Christmas presents and a lifetime of everyone being too busy to celebrate. I'm being petty, I know.

The rest of the evening vanishes in a flurry of excited chatter about midwives and maternity leave, comparing sickness and fatigue, how happy Karl is and how lovely Edward was in his email. Lacey squeals that I'll probably get married now. 'A pregnant bride and bridesmaid!' she announces, and I have to rein her in a bit before I throw up again with how overwhelming all of this feels.

We move to safer ground and talk about all the things we'll do. We'll go to baby massage classes, we'll have lunch in posh garden centre cafés with them, we'll have matching prams, we'll take pictures of both of them in matching outfits (we're talking as though we are both having mini-me girls) and we'll watch them grow up together, be best friends at school together and go on their first holiday together as reckless teenagers. We really let loose with our fantasies and it feels amazing. Now is not the time to imagine the sleepless nights and stinky nappy changes. There'll be time for that later. This is the moment we get to share something beautiful together. I go wild for her, she goes wild for me, we're both exhilarated.

Once she's left, promising to drive carefully over any speed bumps (is that a thing to worry about, or is my baby brain going into overdrive already?), I welcome home a sleepy seven-year-old and we head to bed. I feel the happiest I have in a long time.

This feels right.

THE NEXT MORNING, I wake up jubilant. Lacey is pregnant, Edward is on board, Alice thinks I'm cool, the world is coming good. I almost leap out of bed before I remember it's sicky-uppy time followed by the normal routine of telling Lyla to get her skirt/shirt/socks/shoes on eighty thousand times.

By the time we set off in the car, I'm exhausted. How on earth am I going to manage this daily rigmarole with two children? I suddenly feel quite low again. My emotions right now are like being on a fairground ride. Can I get off?

As we walk through the school gates, I try to tell Lyla I need a bit more cooperation in the mornings. But I can see it's all going over her nonchalant little head. The new mum, Gloria, is walking in with her twins at the same time, one hanging from each hand.

'Verity Mae Straunston, if you don't walk properly right now I'm going to put you back in the car and tell Mr Ravelle you're too naughty to go to school!' I hear her threaten as Verity and her sister, Athena, giggle.

'I think they're all the same!' I say to her in sisterly support. 'Mine doesn't listen to a word I say in the mornings.'

'I may as well be wrangling circus animals sometimes!' Gloria says, half to me and half to the twins.

'How do you manage two?' I ask, hoping she'll tell me some magic secret and being pregnant with my second won't feel so frightening.

'I don't. I just grab each one by the hand and go for it. As long as I have two hands and accept I'm not perfect all of the time, we get by!' she says with a smile, a laugh and two children pulling at her arms.

Well, if badass single mum Gloria Straunston with challenging *twin* children can do it, bloody well so can I!

SIXTEEN

MAY

YOU COULD CUT THE tension at work with a knife. Natalie has pitched and refined and pitched again and now we are awaiting our fate. MADE IT is already booming with local jobs, London shoots and our recent emergence into the film sector, but to have this major London Fashion Week gig would be a real coup. Natalie still hasn't spoken to me a great deal, and I don't know what my job will look like after all this. She's only communicated the essentials but Stuart and Alice fill me in each day on the latest developments.

Since insert-fatty-pic-here-gate, I've been finding more and more ways to be out of the office and out from under

Natalie's feet. The books are laden with local jobs so I've scooped some of them up to busy myself with, plus, in getting back to the coalface, I've realised that I still love the practical side of things.

The big Friday rolls around and while I've been out on shoots, the excitement in the office has reached fever pitch.

Every time the phone rings, Stuart answers it in an increasingly posh voice until Alice snaps, 'Why are you answering like you work at Buckingham Palace?' From then on, normal telephony resumes.

At 3.15 p.m., the phone rings, Stuart answers (in only a semi-royal accent) and, keeping his voice calm and serene with, 'One moment please, I'll connect you to her,' he stands up from his desk flailing his arms wildly and mock-thrusting his laptop. It's quite the scene.

We wait in silence, staring at Natalie's closed door. I think about getting up and shamelessly standing right outside it but notice Skye has already beaten me to it and is 'just checking the noticeboard' very studiously. Right by the door. Good old brazen Skye, you've got to admire her.

Suddenly the door bursts open, Skye almost jumps out of her skintight crop top and Natalie exclaims, 'It's ours! We've won it!'

The office erupts into whoops and cheers, Alice jumps up to give Natalie a celebratory hug, Skye claps, Stuart again faux-thrusts his laptop and makes sex faces (I must ask him why he does this one day, it's so weird) and I continue to stand by my office door, smiling and taking it all in.

My idea did it.

My idea won a major London Fashion Week contract.

I stand there, thinking about how much I can't wait to tell Kath and Lyla, my biggest cheerleaders in life, when Natalie comes over to me with outstretched arms.

'Well done, Robin, you did it again,' she says warmly into my ear. For a few moments I don't move. For all these days and weeks I've been feeling like a grounded teenager whose parents aren't angry, just disappointed (aka the worst thing they could *ever* be). I think of all the slinking around, desperate not to bump into her but also desperate for things to go back to normal, of feeling unspeakably guilty for making such a huge mistake (or rather, for not noticing Skye's mistake before Natalie did) and anxious to the point of nausea (that could be the human life within, admittedly), and here she is congratulating me. As the kids would say, 'Da fuq?'

'What? But you took me off the job. I missed, I mean I messed . . .' I say, shocked at the sudden kindness, my brows furrowed in confusion and probably looking like a bit of a tool.

'Don't think I don't know the score. I know you. I was so disgusted, and so disappointed you didn't manage Skye better and didn't check through the work you were supposed to be overseeing. I handled it badly, you were a fool (a noble one, I grant you) for taking the rap, but I know whose ideas are whose and I know you, Robin. I know what you are and aren't capable of. I'm sorry I flew off the handle, I'm sorry I left you stewing about it. I was under a lot of pressure but I know that's no excuse, especially not after all you've done for MADE IT,' Natalie says, quietly and gently.

Once more, I can feel tears welling up. All I seem to do these days is cry at things – bloody hormones. I'm so relieved! Maybe now we can work together again like last year; maybe I can tell her about the baby. Suddenly asking about maternity leave doesn't seem nearly as frightening, and for a split second I envisage myself at LFW, working with Mara's models, my bump in full bloom, everyone looking gorgeous, me with my glow, Natalie nailing it, amazing!

'Natalie, I—'

'No need to say anything, this is a happy moment. I'm sorry I've been so off, it's been a shock to the system being back and this pitch has meant such a lot. You should know, I *have* spoken to Skye now. I've put her on a six month trial period. She knows she needs to regain our trust, and then some. I should have communicated better with you, but I just couldn't. Forgive me?'

'Forgive you? As if you have to ask. I'm just happy you're happy, happy we've won, happy everyone's so happy!' I gush loudly, instinctively reaching a hand to my not-even-there-yet bump and then pulling it away before she notices. I can't wait to tell her, but I think today I'll let it be just the pitch win that we're celebrating. The baby news can have a whole day to itself, spread out the joy a bit.

'All right, Robs, we get it, you're happy! Now come and have a glass of sparkles with us all!' Stuart shouts jubilantly from the front of the office.

The party has begun. Alice has turned the music up, Stuart's pouring drinks (I didn't even know we had champagne flutes), Skye is dancing with her eyes shut and a glass in her raised hand and Natalie is striding over with a big smile telling Alice to 'Call the others in, we're celebrating!'

Panicking slightly about how I'm going to avoid sipping champagne without anyone noticing, I excuse myself. 'Back in a mo!' I call, even though nobody's listening, the music's too loud and the celebration too big.

Locking the little cubicle door, I sit on the loo and breathe out slowly. *What a relief to have won and to have such a happy ending,* I think. Today couldn't have worked out any better. This month has turned out to be incredible. They say it comes in threes, so I wonder what the next thing will be!

And then I notice.

I don't know how I didn't before. I was so wrapped up in the celebrations of the win. My knickers, the tissue and the toilet are stained with blood.

Bright red, thick blood.

Part Three

THE BEST-LAID PLANS . . .

SEVENTEEN

IT TAKES ME A good few seconds to register what I'm seeing. There is blood in my knickers. I'm pregnant.

You're not supposed to bleed when you're pregnant.

Isn't this bad?

Optimistically, I think perhaps it's 'spotting'. I've heard of this. Spotting is fine. Except this doesn't look like a few spots of blood. I cautiously take some tissue and wipe again, not wanting to but desperate to see at the same time. This isn't spotting, no one could call it that. There is just so much. How did I not notice it at my desk? Surely I should have felt it? Is this real?

My head seems to be working faster than my heart for

once because I'm not registering any feelings right now. I am bleeding, I can hear Stuart yelling, 'Fucking yes, then!' and Alice 'woohooo'-ing in celebration. I need to go home, I need to find a sanitary towel, I need practical advice, I need to speak to a responsible adult. All of a sudden, that person doesn't feel like me.

I roll up wads and wads of tissue to make a makeshift pad and as I do I notice my hands are shaking. Heart is catching up to head. Suddenly it's not about me, my knickers, my stuck-in-the-work-loos location. It's my baby. Is my baby still my baby, or has it gone? Has it already left me? Can it be saved? Can I do something in this exact moment to help it? I don't know what that would be. I need help. Panic sets in.

Almost on autopilot, I pull up my ruined knickers with their tissue wads, fasten my jeans, flush, wash my shaking hands, walk to my office, grab my bag and leave, walking straight past the team whooping and cheering. I can vaguely hear them asking me where I'm going or shouting my name as I get in my car, but it's as if I'm underwater and I can't make out their exact words. Right now, I don't care. I don't even turn my head to acknowledge their shouts. I'm not me right now, I'm not 'Robin Wilde, Natalie's wingman', not 'Robin Wilde, nicest woman in the office'. No, I'm Robin Wilde and I need to save my baby. I turn on the engine and, without thinking, I drive to Auntie Kath's.

I knock on her bright red door and stand motionless with the same blank expression I've had on my face for the past twenty minutes. I still feel nothing. It's like I've put every fibre of my mind and body on hold to protect myself, but the second she opens the door and I see her face and smell her 1980s Giorgio Beverly Hills scent I lose it. In her dusky purple crocheted cardigan over the top of a lacy mustard shirt that clashes entirely with her chunky green glass beaded necklace, she is the most welcome sight I can imagine. All at once, it hits me and I can barely stand. The sky feels like it's falling in, every ounce of feeling I've ever felt in my whole life seems to well up behind the bones of my face, and I let out a huge animalistic cry and fall sobbing into her arms, trying urgently to say, 'The baby, the baby.'

I don't know how long I stand there but by the time I pull away, Kath is crying too. I've been ushered over the threshold into the hallway and Kath is holding me tightly, stroking my hair and hushing me. 'It's all right, it's all right my love,' she says over and over until my heavy tears turn to dry sobs and I'm just heaving through the pain in my heart. Heart has fully caught up and heart *knows.*

* * *

It is the worst day of my life. After being driven to the doctor's surgery where Kath insisted I see the midwife, despite not having an appointment, we have our fears confirmed. I'm having a miscarriage.

'It's very common this early on,' the midwife says in what I assume she thinks is a comforting tone. I nod blankly, not knowing the words for how I'm supposed to respond. In the end, Kath takes the lead, thanking her for her time and asking her what we do now. After being told we just have to let the pregnancy pass and that I should rest, Kath accepts some 'helpful' leaflets and walks me back to her car. Through all the pain and haze I notice the midwife says, 'let the pregnancy pass' and not 'the baby'. She's deliberately not saying 'baby' to make it easier for me. I want to scream at her to recognise that my baby is gone and even if it is *very common*, I'm not just having a medical experience, my heart is breaking.

We drive home to my house, Kath arranges to collect Lyla from school and I crawl into bed, curl up and cry.

I cry for so many reasons. I cry for the immediate loss I feel, and for the loss I know I will feel when I have to tell people my news and pretend I'm 'fine', regurgitating the 'it's very common this early in pregnancy' line. I cry for the physical pain I'm starting to feel and what that means for the life inside me. I cry for the life I won't be giving to Lyla. She never even knew that for a short while she was a big sister; she never even touched on the joy that was to come to her. I cry for the guilt I feel, such intense, immense guilt for not loving this baby, my baby, from the very second I found out. All those lost days thinking the worst and not embracing each second. I cry just because I'm crying. This is an emptiness like no other. The Emptiness I felt last year in those lonely single-mum-dom days seems only a scratch on the surface compared to the depth of The Emptiness now.

TWO DAYS LATER AND little has changed. I can't imagine happiness ever flowing into my life again. I can't imagine sunny days or laughter. It will just be this pain always. I'm broken, mentally and what feels like physically, too. Nobody tells you what a miscarriage feels like. It's brutal. The heavy bleeding that I keep having to change pads for is a constant reminder of what my body is losing. The cramps take my breath away. The physical pain is less than the pain in my heart, though. Far less.

Kath has stayed at our house, called work for me and told Lyla I have a very bad stomach upset. Lyla hasn't questioned this but has come up every so often to sit next to me in bed, cuddling up to watch vlogs of people opening Kinder eggs on the iPad and to tell me she loves me. Her innocent gestures of love are the only things that lift me at all.

I can see Kath's love all around me. The way she comes in in the morning to draw my curtains, open a window and place a warm cup of tea on the bedside table, or the way she carefully French-plaits Lyla's hair and makes sure her socks are pulled right up so she looks smart for school. The way she busies herself downstairs but pops up every so often with a tray of food or the offer of a 'little drive to perk you up', which I decline both days. I can see all her love, but Lyla's love can be almost tangibly felt. She has no reason to love me so hard, she doesn't know the hurt I'm living in, but she freely pours her affections on me with no basis or expectation for anything other than her mother's love in return. I pour love back. I love her for everything she is and everything I have lost. My maternal heart aches with love for both my babies, and the only thing that will soothe this feeling is to hold Lyla close. I smell her hair, listen to her chatter and praise her enthusiastically for the 'Get Well Soon' card she's made me by cutting out pictures she thinks I'll like from magazines (handbags, food, a poodle) and drawing me and her smiling next to our 'new things'.

Like I did last year with The Emptiness, I shield her.

I dry my eyes before she comes home from school, sit up in bed, smile when she bounds in and tell her my tummy feels much better every time she asks. Lying almost feels good. I want to believe it and lose myself in that lie. I cling to it like a life raft in a sea of misery.

EIGHTEEN

On the third day, Kath comes in with warm Nutella toast and a cup of tea, and instead of leaving, she sits down on the end of the bed.

'Lovey, it's time to get up. You can't stay here forever,' she says with a tilted head and kind eyes. Today, though it's starting to be summery outside, she is wearing a green knitted jumper with bits of red tinselly wool stitched into it and a long navy pleated skirt. I love that Kath just wears what she wants, seasons be damned. I wish I could have her to-hell-with-it attitude more often.

'I can't,' I say quietly, looking at my plate of toast.

'You can. You think you can't, but I know you can.' She places a hand lovingly on my leg.

'I need more time,' I whisper.

'You are Robin Wilde, my most fearless girl, you are brave and kind and ready to stand up and continue living,' she says, giving my leg a little jiggle, as if to really make her point. Despite the jiggle, I don't buy it. I'm none of those things. I'm just a sad single mum having a miscarriage.

'Kath,' I go to protest but I just don't have it in me.

'I know how hard this is. I know how heavy your heart is, but we need to face it and carry on. It's the only way,' she says, her voice ever so slightly firmer.

'I don't know how.'

'We're going have to tell the American chap what's happened. He's none the wiser right now and the sooner he knows, the better. I will help you with Lyla, I'll speak to Natalie, too, if you like, but you need to tell Edward,' she says gravely but softly.

I know she's right. I've ignored his texts – nothing that really warranted much response, just funny little memes or the occasional picture of something in New York that's tickled him (last night's was a rainbow bagel), so he's spent the last couple of days completely oblivious to everything that's happened. He needs to know. Unlike the fizzy trepidation of revealing I was pregnant, I feel completely numb about telling him this. I feel like it's just a factual task I have to tick off a list. Not that I'm numb to the pain of losing this baby – it couldn't feel more acute – but the usual dithering I have over big interactions with a guy is completely lacking. I don't care about sounding cool, I don't care about coming across as funny or attractive, none of that matters.

I send him a message, being considerate of the time zone difference as Kath wisely advised. *Hi Edward, I need to talk to you, please could you text me when you are awake and I'll FaceTime you. Xx.* I hit send without mulling over every word, without stressing over the amount of kisses or the exact grammar. I can't imagine ever caring about those tiny things again. Why would I?

Kath spends the rest of the morning at the breakfast bar apparently mixing up liquid soap with essential oils and dried lavender and decanting it into glass bottles with little brass pumps that she bought from the web. I have the first shower I've had in three days and stay in there for a very long time, trying to let the hurt wash away with the blood and hot soapy water. Watching the blood slip down the plughole is strangely mesmerising. A part of me is leaving forever yet I'm still here, watching it happen and acknowledging it, aware that I can't stop it or tame it. I watch it for a long time, hoping that once it stops, I'll stop hurting. Of course, the hurt outlives the amount of hot water I have in the tank and so I step out of the shower still in pain, physically and emotionally, but clean at least.

I get dressed into the same comfy velour jogging bottoms I remember putting on when I first realised I could be pregnant, add a slouchy, long-sleeved T-shirt and thick socks and head downstairs.

The whole house is infused with the calming scent of lavender. Having not been in the kitchen for a solid forty-eight hours, I'm surprised to see it has been turned into quite the craft workshop with sprigs of dried lavender, bottles, dishes, spoons, bath bombs and labels littered over all the surfaces.

'I don't think even Moira and I can get through this many bars of soap,' I joke weakly to Kath as I pick up a small creamy bar and breathe in its delicious fragrance.

'I know. I've been wanting to tell you. I'm going to start selling them at fairs and such,' says Kath sweetly. 'Moira loves all my products and so do the ladies at the Cupcakes and Crochet Club. We talk about it a lot! Everything these days is designed to make you look younger, "appear more youthful" and all that, but that's not what we – well at least Moira and the gang – want. We're quite OK with getting older. You don't stop being a woman just because the menopause hits. We're not trying to turn the clock back – we want to make the most of now. I don't want to slather on chemicals to get rid of my laughter lines. I bloomin' earned those! We just want some nice smellies to enjoy in the bath, a lovely cream here and there to make us feel a bit swish, you know? I don't want all these anti-ageing, surgery-mimicking scientific lotions and potions. So, as they say, I'm taking the bull by the horns and doing it for the girls. Lavender Lovies for all!'

I love this woman. Building an empire downstairs, taking care of me upstairs and doing all the childcare for Lyla: she's a marvel.

'You're a good woman, Kath,' I say with a smile and a little lump in my throat. Everything is so raw and emotional. I want to talk more about it, about her setting up something so wonderful, supporting other women, disregarding her age and proudly going forward, but I can't right now. I'm running on next to no energy and I think talking about another remotely emotive topic will send me over the edge.

'So are you, petal, so are you,' she says as she gets up to busy herself making me some soup and buttered bread. As she and I clear some space at the giant wooden table, I realise that, just like with Lyla previously, today I can feel Kath's love, not just see it. Perhaps this is a step forward.

Hey! I'm awake sweet cheeks! What's up? xxx

Edward's text pings as it arrives just after lunch. Another time I might have taken note of the three kisses but not today. None of that matters today.

Without even considering my gaunt, make-up-free face or my shoved-it-up-wet topknot hair, I hit the tiny camera icon to FaceTime him. Better to do than to think.

'Good morning, Miss Wilde! How are we today?' Edward says smoothly and suavely before taking in my sallow skin and frizzing hair. I see a flicker of recognition in his eyes – he knows something is wrong.

'Edward,' I begin, my voice breaking already.

'Oh, Robin,' he says softly.

'The baby. It's gone. I don't know what I did wrong, but it's gone.' I can't bring myself to say the word 'miscarriage'. It's as if it's a bullet in a gun and I can't bear to pull the trigger on it.

Edward hesitates for a moment before replying and in that time, my numb resolve withers to more hot, fat tears.

'Robin. My poor Robin. You didn't do anything. I'm sorry. I wish I was there. It's not your fault.' Those short little sentences are like a warm tonic to my broken heart. All those weeks and months of keeping him at arm's length, and now suddenly I want him so very close to me. I carry on crying, my hand shaking the phone.

'Listen. I can get a flight over this weekend if you want. I can just come and be with you. You don't have to do this alone,' he offers, ever the man trying to find a solution.

'It's OK, my aunt is here, Lyla is here, I'm OK. They say it's very common at this stage,' I add on, trotting out the standard line to smooth over this, the most hideous of situations.

'How do you feel?' he asks quietly.

'Shit. So fucking shit. I had started to get my head round it, was starting to see the positives in it. My friends were happy for me, I loved that my best friend found out she is pregnant too and due not long after me, and we were going to do everything together . . . and now it's all gone,' I say, barely taking a breath before fresh sobs start heaving up into my throat. This is the first time I've thought about Lacey. I've spent three days thinking of nothing but the baby I'm losing and have entirely forgotten about the baby she's gaining. This is how she must have felt when she found my pregnancy test. How hard it will be to see her baby grow and every time think of mine, that I could not get to know. I realise Edward is talking and jolt myself back to the conversation.

'I've not gone, though,' he says with a loving smile. 'I'm still here, far away but still here.'

'Thank you,' I manage. I don't really know how to interpret that statement or offer or whatever it was, but gratitude seems like the best avenue to take.

'I didn't know how much I wanted it until I saw all the blood and knew it was all over,' I whisper sadly.

'I wanted it too. I know this isn't how anybody would plan something but I was thinking of moving back to the UK and making this work. We still could make something work,' he adds after a pause.

'I don't know, Edward,' I say, that familiar panic of getting too close setting in and the desire to have him right here ebbing away suddenly. 'I think I just need to process what's going on and work things out.'

'OK,' he says quietly with no obvious tone.

'I just wanted you to know. I'm so sorry. I didn't mean—'

'Robin, stop. You don't have to say sorry. It is what it is. I'm here if you need me and I'm going to look into flights to come over. Even if you don't want to do anything, I'd like to just see you. I'm part of this, too.'

'OK. If you're up for PJs and comfort food and not much else, then OK.' If he comes without an agenda, maybe it is what I need. I feel a little glimmer of hope.

'I can't think of anything I'd like to do more. If I could bring you a Sarabeth's brunch, I would.'

'You could bring me a box of airport Ferrero Rocher,' I tease, weakly.

'Deal,' he says.

I don't know where to go from here. I don't have the energy for friendly banter.

'Look, you get some rest,' he says, sensing my weariness. 'I'm here if you need me – day or night – and you don't need to worry about anything. These things happen, there's nothing you could have done, and you're definitely not alone. I'll call or message you later.'

'OK,' I say obligingly.

'OK. Bye, Robin, take care.'

We hang up.

NINETEEN

THE FOLLOWING MONDAY, I agree to go into work just for the morning, to attend the Isso Project meeting.

At first, I'd told Kath I didn't want Natalie to know – after all, I'd just lost a baby she didn't know I was having – and I was determined to explain it away as sick leave, but gradually I realised I did want the people closest to me to know. I wanted them to know this baby mattered. So many people choose to keep it private and I completely understand that – telling people can feel like opening up that little box where you keep all your hurt and pain, all over again. Yet, I knew that despite how raw I still felt, I couldn't keep the sorrow hidden away, even at work. I needed them to know. But when it came to it, I couldn't find the words. What if Natalie thought I wasn't committed to my job, what if she judged me for accidentally getting pregnant by a man I'm not even with? I knew this was just my paranoia talking, but it made my thoughts freeze. In the end, Auntie Kath rang Natalie to explain.

Kath told me everything was sorted with Natalie and that she was very understanding, but I'm not looking forward to going in. I don't want to be back in the place where it happened, I don't want to retrace those zombie-like steps. I don't want to be the subject of pitying looks or, worse still, sympathetic words. I'm not going to make an announcement or even bring it up ('Hey, guys, sorry I bailed the other week, my baby died,' doesn't really sit well in office chit-chat, does it?) but from what Kath said after the phone call, Natalie is going to 'handle it sensitively' and let everyone know. I feel like I need handling sensitively too.

I'm lucky, really. So many women have to suck it up and get straight back out there, never letting on the hurt they are walking with every day, never really being allowed to fully acknowledge the experience because 'life must go on'. Ironic. I was never planning to be working as many hours as I have been. Last year I was doing just one or two days a week, and things weren't meant to get this much. Losing the baby has led to me needing a break, but if I'm honest with myself, some time at home just for me and Lyla would be good too.

So the plan is to go in and do a handover of my accounts and jobs and then take a couple of weeks off to have some downtime. Now we've secured the Mara Isso job, the team are planning and arranging everything down to the letter to make sure it runs smoothly, but at the moment, my heart and soul are not in it.

After pulling up to the office and parking my car, I take a deep breath, remind myself of Kath's 'you're stronger than you think' pep talk that she gave me this morning and walk up to MADE IT. I'm early, so it's only Alice on the front desk, Stuart isn't in yet.

'Hey, Alice, how's it going?' I say, trying to keep things normal.

'Yeah, really good, just . . . yeah . . . good,' Alice says with that pitying look I had dreaded. I feel sorry for her. I suppose it's hard to know what to say to a woman who never told you she was pregnant and now she's not.

'Cool. Well, I'm gonna just crack on in my office,' I say weirdly. I don't need to announce this, but today feels like we all need the clarity.

'Yes! Great plan! Here if you need anything,' she says,

obviously relieved that the strained interaction is coming to an end.

My office is exactly the same as it was just over a week ago. Nobody has been in – not even a cleaner – my half-drunk cup of coffee is still on my desk and my wastepaper basket is still full. I don't know what I expected. So much seems to have happened in my life, so much has changed, but this has stayed the same.

Resolving not to think about it too much, I flip open my laptop and log into my emails. My inbox is heaving.

For a couple of hours, I sift through everything in there, sending brief replies or forwarding jobs to Natalie that she will deal with in my absence, deliberately not mentioning to clients what my absence is in aid of. I find a lovely personal email from Natalie, sent just after she and Kath spoke on the phone. I skim over her kind words about my baby and feel touched. I'll read it properly when I'm feeling stronger. I copy Skye into a few that I know she'll have input on and a lot of the admin, invoices and diarising goes over to Stuart and Alice.

At about ten-ish I start riffling through the bits of paper on my desk, the half-written Post-its and the mail I have been neglecting. If I'm going to be on leave, I at least want my desk to appear organised. Clearing through everything is cathartic and time seems to move much faster here than at home.

By eleven, I'm in the 'big meeting room' (why we call it the 'big' one when it's the only one, I don't know) with Natalie, Skye, Kareem, three junior MUAs and Alice taking the minutes. Natalie is handing out face maps, swatches of fabric and colour charts so that we can start working on the exact looks we'll be doing at London Fashion Week in less than four months' time. Natalie, Skye and I will be leading the team with the regular and junior MUAs assisting. Alice and Stuart will be stepping up to hold the fort here while we're in London, so it's a whole team effort and the air is crackling with excitement.

Deep down I know I will enjoy LFW. I love my work, I love working with models, I love the creativity, but today I don't feel it. I feel very far away from all of this and as if joy can't penetrate through the thick layer of sorrow that I'm wrapped in. Sensing my mood, Natalie doesn't push or press me on anything and allows me to sit peacefully, take notes and nod at the right points. When the time comes I'll be on it, I know I will.

By about noon, after a lengthy and lovely chat with Natalie about taking as much time as I need and not worrying about anything except healing, I'm finishing up and Skye pops her head through the doorway.

Normally I'd be on guard for a snippy comment or have the gusto to be annoyed by her presence, but today my emotional energy levels are at an all-time low.

'Hey,' she offers meekly.

'Hey,' I reply. What else is there to say?

She hovers nervously by the door. 'Don't worry about anything while you're off, I'll make sure it all goes OK.'

'Thanks, Skye. I'm leaving it all in your hands, so don't let me down . . . I'm sure you won't,' I add gently, waiting for her to berate me over something or belittle me somehow. There's a long pause before she says anything again.

'Also, I just wanted to say, I'm really sorry for what happened to you. Like, really sorry.' Suddenly I can see a softer, kinder side to Skye and I find myself having to rapidly blink back the tears that are welling up in the corners of my eyes.

'Thanks, Skye,' I say again. 'Just one of those things. Very common.' This is becoming my defence line. Thankfully it seems to work because Skye gives a little nod and a small smile and walks back into the main office where I can hear her striking up a conversation with Stuart about a job she has on tomorrow. Normality resumes after such an unexpected tender moment with each other. Thank God.

Before I have a chance to really dwell on it, my phone vibrates with a text from Lacey. I feel hideous again. I've been avoiding her and fobbing her off all week because I just cannot bear to tell her what's happened. She's sent me countless excited texts with ideas for our joint baby shower, examples of how she wants her maternity shoot to be and links to baby sales we should go to, and I've responded as best I can with thumbs-up emojis and 'oohhh you'd look lovely in a dress like that', just to throw the situation back on her and not talk about me. Luckily she's been so swept up in her own long-overdue joy that she hasn't read between the lines and worked out that I'm not matching her excitement levels. Either that or I'm just really good at hiding things. I'm hoping for the first one.

I decide to call it a day. Lyla doesn't need picking up for two hours, and so in a rare moment of strength and bravery, I head over to Dovington's florist's to get this over with.

TWENTY

OPENING THE DOOR TO Dovington's, I am instantly hit with the sweet scent of bouquet upon bouquet of beautiful, colourful flowers and the soft daylight streaming through the huge skylights above me. I imagine stepping into Heaven feels similar.

The first person to greet me is Terri, the store manager. 'Hiya, Robin! Heard your good news! Lacey's obviously thrilled to bits, bless her heart!'

It's like being hit in the chest with a lorry. I don't know how to respond, so I stand there limp and say, 'Ha! Yes! Of course! Is she about?' in as cheery a tone as I can possibly muster.

'She is! She's making up bouquets in the back. I've

told her to take it easy, keep her feet up, you know. You should be doing the same. Go and sit down!' She ushers me into the back, excitedly.

As soon as I'm through the doors into the big old workshop, I think I'm safe, free of Terri's enthusiasm, but of course I'm not. I've just thrown myself into a room bursting with more pregnancy enthusiasm than an NCT meet-up in a trendy family-friendly pub on a Saturday afternoon.

'Hello! I didn't know you were coming in.' Lacey bustles, moving some long-stemmed roses out of the way to clear a space for me. I notice she's already wearing a maternity top, despite not even the slightest hint of bump. Of course she's going to embrace every single second of this, why wouldn't she? I need to get it together and control my emotions.

Before I can start, she launches in. 'I've just signed up to all the free baby clubs and I think I've decided which one might be best. You get points on all the baby-related purchases, you know, nappies, food, clothes and stuff and then they also give you a free changing bag. Obviously I'm going to get another nice one from John Lewis as well, but you can never have too many changing bags, can you?' she says without even pausing for breath.

'No, I suppose not. Listen, Lacey—' I begin.

'I know, obviously you already know this stuff because you've done it before and you've had Lyla, but it's sort of like starting again, isn't it? Because you didn't save any of your baby bits and bobs, and you're in a new relationship now. Didn't you sell all those kiddie things you had packed away under your stairs last year? Bloody hell, I bet you wished you hadn't done that now! Although I reckon Edward will buy you a lot of stuff. Oh my God, do you think he's going to move back and marry you? He could live with you in your new house and you'll be the perfect family and Lyla will love him and—'

'My baby's dead!' I say, as forcefully as I can. It's the first time I've used the 'D' word. I haven't even used the 'miscarriage' word much; I've stuck to 'loss' or 'it wasn't meant to be', but something just snapped. It was as though everything she was saying, every little idea or tip or nuance was a stab in the heart and I needed to make her stop. As soon as I say it, I burst into tears. Big, angry, rage tears.

Lacey sits in shock, mouth slightly open, hands still holding the stems and the ribbon she was using to tie them. We sit like that for what feels like a long time.

'What do you mean?' she says at last, slowly. What else could I mean?

'I lost the baby,' I say flatly, focusing my gaze on the flowers instead of her.

'When? How?'

'Last week, and what do you mean, "how"? The usual way people lose babies. I had a miscarriage. The baby is gone.'

This is clearly hard for Lacey to deal with and she carries on with her questions. 'Are you sure?'

I can't handle it. It's like when we were in Year Nine and I told her I'd lost my snogging virginity to Alex Myer and she said, 'Are you sure?' Yes, I'm fucking sure. I'm not a complete idiot. I'm about to snap back at her about blood and cramps and the midwife when I check myself and stop. She can't help it. She is so engrossed in babydom that this isn't her being a bad friend, this is a loss to her, too.

'Yes, Lacey,' I offer gently. 'The midwife confirmed it and I've bled very heavily. I'm still bleeding a little bit. The baby is definitely gone.' I try not to let a fresh wave of tears fall as I say the last sentence. 'I'm sorry I didn't tell you sooner. I couldn't face it. I couldn't face anything.'

'Have you gone through this alone?' she asks, small, pearly tears falling down her face.

'No, I had Kath and Lyla. Natalie's given me plenty of

time off, Edward said he might fly over. It's been OK. As OK as something like this ever could be.'

'Why didn't you tell me?' she almost whispers.

'Because you were so excited. You were so happy, I didn't want to spoil that for you. I wanted you to live in this beautiful bubble and enjoy what we had for a while. I knew telling you would be upsetting for both of us and I just wasn't strong enough for it.'

'Oh, Robin. I'm so sorry. I'm so, so sorry,' she says, putting the flowers down at last, scraping back her chair and coming over to me for an awkward hug, standing over me with one breast in my face and one somewhere near my ear.

Feeling her pain weirdly makes me hold myself together. A bit like when something's gone wrong at home and I have to assume my protective mum role and make everything all right.

'I'll be fine, honestly. I'm going to take some time off and just relax, enjoy Lyla, get some more bits done in the house,' I waffle on.

She loosens her hug and sits back down, clearly at a loss for what to say. I think of how much she must have been suffering every time I gave her a pep talk over the last couple of years, after each failed test, each period that arrived when it wasn't wanted. I thought – I hoped

– she might have some more sympathetic words for me, but this seems to have completely stumped her.

'I suppose all you can take away is that at least you know you can get pregnant. You could try again,' she says bluntly, clearly thinking this is some sort of consolation to me. I feel shock. Then I start to feel rage bubble up in me again. But I keep calm and hide it carefully. She doesn't know that's the last thing I want to hear right now.

'You know I didn't try to get pregnant. I'm not ready to think about the future, and even if I was, I can't imagine Edward would be up for "trying again", and there isn't a slew of other eligible bachelors knocking on my door hoping to impregnate me, is there?'

'Well, no, but I didn't mean that! I meant that at least, unlike me, if you wanted to, you could probably fall pregnant again fairly quickly.'

I grimace. I know she's trying to reassure me but it's not helping.

'All I'm saying is, if I lost a baby and wanted to fall pregnant again, it's unlikely it would happen as quickly as if you tried again.'

'Oh, so it's better I lost my baby than you lost your baby? Is that what you're saying?' I know I'm not being fair to her but I can feel myself getting irate.

'No, it's not! Of course I don't think that. You're

grieving and that's important, and I'm just trying to be helpful but I'm putting my foot in it. I've wanted this baby for years, you know that – but a few days ago, you . . .' She hesitates.

'Go on,' I say, standing up. I think I know what she's going to come out with.

'Well, I was happy when I found out I was pregnant. I was over the moon. It was different for you – you weren't trying for it, you weren't even sure you wanted it. I don't know what to say about all this, Robin.' She seems panicked, like she knows she's messed up here but can't talk herself out of it.

'How about you don't say anything? How about I just go?' I say, picking up my phone and keys and heading for the door.

'No! Robin, don't be like this! I didn't mean to upset you, I just haven't dealt with this before and don't know how to support you.'

Just as I'm at the door I turn on my heel and say, 'Lacey, I haven't been through all your infertility problems, but I never accused you of not getting pregnant because you didn't want it badly enough. I think we both need to cool off,' and storm out to my car feeling worse than I did before I arrived.

TWENTY-ONE

By the time I'm home with Lyla, I am a seething mess. After leaving Dovington's and having more time on my hands than I thought I would, I wandered round Sainsbury's throwing things in my trolley I didn't really need; food that doesn't make a meal – luxury olives and infused balsamic vinegar. I also threw in every single thing I could think of that Lyla loves with wild abandon. Her favourite pork and apple sausages, the mini-yoghurts with way too much sugar in, strawberries, Skips, overpriced kiddie magazines, bubble bath in novelty bottles, all of it. At least one of us is going to be super happy this evening.

Once we're in and I start unpacking the shopping, she sits at the breakfast bar in awe.

'Mummy, why have you bought all these things?' she says, picking up a giant multipack of Shopkins that I bought in the toy aisle. 'Are these for me?' Her face is lit up with absolute delight.

'They surely are!' I say with a great big false-only-to-me smile.

'Really? Thank you, Mummy! Why are we having all these things?' she says, elated and confused.

'Well, I decided it's the Mummy and Lyla Night! We're going to ignore all the usual things, put the telly on, play with all these new toys, eat all our favourite foods, put on these fresh, new pyjamas, ignore your homework, ignore the housework and have a magical night, just you and me!' I say cheerily, this time actually feeling it.

'What?! Mummy!' she squeals, jumping down from her stool and rushing round to throw herself into a huge hug with me.

My God, her hugs are wonderful. She's warm and soft and exudes love. You can't help but not feel every little bit of it. I sink to my knees to meet her height and let her hug me longer, burying my face in her silky hair and squeezing her hard.

'Are you OK, Mummy? You're being really, really squeezy,' she says, still embraced in my arms.

'I am. I've felt so poorly this last week, and it's nice to feel a little bit better because of you.'

'I'll be Nurse Lyla and I'll take care of you,' she says, stroking my hair the same way I stroke hers when she's ill.

You already do, I think.

Our evening is a dream. We have bubble baths, her first and then me while she sits on the bathroom floor rifling through all my make-up and talking about her day, telling me about the new twin girls in her class, about what she and Roo like to play at lunchtime. We put on fresh pyjamas and slide our feet into soft slippers that I left by the radiator for that extra snuggliness. Then we go downstairs where I make sausages, mash, onions and gravy, put on a Christmas film even though it's nearly summer, draw the curtains and cosy down like tiny field mice in their grassy burrow. Lyla finishes her dinner, takes her tray out into the kitchen (as a special treat I allowed trays on laps tonight) and then cuddles into the crook of my arm as we gaze at the TV.

This is more healing than any pill, any leaflet or any 'helpful' chat with an adult. For a few hours I feel normal again. As though everything is as it should be. Just me and Lyla in our little bubble.

By 8 p.m. she's drifted off to sleep and rather than waking her, I scoop her up, all warm in her dressing gown, and carry her into my bed. Tonight's one of those nights where I want her close to me, to feel her warmth, her life.

As I pad downstairs, I feel a vibration in my pocket.

Hey Robin, I haven't been able to reach you these past few days but just to let you know I'll be in London by Thursday and would love to come up to yours for the weekend and be with you. No pressure to do anything, just chill out and relax. LMK what you think, E xxx

I feel a pang of guilt for avoiding Edward for the last few days, despite his regular texts and WhatsApps, but with the strength gained from tonight's cosy-fest, I reply.

Hey! Sorry, it's been a bit of a rubbish week. Feeling much better now (physically and emotionally). It'd be really nice to have you up here and hang out. Let me know if I can get anything in for you, xx

Dropping Lyla at school in the morning, I hope it will be uneventful and that I won't see anyone I know, particularly Val.

Lyla is, as always, bursting with energy and chatter so

I allow myself to be swept along by her happiness as we take her many bags (seriously, so many clubs and groups need so much kit, from junior coding to flipper swimmers, I swear she has a more action-packed day than most adults) to the cloakroom and make our way to the drop-off point in the hall.

'Long time no see!' calls a familiar voice. Lyla is full of glee to see Clara and the pair race ahead. Why are young children like this? They see each other nearly every single day and yet each morning they seem thrilled to be with one another again, as if years have passed by in the meantime. I wish I were that thrilled to see anyone, or that anyone was that thrilled to see me. I turn to face Gillian.

'Hello! Long time no see, indeed! How are things?' I ask in what I believe to be a normal tone.

'Very good, thank you, just plodding along, you know. I was going to give you a ring this afternoon – we haven't seen you at school much lately. It's been your aunt and the hippy girlfriend a lot. Is everything OK?' she asks. I love that in an act of solidarity, Gillian calls Storie the 'hippy girlfriend'. I know she knows her name, so this small act of rebellion is appreciated.

'Oh yes, I've just been a bit sick,' I say, but I can feel the panic in my voice at having to talk about it again.

After Kath telling Natalie, and the disastrous conversation with Lacey, I've realised that although I want some people to know, I can't seem to cope with actually telling them myself.

Sensing my distress like a protective mama bear, Gillian pushes gently. 'Are you sure, lovely?'

I thought I was all right, or at least getting better, but Gillian's concern is setting me off again and I can feel my breath catching in my chest. 'Yep,' I manage, slightly high-pitched.

'Shall we drop the girls off and go and get a coffee?' asks Gillian, kind enough to not make me cry in the middle of the school corridor.

TWENTY-TWO

'It's hard to blurt it out but I think ripping the plaster off and just saying it is best,' I state boldly after a big sip of mint-infused hot chocolate at the local coffee shop. I needed the sugar this morning.

'All right, I'm listening,' says Gillian in her usual calming voice.

'A few weeks ago, I found out I was pregnant,' I begin and notice her sit up and a huge happy smile flash across her face. I carry on as quickly as possible to avoid the congratulations I know I'm about to be confronted with. 'Last week, I found out I wasn't pregnant anymore,' I add, looking intensely at my mug. I don't feel strong enough to use the big words. Even 'lost the baby' feels too sharp today.

'Oh Robin,' Gillian says, immediately reaching for my hand across the table.

'Yeah. It's very common at this early stage.' I wheel out my tried and tested spiel, the phrase that seems to soothe people, make them think you're all right and taking it in your stride. It's a get-out clause for other people, too; they don't ask more or push further.

'It doesn't matter if it's common or not,' Gillian says more firmly than I'd anticipated. 'That baby was a part of you, you had hopes and dreams and expectations and they've been taken from you.' Her hand still on mine.

I look up from my mug and meet her gaze.

'That's exactly how I've been feeling, Gillian. It's not just that the baby's . . . gone . . . but that all my plans and hopes are gone, too. I just wanted it so much, and now . . . now . . .' I begin to cry again.

Gillian sits for a second in silence letting me have my moment of grief before she says, 'I promise you this will get easier.'

'I can't wait to not feel this, to feel better.'

'Well – and I hope you'll take this the right way – you'll never feel totally the same again, Robin. Better than now, yes, certainly, but you don't magically go back to being the person you were before. But that's OK – it'll be part of you, and you'll come to terms with it. You'll learn to love your angel baby in a different way.'

'My what?' I ask, completely confused. I've never heard the term before.

'Your angel baby. When a woman loses a baby, I like to think they go to Heaven as angels and become angel babies. I know it sounds a bit twee but, well, it's what gets me through.'

I blink a few times and realise what she's saying.

'Gillian, I didn't know.'

'It was long before we met. I've accepted the losses but I still remember them.'

'More than one? I'm so sorry.'

'Yes, two. Both before Clara, and then she was our miracle. You never fully recover, like I say, but you do move on and find peace with it. I still love them like they are my babies. I always think, I have three children, one here with me and two in my heart.'

Gillian's words are beyond poignant. I feel a fresh wave of tears but this time they seem different. Almost like relief.

'I'd never considered that I get to keep the idea of "my baby". I'd felt that since it was gone, so was the notion of them as a future person.'

'Robin, you made a baby, you carried that baby, your body nourished that baby and your heart cherished it. It is still, and will forever be, your baby.'

I notice now that Gillian has tears in her eyes, too. We sit and talk for an hour, about how long she and Paul tried and how they have two special days each year to remember each lost baby, releasing balloons or taking Clara on a day trip and telling her how loved she is. My heart aches for Gillian and loves her all the more for understanding the pain I'm in right now.

Long after our drinks have gone cold and we've ordered new ones, this time with panini and brownies for sustenance, Gillian inhales deeply and says, 'I think you need a project, something to focus on.'

'I've just taken a few weeks off work so my project is going to be relaxing and pampering myself,' I joke.

'Well, I need some help. Now I understand why you weren't at the last PaGS meeting, I should fill you in on it,' she says. 'We discussed how to raise funds for the charity that's been helping with home nurse visits for Mrs Barnstorm. The new mum, Gloria, suggested a Ladies' Night with wine and shopping stalls – apparently it was a huge hit in her last school – but I just think it needs a bit more. I know you'll be able to help, you're always so creative. What do you think?'

I still barely know Gloria but she seems nice. She bounds through the school gates each day wearing the brightest outfits over her ample curves, hair bouncing, a smile for everyone. She's literally the physical opposite of Val and I can't help but warm to her. If she and Gillian want to make this Ladies' Night a success, then I want to help.

Gillian's a dab hand at arranging events, having single-handedly raised over five thousand pounds at the village fete she runs every year. She always told us she just did the teas and coffees, but it turns out she's the brains behind the whole thing, it's just she doesn't tell anyone that bit – what a dark horse!

Gillian and I nurse our coffees and I have a brainwave – a Spa Night!

Together we decide to invite local beauticians, independent vendors, catering, entertainment and make-up artists to come in for an evening of shopping, pampering and relaxation. Gillian says she has contacts for some potential local sponsors and she knows I'd be just the person to invite make-up artists in to give makeovers. A brow bar, a smoky-eye workshop, twinkly summer pedis and maybe hand massages for us mums who spend too much time doing chores (or scrolling and clicking on our phones). I'm already getting carried away with ideas.

I love the thought of it all. While sitting in the coffee shop, we ring Mr Ravelle to ask if he'd be up for us doing such a thing and you'd think he'd just won Head Teacher of the Year, he is so excited. At one point he even suggests we invite the local press to report on our community spirit! Steady on, Ravvy!

I feel like I've seen a whole new side of Gillian. Not only her tender, vulnerable side with her – our – angel babies but also a creative, innovative, businesslike side. I'm impressed and totally inspired by her. She's a woman of hidden depths and I'm almost a little bit ashamed that I didn't look further and see that in her. She was so right, the whole drive home I let my brain whir over who I could invite and what I could do, rather than dwell on the pain in my heart. It's not solving it by any means, but The Emptiness suddenly feels a little less empty.

TWENTY-THREE

JUNE

I NOTICE I'M CRYING A little bit less each day.

Not having to be at MADE IT, plus the twin distractions of helping to plan the Spa Night and the fact that Edward is coming to the UK are all working in my favour. I think the key is to keep my brain busy. If my head stays full, it doesn't register that my heart is so empty.

Edward and I agreed over email that he would come up to visit on the Saturday morning to spend an 'easy-breezy' day and night with me. Easy-breezy is one hundred per cent what I need right now.

It's Simon and Storie's weekend with Lyla (thankfully, because there's no way I'm ready to introduce Lyla to

Edward yet; and pleasingly there have been no more foraging 'incidents'), and Kath came over yesterday to help me blitz the house with a duster and hoover. 'You don't want him thinking you live like a slob, lovey,' she said as she arrived with her cordless vac and cleaning caddy.

So, the house is clean, Lyla is safe and well and I'm genuinely looking forward to seeing Edward. I don't want him to feel I've made too much effort, but I still want to look reasonably nice, so I've gone for an indigo-blue maxi-skirt with a white cami tucked in and a really pale shell-pink cardigan to throw on top if I get cold. Hair is in a messy topknot, but that good kind of messy that actually takes a solid fifteen minutes to perfect, and make-up is soft but on.

At about 11 a.m. he pulls into the drive in a neat little electric hire car (he's a man that cares about the environment, then) and I feel a surprising but familiar fizz of excitement in my tummy.

'Gorgeous Robin!' he says as I open the door to greet him.

He steps into the hall for a hug and holds me for a very long time. We go past hug level and I can feel him caring for me. One arm wrapped round my back and one hand holding my head, I feel safe and warm and everything I wanted to feel a couple of weeks ago when the whole awful thing happened. I want to stay in this embrace forever.

We pull away and look at each other. He can see my teary eyes and I don't care. I think we are past the point of trying really hard to be super cool with each other, although I'm not sure we ever did that anyway – that's why it's always worked so well, why it's been so 'easy-breezy'.

'I'm glad you're here,' I say with a big breath out.

'Me too. I missed you!' He laughs.

'I must be getting under your skin,' I tease, and just like that, old comfy banter resumes and we leave his bag in the hallway and head through to the kitchen because we are British and we cannot possibly have any kind of interaction in a home without a cup of tea.

As agreed, we spend the afternoon on the sofa doing very little. I didn't want him coming all this way with the wrong impression, so I explained to Edward on the phone a few nights ago that I don't feel at all physically ready for any kind of action and he was so understanding and respectful, it made me feel completely comfortable about inviting him all the way across the Atlantic just to hang out on the world's squidgiest sofa. But even though sex is off the cards, there is a comforting level of sexual chemistry, and as we chat through some of my beloved Netflix films (that Edward describes as 'utter dross'), I feel myself leaning into him and his arm scooping around me.

We stay like that for a long time. Sitting side by side, saying very little but just being, it's good. It's healing. We don't talk about the baby, but I feel like we don't need to. I don't need to explain anything to him; we just sort of get it and enjoy being with one another.

By evening, we're both shattered. How is it that when you do nothing, you feel more tired? Admittedly he can claim jet lag, but I can't. We order Chinese takeaway and while we wait for it to arrive, we flick through Saturday-night TV, talking about the stuff we used to do in our 'youth'. It turns out Edward was much less of a rebel than I was and had regular 'TV nights' with his mum and dad. They'd order pizza every Saturday as their one takeaway a week and all sit down together to watch *Noel's House Party*, *Challenge Anneka* and *The Generation Game*.

'How wholesome you were! Did you then all say how much you loved each other before you went to bed in matching striped PJs?' I joke.

'Errm, yeah, kind of! I mean, we didn't have the matching PJs, but I always told Mum I loved her lots before going up to bed and still say it every time we finish on FaceTime,' he says, as though it's perfectly normal to be that happy and get on so well with your family.

'That's really sweet,' I say seriously, sensing it's not really a thing to mock. 'My family weren't quite like that. Dad lived most of his life in his shed at the end of our garden allotment, probably hiding from us. And Mum, well, Mum has very high standards and I'm not sure we ever really met them, especially not me. She was always disappointed that I wasn't slimmer, didn't take up an instrument and didn't share her passion for her charity work. She was always organising lunches or fundraisers and bossing everyone around.'

'So not like you and this Spa Night you're doing? That's not organising a fundraiser?' he ventures.

'Ha! Well yes, it is, but I'm not going to be bossing people around and I don't have impossible standards like she did. That's why I'm here with you!' I say, poking him fondly in the arm. *Quite firm, muscular arms,* I think before I drag myself back to his words.

'Are you with me?' he asks suddenly, the tone changing completely.

'Well, I'm here, aren't I? And you are here with me, aren't you?' I say, smiling to try to encourage the easy-breezy atmosphere back but realising what I've just said and wishing I could gobble it back into my mouth again.

'So, in your mind you're not "*with me* with me"?' he says, almost as more of a statement than a question.

I feel trapped and panicked. I like things how they are, with no labels or boundaries or expectations. The last time I expected things of a man and thought about things like this I got really bloody hurt and I can't have that this time.

'Edward, I don't really know. I don't know what we are, but I know I'm enjoying spending time with you and I enjoy what we have at the moment,' I say, knowing really this isn't enough.

'But what do we have? I thought we had something with a bit of substance,' Edward probes. I wish he wouldn't.

'Well, we have a good friendship, and . . .' I trail off.

'We have a good friendship? Robin, we made a baby and I was in it for the long haul with you!' he says passionately, making me almost wince at the 'B' word.

'I know,' I say, looking at my lap. I want so much to be enthusiastic but it's as though Theo completely damaged me and I'm now incapable.

'I don't like playing games and I don't like messing people around. I like you. I really, really like you. I think I'm seriously falling for you. I'm saying I could move back to the UK and try to make this, whatever this is, work,' he says, picking up both my hands as he says 'this'.

I feel like I'm going to be sick. I can't handle this level of emotional pressure. This was meant to be a night of nothing, and all of a sudden it's a night of something. Something big. My mind feels like it's gone into overdrive. After weeks of everyone walking on eggshells around me, this is way too much. I can feel my anxiety squeezing around me like a fist. I should be delighted. But his declaration has set my pulse racing for all the wrong reasons. I can't speak; I can barely breathe.

'Edward,' I manage. 'I can't do this right now.'

I'm saved by the doorbell ringing. We may have gone from wanton sex to wonton soup in a matter of weeks, but I practically jump off the sofa to avoid Edward's gaze and collect our food. Never have I been so glad to see a takeaway arrive.

TWENTY-FOUR

Edward and I did a good job of being friends, hanging out, until he left on the Sunday lunchtime. The weeks since have ticked by and although we've kept in touch by text and banter has been as it always was, there's been a peppering of serious moments, too, where we touch on real life. Unfiltered moments, like his dad being taken into hospital for tests and how hard it can sometimes be for him to live so far away, or when I told him about the day I just sat in the supermarket car park crying about what could have been with the baby. He never fails to be supportive and I feel like a real friendship is developing, like roots are growing in where I least expected them to and it's good. We haven't spoken any more about his offer of moving back and the 'falling for me' situation. That feels like the big scary monster looming in the corner, and I can't really handle facing that right now.

Lacey is blooming. She is the only person I know who enjoys morning sickness, or rather, I think she enjoys boasting about it to anyone who will listen ('Yeah, it's so bad, I was sick eight times this morning – eight!'). Despite having no visible bump at all yet, she insists on wearing completely and only maternity wear and I'm sure she's faking a slight waddle as she walks. But she could be wearing a (maternity) sack and still look amazing, thanks to the almost permanent smile she wears as she rubs the small of her back.

After my storming out of Dovington's, we didn't speak for a couple of days. I don't think either of us knew how to move forward from that. Once I'd cooled down, I could admit to myself that I knew she didn't mean what she said. Maybe the fact that she's always got her foot in her mouth and I wear my heart on my sleeve is part of what makes us friends. Normally, I'm the one who'll let the tears flow at anything (I think of the goldfish funerals I led for us as children, or the weep-fests I had over teenage crushes), and she's always been just a teensy bit emotionally stunted, I guess. Keeping things on her level, I sent her a couple of heart emojis followed by the dove emoji. She took the peace offering well and we haven't spoken of it since. Nothing like just completely sweeping things under the rug to keep relationships healthy, eh?

Her knock on the door is a welcome distraction and so I hop up to let her in, lead her through to the kitchen and put the kettle on. Lyla is on a play date with Honor and Roo and since it is Saturday and nobody is required to exert themselves in any fashion, I've not even got dressed yet.

'Oh God, I'm so hot!' Lacey says, flumping down dramatically onto one of the dining chairs and dropping her bag, keys and phone as loudly as possible on the surface.

'Really? It's not that warm, is it?' I say, thinking maybe I'm going mad.

'Well,' she says, drawing out her words, 'it'll be the baby, won't it? All pregnant women are too hot. I've got an app and it's one of the things it says.'

'Oh, right. I'll open the back doors then, give you a bit of a breeze.'

'Thanks, Robs. It's hard work being pregnant!' she adds sagely.

I'm trying to be graceful and I don't want to stop her

talking about the baby or how excited she is, but I can't help feeling my hand hover over my stomach for just a second, feeling for the baby that isn't there anymore. I would have been sixteen weeks pregnant by now. My life feels ruled by weeks. Ten weeks till the Isso Project at LFW; sixteen weeks is how far along I would have been; ten weeks is how far along Lacey is; thirty weeks till we meet her baby; thirty weeks to get over my loss.

'I'm glad you popped by,' I say, attempting to change the subject. 'I was meant to be tackling the house today, and the last thing I fancy is getting all the cleaning stuff out and doing it.' This isn't true. I wasn't going to do anything, but I needed to say something to break my chain of thought.

'Bloody hell, no! Just the smell of all the products is enough to trigger my morning sickness. Karl says while I'm pregnant we can hire a cleaner but to be honest,' she laughs, 'I'm going to keep her on once the baby's here and say I still have smell aversions! So, what's your news?'

'Well,' I say with as much enthusiasm as I can muster for a woman who's living the life I didn't know I even wanted until a few weeks ago. 'You know I'm organising a Spa Night at the school with the PaGS? Well, it's turning into a real project! People have really dug deep and got involved. Even Kath's going to set up a stall for her lavender creations. She's actually doing really well with them. After Moira's frankly disturbing endorsements, all the women from her Cupcakes and Crochet Club have put in their orders and I think she's even sent a batch down for Mum and her Rotary Club ladies!'

'Who knew Kath was such an entrepreneur!' Lacey smiles, sipping the tea I've put in front of her.

'I know! She's branched out from creams and bath bombs to liquid and solid soaps, bubble bath and hand sanitiser, all infused with lavender. She puts the liquid soaps in little glass jars and leaves a full sprig of lavender in there so it actually looks really pretty in your bathroom, too. She's a powerhouse, Lacey!'

'I bet Lyla loves it, doesn't she?' says Lacey.

'Oh, she's a proper little assistant! Kath often enlists Lyla's help and they sit doing it for hours. Lyla feels so special, popping in the sprigs or sticking labels on jars, it's so sweet to see. And apparently, Kath's made quite good friends with a chap called Colin from the wholesaler where she buys the lavender, and he's helping her turn the garage into a workshop. I absolutely love how driven she's being, how much she thrives on it, you know?' I say, genuinely enthused.

'Yeah, she's doing brilliantly. Do you think the bubble

baths would be suitable for pregnant women?' Lacey asks a little absent-mindedly.

'Probably, I'll ask her. Don't you think it's impressive that she's taking life by the horns and making a little something for herself, though?' I ask, wondering if everything I say will keep coming back to being pregnant.

Sensing my frustration, Lacey snaps out of it.

'Absolutely! She's a woman on a mission. Maybe she could make up packages, and I could put them next to the till at Dovington's? I bet all the men in the doghouse buying "I'm sorry" bouquets for their wives and girlfriends would love to pick up one of her products, too!'

'That would be amazing. I'm sure she'd love that. She's really on a roll now. I'm going to help her make some business cards and leaflets, too.'

'Perfect. Oh, by the way, are you free the week after next?'

'I think so. I've cut back my hours at work for it to be more manageable and to spend more time with Lyla for a little while, so I should be free. Do you fancy doing something nice?' I ask, excited that I've finally got my Lacey back and it's not all about the baby.

'Well, yes! The hospital have booked me in for my twelve-week scan and Karl is running a training day that he literally cannot leave. We've already had two private scans just for peace of mind so he's not going to miss out on much, but I don't want to be that sad sack that has to go alone, so I wondered – will you come with me?' she asks, smiling.

'Oh. Um, doesn't your mum want to go?' I ask, shocked at her request. She seems completely oblivious to what she's asking of me.

'It sounds silly, but we've already had a scan together. I'm addicted to this private scan place. Eighty pounds and you get twenty minutes just looking at the baby and all the little features and movements. I mean, not that it has a lot of features yet, but you can see it's a baby, you know? Anyway, it's at 11.30 a.m. and I could drive us if you like.' Lacey carries on, absorbed in her own excitement. I shouldn't be so surprised. Her heart's in the right place, but she doesn't always engage her brain in time. When we were fifteen I got dumped by my first 'boyfriend' at the end-of-year school party but that night all she talked about was how three different boys had asked her out and she wasn't sure who to choose. I think she was trying to distract me. I'm a grown woman now, but part of me feels like that fifteen-year-old girl all over again. I know my lovely Lacey doesn't mean to hurt me, and it's all part of something she's waited so long for, but right now I want to shake her. She's always been such an amazing friend so I need to find the right words to show that I really am pleased she's pregnant, but there are some things that are just too painful for me at this stage.

'Lacey, I really want to support you and help you, but I don't know if I can manage this,' I say, sitting down at the table with her and our big mugs of hot tea.

'I thought you said you were free?' Wow, this isn't going to be easy.

'I am free. But, Lacey, come on, you must know how hard this would be for me. I should be having scans, too, I should be looking at little features and movements. But I'm not. My baby doesn't exist anymore,' I say, leaving the last line hanging heavily in the air, not really knowing why I said it or how much weight it held in me.

Lacey's face softens.

'I know it's hard, Robs, I've been there. All those months desperately waiting for this little baby,' she says, tapping her stomach. 'But it was early on, wasn't it? And you can get pregnant again, you've proven that it wasn't hard for you to conceive. Edward will move back over here and Lyla will finally have the family unit she needs. It'll be fine, I promise.'

I'm stunned. Everything she's just said has completely knocked the wind out of my totally unpregnant sails.

Facing infertility and having a miscarriage are both awful, but they're not the same. I'm not looking to engage in some kind of competitive grief. They're different, even if equally painful, experiences and yet she's thinking I could just get knocked up again instantly (maybe I shouldn't have let it go the first time she suggested this). Never mind whether I'd want to, if I'm ready or the fact that the man she's talking about lives on the other side of the planet. But it's the suggestion that Lyla isn't getting what she needs that really stings right now. Was it a slip of the tongue, or does she really think I'm not enough for my little girl? I'm so astounded that I just sit there, gormless, like those people who open the door to surprise TV shows where the presenter is holding an oversized cardboard cheque. Except, there's no cheque or camera crew, just my ignorant, pregnant, cow of a 'friend' who I'm fighting the urge not to throw milky tea all over.

'Are you for real?' I manage at last.

'Huh?' she says, surprised that I'm not thanking her for her infinite wisdom.

'Are you for fucking real?' I say again, a bit louder and clearer.

'Look, I'm sorry if you're upset by me having a scan – you don't have to come. I just thought you'd like to be asked and I thought you wanted things to go back to normal,' she says indignantly.

'Back to normal? What's normal?' I say, still reeling from the Lyla comment.

'You know what's normal! Before things happened, before last month . . .' she says, tailing off at the end.

This isn't *my* Lacey talking. This isn't the woman who stayed by my side – apart from loo breaks – for four solid days when Simon left; the woman who could make me smile even in the most frightening days of The Emptiness; the woman I've always trusted with the most breakable parts of me. What has happened to my best friend?

'You can't even say it, Lacey! I'll say it for you. Before I had a miscarriage. Before I lost something I didn't even know I loved until I watched my body reject and destroy it.' With that, great heaving sobs rise up through my body and I slam both fists down on the table.

'That's not what I meant. All I meant was—'

'And, while we're at it, what does Lyla "needing a family unit" mean? Have you not met Kath or Simon or me? I'm enough, Lacey! It's 2018. Not everyone has to be in an identikit nuclear family with a matching husband and matching house with a cleaner and a job they can swan in and out of whenever they fancy it. I make this work.

My family unit doesn't look like yours but it's still a fucking good family fucking unit!!' I'm on the edge of hysteria but it feels like a release. All those worthless, angry or sad feelings I've been harbouring for all these weeks are bubbling up and spewing out of my mouth and I finally feel a little bit alive again. It's not just that I can't stop them, I don't even want to.

'I'm not going to stay and listen to this. I don't need the upset,' Lacey says, getting up to leave.

'Thank God. If I have to hear one more thing about you being pregnant, I'll scream. No wonder Perfect Karl is working so many extra hours, he's probably sick to death of you.'

Instantly, I know I've crossed a line. I can see the sting in her eyes as she picks up her phone, keys and bag and walks out of the house. I know I should say something, but I can't. Right now I'm relieved. Relieved not to have the opportunity to be hurt – or to hurt her – more.

For a few seconds I sit at the table staring at her empty chair and then, as if everything is all right, I stand up, wipe my eyes and nose with kitchen roll, go upstairs and run a bath, chucking in one of Kath's lavender-infused bombs and plonking myself in, just in time for a huge, fresh wave of tears to fall. Fuck.

TWENTY-FIVE

JULY

The early-summer weeks pass and the day of Lacey's scan has come and gone. I don't reach out to Lacey, nor her to me. I think about her on the day of the scan, all day, wishing things could be some sort of normal, that I could be on the end of an excited text with the scan picture attached, telling her it looks so cute and I'm so thrilled, but I'm just not. I'm still angry, but now as well as that hot rage, I just feel sad.

I think I can get over almost all of the comments she churned out and put them down to the fact that her baby brain is firmly engaged (I mean, I remember feeling and saying some daft things when I was pregnant with Lyla, though I don't remember any foot-in-mouth calamities of this level). But the remark about Lyla needing a family unit got to me. It plays on repeat in my mind as I make Lyla's packed lunch, or wait for her to come out of school. I thought I'd nailed motherhood at last and that I was enough, that I was doing enough, but now doubt has crept into the cracks I didn't know were there and I think about it all the time.

Kath unexpectedly pops round on a sunny afternoon in half-term with another batch of lavender creations to show me on the doorstep like a travelling salesman. 'I don't think all your posh mummy friends will want these, will they?' she asks, showing a rare insecurity.

'Of course they will! Look how much Moira and the crochet ladies have enjoyed them. Everyone at school will love them, too, and besides, they're not that posh,' I say.

'What about that horsey one with the same jacket as Princess Anne?'

'Yes, OK, Finola's a bit posh but everyone else is fairly normal! Now, don't stand out here, come in, come in!' I say, stepping back and moving towards the lounge.

'I can't stop, Colin from the warehouse is in the car, we're going out for a stroll and then dinner,' she chimes, not making eye contact with me. Instead she fiddles about with the little cellophane bags of lavender bath salts she's tied with purple ribbon and arranged in the shallow box she's carrying in the crook of her arm.

'Oh, hot date is it?' I laugh, trying to put her at ease. Obviously she feels weird about going to dinner with a man – she hasn't dated anyone since Uncle Derek died a few years back – though she probably just wants to talk to him about her lavender business.

'Ha, yes! You could call it that! Colin's a bit of a dish, I suppose,' she says, blushing from forehead to bust.

Good God. 'Kath, are you seeing Colin?' I say, shocked.

'I can see him, yes, love, he's in the car,' she says, waving him to get out and come to the door.

'No, no! I meant are you actually seeing him like . . . *dating* him,' I rattle off quickly, now Colin is on the move.

'Well, we go out for lunch and dinner, I watch him play bowls on Wednesdays and we've enjoyed some special time together, so yes, I suppose we are dating,' she says, slightly flustered, but excited like a teenager as he walks over. Jesus Christ, what sort of 'special time' has my aunt enjoyed? Actually I don't want to know.

Bald, with crinkly blue eyes, Colin walks up with what I detect to be a swagger and puts his arm comfortably around Kath's waist, causing her to blush even harder and necessitating even more furious rearranging of the bath salts. Colin is wearing tan Hush Puppies, a pair of very faded blue jeans with a pink paisley shirt tucked in and secured with a conker-brown belt that looks a wee bit tight. I think he thinks he is a 'cool guy'.

'You must be the wonderful niece I've heard all about!' Colin says, beaming.

'Aha! I must be! Now I know you're off for dinner, but come on in, if you've got time, no need to stand on the step,' I say, also slightly flustered, somehow catching it off of Kath.

I walk through to the lounge and they both follow and sit on the double sofa, and Kath puts the box down on the footstool. Hearing people coming in, Lyla bounds down the stairs and stops in her tracks when she sees a strange man sitting in the front room.

'Look, Lyla, Kath's brought a friend round! This is Colin! He helps Kath make her lavender things,' I say in a children's-TV-presenter tone.

Lyla goes into typical child mode, completely ignores Colin and climbs onto the sofa next to me, hiding her face in my back and shoulders.

'She's shy,' I say with a smile and shrug and Kath nods.

'Colin and I weren't going to stay,' Kath says.

'No, I like to meet your friends. Colin, Auntie Kath tells me you work at the wholesaler's, that you've been really encouraging her to make more of her products,' I say brightly. I feel as though this is a glimpse into the future, where I will have to vet Lyla's boyfriends like this.

'Any excuse to spend more time with this gorgeous creature!' he says, mock-tickling her sides and causing her to squirm and giggle.

'Yes, I'm sure. So do you, er, source your lavender locally?' Wow, I'm really scraping the barrel for conversation here.

'All over, really. That bubble bath she gave you, I must say I'm rather proud of it too. I had the great pleasure of being Kath's, shall we say, guinea pig, with a lot of her products. Any excuse to get a bit sudsy, eh?' Colin the Cool Guy says, now heartily laughing. I want this thread of conversation to end immediately.

'What's sudsy?' Lyla pipes up. 'Like Pudsey?'

'No, lovely, Colin just means a bit soapy,' Kath interjects far too quickly for someone faking breeziness.

'Why is that funny?' Lyla persists.

'Well, sweetheart, because I had a wonderful assistant to help with my suds,' Colin replies, with a rather repellent waggle of his eyebrows.

'I don't need help with *my* bath. I'm seven. I can do it myself and wash my own hair, can't I, Mummy?' she says proudly, mercifully not cottoning on to the adult nature of Colin's cringe-inducing remarks.

'And you know, Robin, Kath tells me you're a single lady about town—'

'I'm not "about town", but yes, I'm single,' I interject.

'You want to give the lavender body butter a try. It drives the men absolutely berserk. I should know!' he says with a wink and a pat of Kath's thigh.

'OK! Great advice!' What's wrong with him? And why did I let this randy old goat into my living room?

'Yes, my lovely lady here is quite the whizz with her new lavender line,' Colin starts.

'She's not *your* lady,' Lyla says bluntly, and Kath shifts uncomfortably in her spot on the sofa.

'Well, no, she's her own lady but she's my lady friend. My girlfriend, I suppose,' Colin says with all the tact of a bulldozer down a village high street.

'No she isn't! Kath isn't a girlfriend! Kath loves me and Mummy and Derek!' Lyla peaks, distress rising in her small voice.

Sensing the meeting is not really going well for anyone, Kath stands up. Colin, the only person oblivious to his mistakes, stands up too.

'I do, lovey!' Kath says, putting her arms out to Lyla, who instinctively gets off the sofa and goes over for a cuddle. 'I love you to the moon and back again, and Mummy too. But we have to go, because we have a table booked. Shall I pop round tomorrow after school and we can make Mummy's favourite scones for her?'

'Yes! And biscuits too!' she negotiates.

'Biscuits too, then!' she says, cuddling her tightly back and looking at the floor with pursed lips.

They make a speedy exit and, as I close the door, I turn round and lean on it to take a big breath, not noticing Lyla sitting directly opposite me on the stairs.

'Kath's boyfriend is a worm.'

TWENTY-SIX

It's twenty minutes until the Grand Opening of the Hesgrove Pre-Prep School PaGS Spa Night. After myriad phone calls, an overcrowded WhatsApp group, a few coffee shop planning meetings with the other parents and two or three nervous but excited, 'Are you sure they'll like my products?' messages from Kath, the big night is upon us and I'm excited.

I feel like such a mum tonight, but in a good way. The kind of mum I always wanted mine to be. The kind that is friends with all the other mothers, is part of the school community, has a calm, maternal way about her. I don't know whether it's the buzz of being involved in a new project, or the super soft white slouchy cardigan I bought from ASOS last week and have thrown on over my slouchy jeans and trainers, either way, I'm digging it.

Gillian, Gloria, Matthew and Laurence, Stephanie from Year Five and Ros from Year One have spent the afternoon setting up the facilities with me. We've turned the utilitarian dining hall into an inviting, serene, well-laid-out 'spa'. We have used medical-style room dividers draped with silk and taffeta from the art department to measure off treatment 'zones'. Gloria has booked in ladies to offer hand, back and shoulder massages, we have a person coming in to provide Indian head massages, one of the school dinner ladies 'does a bit of reiki on the side' so we've solicited her services, and Matthew's favourite chiropodist is attending for two out of the three hours, too. I've tried not to ask why this one is his favourite and how many he actually has to warrant a favourite, because he made it all sound so normal when he mentioned it at the coffee shop meeting a few weeks back.

In the beauty zone we have Skye and one of her millennials offering mini makeovers and a lady called Nicky doing gel nails for £5 less than she would in her salon. We've also booked in a body artist to offer metallic temporary tattoos and hand art with body paints. Skye offered to help for no fee as a 'thank you for taking responsibility for my huge mistake', which I thought was noble of her. I had already forgiven her, but I won't tell her that and will take all the help we can get for tonight. In fact, since the whole insert-fatty-pics-here debacle, Skye seems to have been something approaching humble. I wouldn't say we are best buds ready to swap gossip and share a glass of wine (I wonder if she drinks, or is this against her principles, too?) but I think she has learnt to respect me a little, step down off her pedestal sometimes, and I appreciate it. It's quite comforting to have her here tonight, we've become a bit more of a team since working closely on the Isso Project.

Over on the far side of the hall, we have our shopping stalls and wine kiosks. We have the local delicatessen serving mini samples of wine from around the world as well as olives, cheeses, overpriced crackers, chutneys and the most beautifully ornate truffles I've ever seen in my life.

There are also stalls from artisan jewellers, children's book initiatives, knitted clothes, wood crafts (I can't help but think how much Storie would enjoy this stand) and in pride of place (thanks to a little bit of meddling on my part this afternoon), Kath's 'Lavender Lovies' stall. I had a professional banner designed and printed with sprigs of lavender and the name in a swirly font. I've covered her table with a sage-green silky fabric that I think will really make her purple creations pop.

At 5 p.m. the vendors trickled in to set up, ready for our 6 p.m. grand opening. Mr Ravelle has agreed to open the event, something Gloria seemed insistent on. She's a really nice woman but she's fearsomely pushy when she's on a mission. She even brought her own clipboard in. Who has a personal clipboard at home ready to use for events like this? Gloria Straunston is who. We've all accepted her as our leader for tonight. She who holds the clipboard, leads.

Gillian has become quite friendly with her these last few weeks. Apparently she's been a single mum to her twins since she divorced her American husband three years ago, and ran her own very successful online business in PR until she recently sold it. Gillian seems impressed at how well behaved her children are and how tastefully decorated her country home 'with room for six or seven cars on the drive and Jacobean panelling in the entryway' is. I suppose the bossiness correlates to the well-behaved children (maybe she has clipboards for them, too?), I certainly want to stand up straight and behave better when I'm around her. I think Mr Ravelle is under her spell as well, since he's been flitting about all afternoon helping us set up.

By 7 p.m. the hall is heaving. Mr Ravelle opened the event with a ceremonial lifting of his disposable wine glass from the drinks stall and the guests poured in, full of merriment.

My Gloria-assigned volunteer duty is to 'ensure all vendors and service providers are content', and also to 'manage bin bag collections'. I think this means check on the people and pick up rubbish at the end. I can totally handle that and I'm just glad I'm not poor Ros, who is stuck on 'assist with surplus parking requirements' and is currently standing outside in the car park wearing a hi-vis jacket.

I walk slowly round the hall and note that all the masseuse 'cubicles' are full and their waiting lists outside them (on little tables adorned with sprigs of lavender that I borrowed from Kath) are full, too. So far, so good.

I meander over to the beauty zone. Skye is giving one of the nice mums I recognise from Year Four a makeover and answering questions about contouring, her millennial MUA assistant Maci is giving another woman a 'full brow lift' with her powder kit, and Nicky the nail lady has a queue forming. The only fly in the ointment is the fact that the body artist isn't there. Instead, there's a sad, empty table with 'body art' written on a slip of paper Sellotaped to it. Where is she? It's my job to ensure all the vendors are OK, but I can't ensure they're OK if they aren't here. I've invested so much time and energy into this event that I start to feel a bit panicked at the thought of anything tarnishing it. I look around for Gloria and her clipboard but she's nowhere to be seen.

Sensing my discomfort, Skye stands up and comes over, leaving her customer with her contour half done. On one side she's a chiselled masterpiece and on the other she's a plate.

'You OK, hun?' she asks. To anyone else she'd sound nonchalant, but now that I know her, this is true care.

'I am but the body artist hasn't shown up and I can't see Gloria, who has the list of names and contact details.'

'Want me to fill in?' she asks as if it's no big deal. This is what I like about Skye. As frustratingly condescending and opinionated as she can be, she isn't afraid of hard work.

'If you could, that would be amazing! Do you have the kit?' I say, so relieved.

'Yep, I live for body art, so I always have a stash of adhesives, paint and glitter in my box!' she says with such a can-do attitude that I could hug her.

'Thank you, Skye, you're a star!'

'No worries, bae, I've got your back.'

She says that so sincerely that I grin back at her. I'm

not entirely sure what the deal with 'bae' is, but it's said warmly and it's good to know someone has my back. My back is had. I like it.

After a few minutes spent quickly redesigning the beauty zone to remove the spare table and relabel Skye's spot as 'Mini Makeovers and Body Art' while she finishes off the other side of plate-face, I wander across the room to Kath's stall, making sure to pick up a couple of glasses of wine on the way.

Kath's stand looks gorgeous. She's brought Colin along (I won't tell Lyla!), who has made the most beautiful wooden pergola, with faux vines and flowers intertwined and little strings of battery-operated fairy lights draped through as well. The silky sage table is heaving with the most wonderful-looking jars, vials and pots of her lavender creations. A wicker basket is overflowing with purple bath bombs and on a mottled silver tray lie a selection of open jars and pots for customers to sample.

'Kath, this all looks amazing!' I say, handing her the second glass of wine and begrudgingly handing Colin my glass that luckily I hadn't sipped out of yet.

'Thank you, lovey,' she says, beaming.

'This wooden thing is fabulous!' I gesture to the pergola.

'Yes! Colin erected it for me himself!' she says proudly.

'Even at my age I can still erect, ha ha,' Colin chuckles.

'You did a fantastic job, that wood was really quite heavy,' Kath replies warmly, clearly missing his joke. I wish I'd missed it too.

'Well, I'm so impressed. I think yours is the best stall here.'

'Oh, Robin, you would say that, you're always so supportive.'

'No, I really wouldn't say it if I didn't mean it! Have some faith in yourself, Kath, this all looks absolutely amazing!'

I look up to see Finola striding over, still in her muddy jodhpurs and battered old green waxed Barbour jacket.

'Ah, Finola! You came!' I say, going over to greet her and noticing an unusual look on her face.

'Yes, dear, I've come to support the troops. You and Gillian have worked so hard over all of this, I couldn't let the side down.'

'Well, I'm thrilled you're here! Are you all right, though? You seem a bit . . . off,' I suggest, not really sure how else to describe it.

'Absolutely fine, my dear! Fit as a fiddle! I'm perhaps a little out of place, though. I'm not really one for all these lotions and potions. I don't know the first thing about everything you girls do to make the face pretty! I tried that eye shimmer thingamajig you gave me last year with the lip gloss, but Edgar said I looked "frilly" and I haven't tried it again since. I'm not really sure I belong in this world of fancy blushes and whatnots.'

My heart just melts for Finola. Always one to be strong and forthright in everything she does, here I can see a softer, more vulnerable side and I just want to scoop her up for the biggest cuddle and tell her how much I love her. Instead, though, I do the next best thing.

'Come and meet my Auntie Kath, she makes a wonderful range of organic lavender bath bombs, creams and soaps that you might like.'

I can see her interest is piqued. I lead her over and slip away from the conversation just as I hear Finola say to Kath, 'So this just explodes in your bathwater, does it? How exhilarating!'

TWO HOURS LATER, AND the evening has been a resounding success. Every vendor has a full money tin, the hall was busy all through the evening and Gloria and her clipboard ran a jolly good show.

Just as we're finishing up the evening and saying goodbye to the last remaining customers, I see Skye with a familiar face at her stall. Gillian and I exchange a look of excitement and almost skip over like giddy schoolgirls.

'Finola, you look absolutely gorgeous!' Gillian says.

Skye, as a favour to me, squeezed Finola on to her

treatment list and gave her the full works. Always up for a good transformation, Skye has done a beautiful job. Finola's skin is soft and glowing with a dewy blush and golden highlighter. Her eyes seem softer even though they're now defined with perfectly applied brown shadow and light, fluttery false lashes that complement the precise arch of her eyebrows so well. Skye has blended warm taupe tones on her eyelids and lifted the brow bone with a radiant cream colour. For lipstick, she's opted for a neutral warm pink, one of those 'my lips but better' shades, and all tied in together, Finola looks absolutely sensational.

'Wow. Just wow. You look amazing!' I say, gobsmacked. I knew she'd look nice but this is incredible. 'Not that you don't look lovely normally – but it's nice to have a look like this stashed away for nights out or if you just fancy a bit of a change,' I say, anxious to make sure she knows I love her barefaced as much as I do with this gorgeous Oscar-worthy face on.

'I feel like a million dollars.' Finola beams as she stares at herself in the hand-mirror a very proud Skye has given her.

'I feel like one of you young, pretty mums,' she says, gesturing at Gillian and me.

'You are one of us young, pretty mums, you silly thing,' Gillian laughs sweetly.

'I don't think so, dear. I'm always the outdoorsy one. I accepted that was my label and left the looking glamorous to you trendy ones, but this feels marvellous. I must remember I don't always have to be the horsey one just because I was scared of trying something new,' she replies.

'Finola. I have never thought of you as any different from the rest of us. If anything, I assumed you were more confident because you didn't need all the creams and glosses we turn to. In fact, I used to be quite intimidated by you because I thought you were so ace!' I add, laughing.

'You were intimidated by me? I was intimidated by you and your glamorous swishing about!' she retorts. 'Good golly, you're a make-up artist, while until tonight, I've been happier grooming horses than grooming myself.'

'Well, thank God we all love each other now, then, with or without makeovers!' I say, helping her pick up a surprising number of shopping bags (maybe we're going to see quite the change in Frilly Finola) and ushering her towards the door as we're starting to clear up.

'Thank you, Skye, you absolutely nailed it. I owe you,' I say as Gillian walks with Finola to the door.

'No you don't. I owed you. It was lovely seeing your friend feel so good about herself. Sometimes make-up's just creams and colours, sometimes it's a mask to hide behind but sometimes it's a woman's greatest tool. I love this job, you know?' Skye muses.

Earnest, but I'll take it.

'I do know. I really, really do.'

KATH HAS COMPLETELY SOLD out and has a list of bulk orders for people who want to gift friends and family or sell her products in their own businesses. She's absolutely bubbling with excitement and completely oblivious to Colin, who is struggling to get his pergola down. I back away before he tries any more erection jokes.

As is my assigned duty, I wander off to pick up some bin bags from the huge supply cupboard just outside the foyer office. There's a keycode for the lock, so to see the door left open after hours is a bit unnerving. I suddenly wish I hadn't watched so many thrillers on Netflix because I'm starting to imagine this is where a killer is hiding, ready to jump out and bludgeon me to death with a pack of exercise books.

I creep up very quietly and hear the faintest little moan. With fake confidence, in one swift movement, I pull the door open.

My brain cannot compute it. I stand open-mouthed, blinking repetitively like a fish with dodgy contact lenses.

There, in the cupboard, up against the poster paints and sugar paper supplies, are Mr Ravelle and Gloria, snogging like overzealous teenagers!

I'm still standing there, gawping, when Mr Ravelle pulls away, sees me and finally stutters, 'And that's where we keep the bin bags and tidying supplies, Ms Straunston,' as if I haven't just seen him with his mouth attached to her face and her hand over his groin.

'Don't mind me!' I say when the power of speech returns to me. I close the door in a hurry. *Good on them,* I think.

My God, what a night. I retrace my steps to the hall, smiling to myself. I can't wait for a debrief with Gillian and Finola. I can't wait to find out how much money Kath has made, and, I realise, I can't wait to go full steam ahead for LFW in six weeks – with Skye. And suddenly, tonight, it seems as if some light has seeped back into my life. I feel that familiar fizz of happiness knocking at the door.

Hello, I've missed you.

Part Four

STRIKE A POSE!

TWENTY-SEVEN

AUGUST

No one ever said balancing work and being the best mum to Lyla would be easy. Does anyone ever get it right?

As the days speed by in the run-up to London Fashion Week, MADE IT feels electric. Imagine that feeling a primary school has the week leading up to the Christmas play, times it by fifty and that's what we're dealing with. Stuart constantly looks a little bit sweaty and I'm sure Alice is moving about a hundred per cent faster than usual, like a hummingbird.

The job has been fully planned out. We know who's on it, who's leading (Natalie, of course, but with myself – hurrah – and Skye as her deputies), we know what kit we're taking. The face charts are ready. The trial runs are done. And Alice has organised all the logistics. But being ready has only made us all the more eager to get started. I'm counting down the days, and it feels good. I didn't lose my job, or Natalie's respect, in the end. But I'm damn well going to shine as part of this awesome team!

I've been taking on more jobs, after my time off. The Spa Night really made me see how much satisfaction I take from working on something, seeing a job through and being proud of myself, so I've upped the ante. Lyla hasn't been thrilled about it. I spent the first part of the summer being really hands-on with her, showering her with love (for both our sakes) and now, when I need to face life again and flex my muscles professionally, Lyla is not so keen. Kath has been having her two days a week but, much to Lyla's horror, Colin has been there a few times and that has really upset the applecart.

Yesterday was the worst day. I went to fetch her after a long day of trial runs for Project Isso and I could see Kath had been crying. All the soft skin around her eyes was raised and red, and instead of inviting me in and trying to stuff me with home-cooked food and sending me back with a foil-wrapped batch of scones, she said, 'Lyla's had a good day, I'm sure she's quite tired now,' and handed me her already-packed rucksack on the doorstep. Lyla had her shoes on ready and didn't say much as we said our thank yous and goodbyes. It's never normally this quick a turnaround. Usually I budget a solid twenty minutes to get in, get the goods (my child) and leave. This was all done and dusted in under five.

In the car on the way home I glance at Lyla in the rear-view mirror a few times. She looks absolutely fine.

'How was your day with Kath then?' I venture.

'Good,' she says, looking casually out of the window. Kids can be so aloof when they want to be.

'What did you do?' I push.

'Not much.' See? Aloof AF.

Why do children do this? When you want forty nano-seconds of silence, they want to tell you every detailed thing in their brains, but should you ask how their day went or what they learnt at school, it's as though selective amnesia has set in, and obtaining any information at all is akin to drawing blood from a stone.

'OK. So, did you make any scones today?' I try a different approach, knowing full well hardly a day goes by at Kath's where she doesn't bake some of her amazing scones.

'Yeah.'

'And what about shortbread?' If she thinks I'm going to give up, she's wrong.

'Yeah, with lavender in though.' Oh, some detail!

'Well, that sounds nice,' I offer warmly.

Silence.

'Was the shortbread nice with lavender in?' God, she's hard to crack tonight.

'No. Gross. It tasted like a garden,' she says with venom.

Yes, we're getting somewhere at last. 'Oh dear!' I say, hoping she won't be able to resist telling me more.

'Colin said it was the best shortbread he'd ever tasted, Mummy.' She seems really disgusted by this last statement. As if Colin's off his rocker a bit. Which maybe he is, I don't know.

'Did he? So he popped over, did he?'

'Yes. I watched Kath's videos. Your old ones. I don't like him so I thought about what you always say – if you don't have anything nice to say, don't say anything at all, right?'

'Well, yes, but we musn't ignore him entirely.' I'm impressed at her politeness (and if I'm honest, a bit envious of her bluntness), but sometimes a little guidance is needed in etiquette.

'I didn't. I was very forthright.'

I notice an emphasis on the word 'forthright'. 'Oh. What does "forthright" mean, then?' When did my seven-year-old become so eloquent?

'It means saying exactly what you think, even if it's a bit bold. That's what Kath said. She was crying but not cross. She just said I'd been very forthright and then she put your old *Lion King* video on for me. I told her I didn't want to watch it but she said, "Lovey, I need a break, just sit and watch this, please", and I thought that maybe she did sound a bit cross, actually.'

Good grief, this doesn't sound like Kath.

'Wow. That's a lot of information there, Lyla. What did you say that was so forthright?'

'Don't want to say,' she says, squirming in her booster seat.

'You can say it. I won't be cross. Just tell me the truth.'

Silence.

'Please, Lyla. I'm on your side. Always,' I add gently.

'OK.' She pauses as though struggling to let it out. 'I said that Colin shouldn't be trying to be Kath's boyfriend because Kath had a boyfriend and then a husband called Derek and we love him and he loves Kath forever and is waiting in Heaven for her in a house made of flowers and shells and when she gets really, really old and dies and goes to Heaven, Derek will be there at the end of the tunnel, smiling, with his arms out like this.' She gestures wide open arms from the back of the car. 'And he will hold her and love her and they will live in their flower and shell house and Kath will tell him all the things she's been doing on earth while he's gone. They'll go through their holiday albums again and dance again and Derek will tell all his jokes again and Colin can't come! Colin can't come into the flower and shell house and Derek would hate Colin!'

Shit.

No wonder Kath was teary. All those years she's spent portraying this magical version of where Derek is have certainly come home to roost. I could kick myself for not having had a chat with Lyla that first time she mentioned Derek in front of Colin.

'Oh my goodness,' I say, exhaling dramatically.

'What?'

'I think that might have upset Kath, because she might like Colin being her boyfriend.'

'But Derek was her boyfriend and then her husband. They got married and had pink cake and champagne and Grandad Wilde was there and—'

'No, I know, I know they got married and I know Derek was Kath's boyfriend before that, but, now he's gone, I think Kath would like to have someone in her life. Colin makes her happy.'

'But Derek isn't gone. He's waiting. In Heaven,' she persists.

'I know, I know, baby, but, just for now, while she's waiting to see Derek again, I think she would like to enjoy spending time with Colin.' I try to talk slowly and gently because clearly this is a big topic for my sweet black-and-white thinker.

'Then she should put all of Derek's photos away and tell us that her heart doesn't belong to Derek anymore,' Lyla says matter-of-factly. How I wish I could see love as straightforwardly as she does.

'Oh, Bluebird, love isn't really as simple as that. Kath's heart is big enough for both. She loves Derek and I'm sure is looking forward to seeing him again, and also, right now, she's enjoying spending time with Colin and has space in her heart to enjoy that, too.'

I check the mirror and can see the little cogs turning in her mind.

'So does Kath have space in her heart for every man in the world, or just Derek and Colin?'

'Ha, I think just Derek and Colin for now,' I laugh, imagining Kath with a slew of suitors at her door.

'OK then. But he's still a worm.'

LATER THAT NIGHT I text Kath, apologising for Lyla's unintentional insensitivity. I want to make sure she knows how loved she is, and that Lyla and I will support her in everything she does. I settle on a slight lie: *Colin is lovely and we're happy you're happy.* As well as texting, I go online and book Lyla into the school Summer Club for the last week of the holidays so that Kath can have a break and I don't have to worry about any further diplomatic incidents while I'm at work.

Look at me, putting out fires and solving problems without crying or having to eat half a kilogram of brie on sourdough. I'm basically nailing life again.

TWENTY-EIGHT

As August rolls on and I'm relieved that I can smile again, the temporary high of the Spa Night success has worn off. I know I'm still not tackling some of the big questions facing me, but I'm doing my best. There's a lot to be said for just putting one foot in front of the other. 'Just focus on enjoying summer,' people keep saying. So I will. No need to think about baby loss or my strained friendship with Lacey or what Edward wants, if I'm busy 'enjoying summer'. I'm not sure I'm very good at it, though. Spending my time appreciating the inner-thigh sweat and sickly 'fun' flavours of fruit cider is not my idea of a good time. I will say, though, packing The Emptiness tightly into a box feels much better than wallowing in it, feeling as though I might drown in nothingness. I've decided I won't be unhealthy and suppress my feelings – I've read enough blog posts and life-affirming quotes in beautiful typography to know that at some point I need to 'find my peace' and move on – but, right now, this is working. I will deal with the box of Empty (it's mad how a box called 'Empty' can feel so horribly full), but for the time being I'm really focusing on 'enjoying summer' and, most importantly, Lyla.

Lyla turns eight in two weeks and this year, I'm throwing her the birthday of all birthdays. We always celebrate with something. We've done all the usuals: the tedious two-hour session at soft play, the bouncy castle in a community centre, the horrific DIY-twenty-kids-to-your-house-for-cheese-sandwiches-and-party-rings, but this year, this year will be different.

First of all, I have a little bit of extra cash to play with for the first time in forever. I wouldn't say money buys you happiness, but it certainly buys you options and those options make me happy. I also have an overpowering desire to spend every waking minute pouring love into Lyla. Loving her feels healing. It's as if my maternal heart is aching and the cure for that hurt is to love my baby, the baby in my arms as well as – as Gillian so perfectly put it – the baby in my heart. By loving Lyla this hard, I feel like I am loving both of them, easing my niggling guilt for not being instantly thrilled about the pregnancy. This way I can try to fill my mind and heart with happiness instead of sorrow.

Lyla and I have talked a lot about the Big Birthday. When you're in single figures every birthday is a big one (plus it's a handy distraction so I don't have to think about my own Big Birthday, coming at the end of the year). We've decided we are going to do two separate celebrations, one just for us and another for everyone.

The two of us will have a lovely day doing all our favourite things, then for everyone we are hiring out the local parish hall and everything must be 'mermaidy', Lyla has insisted. Having grown up in the 1990s when Ariel was my idol (although I never did achieve the fringe volume that she did, dammit), I'm all over this.

We've spent many happy nights on the laptop and iPad, trawling through Pinterest for mermaid party ideas and saving them all on to a Master Mermaid List, ready for me and Kath to put into action.

I've hired a specialist balloon company (not just a shop that sells helium and foil balloons, but a specialist-moderately-famous-on-Insta balloon company), who are completely covering the parish hall walls with balloons of every under-the-sea colour you can imagine. There'll be pale blues, aquas, turquoise and pearly whites, as well as crystal-clear smaller balloons hanging from the ceiling to mimic bubbles. Throughout, tiny blue and gold fairy lights will intertwine to give a sparkling sea vibe, and on every table (decorated with fishing nets and sparkly green cloth) there'll be bowls of sweets, pretzel rods dipped in white chocolate covered with blue sprinkles, miniature sandwiches cut into starfish shapes and lilac plastic goblets filled with 'mermaid mocktails' ready for the children.

Lyla has decided to wear her holographic silver leotard tucked into a turquoise tutu (the spirit of dance is always within her, it seems) and I've decided to go wild, abandon my jeans/T-shirt combo and have treated myself to a silky vintage tea dress in deep periwinkle, with a fun shell print dotted all over it. It came in the post the other day and when I tried it on Lyla said, 'Oh, Mummy, you look like a seaside princess! I wish you'd wear silky dresses every day.' I let her be in awe for a while and then reminded her that even princesses like jeans and T-shirts, and thankfully my tiny feminist didn't protest. 'Yep, you don't have to be a princess and wear big dresses or tutus, but you can do THIS in them,' she said, jumping onto my bed and flicking her tutu around like a mad thing.

When do we adults stop doing that? At what age do you suddenly stop finding joy in jumping on a bed, flapping your limbs around and flipping your skirt up and down while you twirl and shout? *Maybe I should try it,* I thought, and before I knew it, we were both flailing about on my bed, flicking our dresses and singing songs that made no sense and had no tune. Turns out, you don't actually lose the joy in that, you just sometimes need a little person to remind you of it.

'Mummy, I love it when you stop being a grown-up,' Lyla said once we'd flumped down onto my now very crumpled bed. 'It's like there are birds in you and you don't have to be normal.'

I don't know if I like the idea of birds in me, but I like the fact that Lyla loves it.

'Oh really? Well, this bird is hungry and is going to peck this little tiny bug for her dinner,' I exclaimed, grabbing hold of my giggling ballerina girl, squishing her up and pecking her with kissy lips all over her face while she wriggled and squealed and laughed with sheer delight.

In that moment, the box of Emptiness was shut. I felt so full I could barely even remember what empty was.

TWENTY-NINE

THE ALL-IMPORTANT SATURDAY ARRIVES, with bright sunshine streaming through my thin curtains and the most excited not-quite-eight-year-old jumping on my bed singing, 'Party tiii-ime, party tiii-ime, party tiii-ime!' with no regard for the fact that I'd stayed up till 1 a.m. with Kath cutting bits of bread into fecking starfish shapes or printing, cutting and gluing tags saying 'Thanks for swimming by' to giant bubble wands as favours for the boys and girls who attended.

At one point, even Kath, craft-lover extraordinaire, ran out of patience spray-painting thirty plastic forks silver with blue sparkles (Dinglehopper decorations, of course).

'In my day, we just tipped some choccy biscuits onto a paper plate, threw you all in the back garden and called it a good time!' she'd said with exasperation.

If Lyla had her way, we'd have started the party at 8 a.m., but unfortunately for her, the invites said 1 p.m.–3 p.m. and there was still a lot to be done. Kath had agreed to come back over in the morning, so her 'cooee' was a welcome sound at ten, by which point Lyla was practically bouncing off the walls in excitement and I'd already burnt two bags of microwave popcorn and was wholeheartedly regretting the 'blue caramel-covered popcorn treasure bucket' idea.

'Auntie Kath! It's my birthday!' screams Lyla as she jumps down off the kitchen bar stool from where she has been overseeing all my efforts.

She reaches Kath in about half a second flat and I hear the familiar sound of Kath greeting her and singing 'Happy Birthday'. What isn't familiar, though, is the sound of Colin saying, 'Mainly happy returns of the day, Lyla,' with a chuckle at his own joke, and stepping over the threshold.

'Cooee,' Kath chimes as she walks into the kitchen holding a box of tiny silver vases with sprigs of fresh lavender in them. I hadn't asked for these but the colours work and I don't want to be rude, so I take the box off her with an 'Oh, lovely, thanks Kath,' and a slightly stiff 'and hello, Colin, wasn't expecting to see you today.'

'Many hands make light work!' he says, using one hand to give Kath a gentle tap on the bottom, sending her into a fit of blushing giggles.

'You're not supposed to touch people's bottoms, Colin,' Lyla announces in disgust, completely silencing us all, especially Kath and her giggles.

'I don't think Auntie Kath minds,' Colin says with a smirk.

Jeez, has no one ever told this guy there's a time and a place for these things? And that an eighth birthday party is definitely not the moment?

'Well you don't know that because you didn't ask her. You can't touch people's private parts without asking for their content. It's not allowed, and bottoms are your private space,' Lyla replies indignantly.

'Consent, darling,' I correct, but am impressed by Lyla standing her ground. 'And you are exactly right. I'm sure Colin is sorry and is going to be more mindful of where his hands go for the rest of the day, aren't you?' I say, shooting him a hard glare.

'Er, yes, I suppose I am. Very sorry, Katherine. Very sorry all,' Colin mutters.

I couldn't help but feel incredibly proud of my

switched-on daughter. *One–nil to the mermaid in the tutu,* I think. *Atta girl, Lyla*!

After a strained hour of dealing with Colin trying to be 'helpful', Kath dithering around, far more flustered than I've ever seen her before, and Lyla safely sedated by technology (God bless the iPad), we are ready.

Despite his awkwardness, I am glad of Colin's help loading my little Nissan with all the party gubbins, and the fact that he has a large Ford estate to heave the rest into, not forgetting Kath's lavender posies ('made fresh today, straight from the warehouse', as Colin has reminded me several times, as though that was some kind of peace offering for bottom-gate). I have to admit, despite having such a hard time from Lyla, he is trying.

With Kath and Colin in the estate and Lyla and I gussied up and in my car, we head to the hall to set up.

'I don't want Colin at my mermaid party. He's not even a merman,' Lyla sulks.

'I know he's not, but he's Kath's friend so we're going to be nice to him.'

'I'm not. I'm going to use my mermaid powers to get him.'

Not wanting to enquire what 'get him' means or start an argument before the main event, I turn up the radio and hope she'll forget about him. With the balloons, the magician, the face-painter and all the other junk I've hired (the smoke and bubble machines seemed like good ideas too), she won't even notice he's there.

I can't help but think about the people who won't be there, though. Lacey and I haven't really been in touch since the big fight. She's sent Lyla a sparkly mermaid card with £20 in and a boxed helium mermaid balloon through the post yesterday (I've clearly talked about mermaids too much on Twitter), but there was no mention of coming today. Rather sweetly, Edward FT'd me last night while I was in the midst of mermaid-craft hell and we chatted for a while about our childhood birthdays and all the things our own mothers did for us (mine were rather low-key, but his seemed to be full of sessions at Laser Quest or days at theme parks). It was warming to chat so easily and happily to him with no awkward questions about 'us' or anything further ahead than this party. I was glad to wake up to a 'good luck today, super-mum' message this morning. Sort of, a little bit, maybe, I wish he was here.

THREE HOURS LATER, THE parish hall looks like the most Pinterestable party you've seen in your life. All the children have taken the 'under the sea' dress code on board, especially Roo and Honor, who have body glitter on their arms, streaks of silver spray in their hair and little dots of iridescent pearly eyeliner on their cheeks like magical mermaid freckles (maybe Finola really is getting into the make-up thing). The hall is packed with tiny mermaids and mermen, a couple of Flounders, two crabs, four sharks, a jellyfish (that mum had gone to town on the crêpe paper) and one little boy 'tangled up' in old plastic bottles and string – 'the effects of single-use plastics on the sea,' he tells me morosely. Naturally, at that moment Simon and Storie happen to be standing nearby (having arrived at 1 p.m. on the dot, offering to help when it's clearly all been done) and Storie almost weeps with how much she loves the costume. She'll no doubt hunt down the boy's mother and ask her out for green tea.

By 2.30 p.m., games have been played, snacks consumed, the face-painter has done the exact same job on everyone whether they liked it or not, the magician has attempted to impress but Corinthia (of course) pointed out that the magic coin was in his other hand so loudly that one of the crabs cried in disappointment and we are now wrapping up the final half-hour with the DJ playing a selection of chart hits that every eight-year-old in the room seems to know all the words to. How do children do that? Where are they learning such intricate songs? Yet they cannot do anything of real use like the laundry or put their school shoes on when asked?

One by one, mums and dads start turning up to collect their sea-themed offspring after having a blissful few hours by themselves swanning around retail parks or drinking coffee silently in Costa without being nagged for a babyccino. Every time one of them gasps at how amazing the hall looks, I swell a little bit. Mentally, not physically, I mean (although with the amount of blue caramel popcorn I've nibbled, I wouldn't rule it out).

Even Finola, who's been known to call party decorations 'fluff and piffle', says, 'Well, this certainly is quite the show pony, isn't it! First class, darling. Did you erect this beast all by yourself?'

Finola is very casual with the word 'erect', much like Colin.

'Aha! No, I had help from Kath and Colin,' I say just as Honor, Roo and Lyla skip over.

'Yeah. Colin is Kath's boyfriend! He touches her bottom and puts his tongue in her mouth and it makes me sick!' Lyla shouts over the music. Christ on a cracker, why did she say that! Finola's eyebrows rise so high she almost loses them in her scraped-back, sensible headband.

'Bluebird, what do you mean, he puts his tongue in her mouth?' I ask, shocked.

'In the courtyard outside, just before. We all saw, he was kissing her but his tongue actually went inside her mouth and Kath said, "Colin, you naughty boy", and Colin said, "Only as naughty as you want me to be, Mrs Lavender",' Lyla says, the music having come to an end now.

'Well, it certainly sounds like they've enjoyed the frivolities of the afternoon!' Finola exclaims.

At this exact moment, in walks Val with Gillian by her side, chatting politely. I know how Gillian really feels about Val, but I also know that her deep desire to be nice to everyone will always override it. Val looks different. Still Val, but Val with wider eyes, fuller lips and even straighter hair than she usually has. Enhanced Val. If you put Val and an old Barbie into a mixing machine, Enhanced Val is what you'd get. I can't stop looking at her but Gillian snaps me out of it.

'Wow, it looks beautiful in here!' Gillian says, taking it all in.

'Mmm, very nice,' Val manages, the skin around her mouth barely moving. She waves to Corinthia to come over.

Lyla, not sensing how much I want her to not speak

about it, says, 'Why does Colin want to be naughty, Mummy? Why doesn't he want to be good?'

'We'll talk about it later, sweetpea,' I say hurriedly. 'Why don't you go and find Clara and tell her her mum's here?'

'I still think Colin's gross,' she says, giving me a parting look indicating she knows she's been shut down but obliging with her Clara search anyway.

Once everyone has gone home, the balloons have all been popped (the ones I can't fit in my car to bring home to 'love forever', as Lyla suggested) and we've said our thank yous to everyone, we head back to the house.

I looked for Kath and Colin (tentatively, even in the courtyard) but they were nowhere to be found. A text pings onto my phone as I reach home. *So sorry, lovey, had to nip off, bit of an emergency, speak soon! Lovely afternoon! K xxxx*. This is the least Kath-esque text she's ever sent, and it makes me instantly think she's gone home for some afternoon delight. Good for her, I suppose. At least someone is having some 'adult' fun.

THIRTY

IN THE MANIC LAST week of August, and with my own little mermaid safely (and I think fairly happily) ensconced in holiday club, I can throw myself into work. With the Mara Isso job looming, the office is on high alert and on top of that we have our usual jobs and bookings to contend with, so it's been long, busy days and I've been out on lots of jobs.

I have to say, I've loved it. I love working with people and seeing the joy on their faces when they look in the mirror and see the difference my brushes and powders have made. I know inner beauty is what counts, but having that boost, that lipstick an extra shade brighter, those lashes a tiny bit longer, can make all the difference to a person. I've even noticed that since the PaGS Spa Night Finola has been wearing a pearly-pink lipstick and some eyeliner from time to time. She doesn't seem to have progressed to mascara or filled brows, but she's having fun with it. I'm proud of her. There's even been a selfie uploaded to Facebook, which I think must be a first for her. Make-up certainly doesn't make a person, but sometimes it does make them feel good.

Skye is thriving on the buzz and hectic pace. In the office she's smiled at me on at least three occasions and I haven't endured a single telling-off for eating a panini from a chain coffee shop or the time I forgot my keep-cup. We've partnered together on a couple of jobs and rather than my usual under-the-skin annoyance that I used to feel, it's actually worked well. It almost feels like the olden days, the Robin and Natalie days where we found a rhythmic groove and were an amazing team. As much as I wish the insert-fatty-pic-here saga had never happened, good has definitely come from it.

I've been focused and motivated and I feel great. That is, until I collect Lyla on the last day of Summer Club, walk into the foyer and see her sitting ominously with a stony-faced Mr Ravelle. Oh God.

'Good evening, Ms Wilde,' he says, standing up in his 'casual wear'. Instead of his usual tawny-brown suit, we have straight jeans and a short-sleeve bottle-green check shirt, tucked in, with brogues and a brown leather belt. So casual. There is not a single crease in any of his apparel. I wonder if he has a secret iron in his office to ensure that even on 'casual' days, he doesn't look casual. More to the point, I wonder if there is a secret Gloria in his office. Stop it, brain, now is not the time to let a little smile out, this all looks very serious.

'Hello! Everything all right?' I ask breezily and perhaps optimistically.

'Ms Wilde, Lyla has exhibited some very . . . challenging behaviour today during tennis,' Mr Ravelle says, so gravely you'd think she'd bludgeoned someone to death with a racket.

'Oh dear. What's happened?' I say, raising my eyebrows at Lyla, who looks sheepish.

'There wasn't that much blood, Mummy,' she says. Jesus, she hasn't really bludgeoned someone, has she?

'This afternoon Lyla became frustrated with her tennis partner and rather than using her words to express herself, she decided to use her tennis racket to exert physical force upon the situation.'

So, yes, she has indeed bludgeoned someone with a racket. Brilliant.

'Oh, God! I'm so sorry! Is she all right? The other girl, I mean?'

'Yes, she'll be all right. She has suffered a minor cut to her lip, which did result in some blood loss, but Nurse Fernlie has seen to her and assures me she'll make a full recovery over the weekend. I don't think I need to tell you what a serious matter this is, Ms Wilde. Here at Hesgrove we do not tolerate violence of any kind. I don't know what behaviour you find acceptable at home, but another incident like this and we will have to have a serious discussion about Lyla's future with us.'

Wow, he's really gone in at full throttle. I was about to get in a flap about my delinquent eight-year-old, but his tone has ruffled my feathers to such a degree I kind of want to hit *him* in the face with a racket now. He's speaking to me as if I condone this behaviour, as though I encourage Lyla to whack people with sporting equipment. I'm not that mother, Mr Ravelle, I'm a good, decent woman with standards and morals. You don't see me snogging people in cupboards, eh? Naturally, I don't do or say any of those things.

'Right, of course, well, that's understood then,' I say, nodding excessively.

'It's not like Lyla to behave this way,' Mr Ravelle says,

a little more softly this time. Perhaps he's realised he was a bit much, or perhaps he noticed my hard stare.

'I know, she's usually a very good girl and we'll certainly talk about this at home,' I say, trying to keep my voice steady. I'm a ball of worry, anger and confusion inside. I need to hear the whole story, I need to hear what would make my sweet girl behave like this before I go off the deep end, berating her for this, or me for failing to teach her that violence is never the answer. 'It won't happen again,' I promise, wondering if that's actually true.

THE WHOLE (SUPER QUICK) drive home I think about how to handle this. Obviously something's bothering her and I don't think a standard 'telling-off' is the way forward. I'm not buying the usual 'kids will be kids' line. There has to be more to it.

Once we're in, I ask Lyla to get changed into PJs, wash her hands and 'try for a wee' (our standard evening routine), and after a few minutes she plods down the stairs looking much more downcast than I anticipated.

We scooch onto the sofa together and she nuzzles into the crook of my arm.

'So what's happened then, Bluebird?' I ask as softly as I can. Softly, softly, catchy monkey, as they say.

'Chloe was playing tennis and she kept missing the ball. I asked her kindly lots of times to try harder but she didn't and so I got really, really cross because we were losing,' she says in a despairing tone.

'OK, and then what happened?' I ask gently.

'I said "stop the game" to Alfie and Tamara, walked over to Chloe and said, "Why aren't you trying very hard?"' she starts.

'Right.' I nod. So far, so coherent.

'And she said, "I am, you're the one who's rubbish",' Lyla says exasperatedly.

'OK . . .' More nodding.

'And I said, "No! I'm hitting the ball and you've missed it four thousand and fifty-five million times!"'

'That seems like a lot of times,' I say quietly.

'And then Chloe said, "My dad takes me to tennis lessons every Saturday and your dad smells like wee because he only eats mushrooms from the floor".' Lyla's voice starts to tremble. 'So I said he only ate them because Storie said they were from Mother Nature, and he doesn't smell like wee, he uses organic natural cleansing products from a special shop that doesn't hurt the planet, and she laughed and so I got my racket and hit her in the face and then her mouth was bleeding and she screamed.'

By this point, Lyla is crying and I want to cry for her, too.

'Oh, Lyla. It's not OK to hit people but it's OK to feel upset, my baby,' I say, cuddling her into me and rocking back and forth as though she's an infant.

'And Kath doesn't want me to play anymore because I said those things about Derek and you don't want to look after me because you want to go to work and Lacey doesn't want to see us anymore because she's having a baby,' she wails.

Wow, this is a lot to take in. As if having some crappy tennis player called Chloe telling you your dad smells like piss isn't bad enough, she's carrying all of this on her tiny shoulders and I didn't realise. I need to tackle this one by one.

'OK, let's make a list of problems, shall we?' I say calmly, stroking the hair out of her face that got swept across when she squidged into me. She nods meekly.

'Firstly, we cannot go around hitting people with rackets or anything else. It sounds like Chloe was really hurt. Imagine how you'd feel if you'd been hit. We'll write her a card saying sorry, shall we?'

Lyla nods.

'Secondly, it was really unkind of Chloe to say Dad smells, so I can understand why you were upset about that. I think we should mention this to Mr Ravelle and he can have a word with her about saying unkind things. That and your nice card will sort that out.'

'Dad does smell a bit like wee, though,' Lyla whispers, looking at her hands. 'But I didn't want her to say it.'

'Oh, Bluebird. You don't have to stand up for me or Daddy. We're both grown-ups and we don't care what people say about us. You don't smell like wee. You smell like shampoo and my big kisses,' I say, smattering her with kisses all over her face, making her laugh and taking her mind away from her frankly pissy dad.

'Thirdly, Kath loves you so much. Kath loves you more than all the lavender in all the world—'

'Which is loads!' she pipes up, cheerily.

'Exactly! Loads! She's not cross about you talking about Derek. It's hard for Kath because she loves Derek very dearly and I know she can't wait to see him again in Heaven, but right now, she's not in Heaven, she's on earth, with us, and it would be nice for her to have a boyfriend to go to dinner with and share jokes with, wouldn't it?'

'I suppose so, but who does she love the most?' Eight-year-olds are so black and white.

'Love doesn't work in mosts and leasts. Just because she loves Colin doesn't mean her love for Derek has halved, it means her heart has doubled. She can love them both and love you and me and her friends and Mollie the dog. If there's one person I know who's got enough love for everyone, it's Auntie Kath. OK?'

'OK,' she says firmly and measuredly.

'Now, fourthly, Lacey. I know we haven't seen much of her. We had a little disagreement, but that's what's special about friends – you always make up again, so when that's sorted, she'll be back and it will be fine,' I say, hoping she doesn't press for more information.

'Maybe you should write her a card as well, then. Like I am going to do for Chloe,' Lyla says, totally switching roles and suddenly transforming from sad, feeble, teary child to caring, problem-solving young woman. When I see glimmers of her like this, I'm excited for her as a teenager and then want to scoop her up, fly off to Neverland and not let her grow up.

'Maybe I should,' I say, getting up off the sofa to find a blank card for Lyla, but knowing full well I won't. It's always easier to give advice than to take it.

THIRTY-ONE

SEPTEMBER

It's 5 a.m. After months of planning and anticipation, we are finally here. London Fashion Week 2018.

Skye, Natalie, the team and I stayed in a nearby Premier Inn last night, and we're ready.

The atmosphere at Somerset House, even at this early hour, is electric. It's still dark but the floodlights are on, technicians are tinkering with the flashing billboards and promo signs, catering staff are rushing back and forth with huge metal trolleys laden with food for designers, models, hospitality and entourages, security staff are having briefings with walkie-talkies and serious faces, stylists are scuttling in with arms full of fabric and make-up artists are marching through, cases heaving with lotions and potions to make even the most stunning more beautiful. If it's like this now, I wonder what it will be like by 9 a.m. when the venue opens to the public, journalists, bloggers and the fashion elite. Like that feeling you get when you step off the plane on holiday, my tummy does a happy flip of excitement. This is going to be an amazing day.

As well as the buzz I take from my work, I have even more reason to be excited today. Finola and Gillian are coming down to support me and watch the show. Mara Isso offered her team the entire back row of the show for friends and family, so I invited them along to have a little peek at my world beyond the school gates. Finola is bringing Roo (Honor can't make it because she's competing in another horse show. I asked Finola if she minded missing it but apparently they're 'ten a penny' and she'd rather see what all this 'fashion fuss is about'). She's also bringing Lyla and taking care of her for me. Gillian is bringing Clara, of course, and a little bit out of left field, Corinthia. Ever the sympathiser, Gillian told us that Val is really struggling with the split and so she offered to look after Corinthia for the weekend. A small part of me, very deep down, feels sorry for Val. I've been there, newly single and afraid, I've lived in The Emptiness and as much as I think she's poison, I wouldn't wish those dark days on anyone. I'm particularly glad Corinthia is coming to the Mara Isso show, full of gorgeous, empowered, plus-size women – it'll do her good to see that beauty isn't just limited to thigh gaps, Botox and boob jobs.

As well as the PSMs, I invited Edward. He hasn't been to London since we last hung out, since he said he wanted more and I said – well, I said nothing. It's a funny one because with no relationship status to hang your hat on, it's hard to know what we're doing. My problem is that I like where I am right now, so much so that I don't want to look too far into the future. I like having him around, but I'm not ready to label that anything other than friendship. I know I've hurt his feelings, but I figure I'd have hurt him more if I pretended I was ready for something I'm not. So we've not really spoken about it since then but I thought he might like to come along and we could perhaps hang out after the show. I texted him about it and mentioned it on FaceTime a couple of weeks ago. I figure it would be fine to introduce him to Lyla as my friend. He said he'd 'see what could be arranged' and I sent him all the details. Not wanting to sound desperate or needy (especially after my big thing about not wanting to have a full relationship), I haven't chased. We'll see. Either way, I can't let myself overthink it.

I didn't invite Lacey.

None of them is getting here till gone 9 a.m. anyway, when they will be ushered into a hospitality suite and then to the runway seating for the 11 a.m. show. But for now, it's work time and I've got a lot to do.

We find our way to the backstage area. Weirdly, backstage is in the actual building but the runway is in a glorified marquee in the large courtyard. Our room in the huge stately building is just springing into life. Along one side of the room are racks and rails full of clothes and shoes, all with bits of A4 paper attached to denote who will be wearing what and when it goes on. In the middle of the room is a set of desks with sewing machines, laptops, folders and water bottles. On the furthest side is one long row of trestle tables, all set up with fold-out, lit-up mirrors on top. That's us. We dutifully walk over and start taking out our kits. On the job we have me, Natalie, Skye, Kareem and four junior make-up artists, then we have four more assistants as well as eight hairstylists and Stuart from the office who has offered to act as runner. I'm not sure we really need him, but I've never seen a man so keen on anything in my entire life as Stuart pitching the idea to Natalie last week. I think she agreed just to stop him giving himself a hernia.

So, we unpack our kits, brief everyone one more time on what we're doing and stick our face maps and set list to the mirrors so they're to hand. We've rehearsed and rehearsed this. We know we are on a time crunch, we know this is our big break, we're not going to let the side down. 'Warpaint' has never felt more apt a term. I feel like a woman marching into war. I feel like running naked into the marquee and screaming, 'BRING IT ON', as I wave my make-up brushes in the air. I feel like climbing to the top of Big Ben with my brush belt attached and shouting, 'I am Robin Wilde and I am—'

'Earth to Robin. Hello, Robin. Come in, Robin,' Skye is saying, waving her hand-mirror in my face.

'Sorry, I was miles away, just going over the visuals for the look in my head, you know?' I lie.

'Robin, I know you're anxious and forgetful, but you've got this. You're going to do a really good job, it's going to be lit,' Skye says with one hand limply on my arm. I think in Skye's world that was a major compliment and I don't feel like now's the time to tell her I'm not anxious or forgetful. I've even brought my keep-cup in my bag.

After set-up and briefing, the models arrive in joggers and casual wear, ready to sit in our chairs and be transformed from already beautiful to still just as beautiful. I'm so glad they went with the natural vibes. These women are so stunning that it would be a crime to cover them or distract from what they already have.

We set to work. The junior MUAs begin with priming and prepping each model while the assistants give the models shell-pink manicures, moisturised legs and arms and offer support to our hairstylists. With the models busy being prepped, Natalie and I take a sneaky peak at the collection.

Hanging on unassuming white wooden hangers are the most beautiful, delicate pieces of fabric I've ever seen. Lace, chiffon and golden taffeta all intermingle like fish swirling effortlessly. It is hard to see where one bit of fabric begins and the others end, such is the intricacy of the designs and stitching. On hangers it is hard to really make out the shape of each garment because they seem to be floaty shreds of beauty, rather than something so conventional as 'a dress' or 'a top'. I stand and try to envisage how these light slivers of cloth will sit on our curvaceous, beautiful models, but can't.

'Wow, what a talent Isso is,' Natalie remarks. I don't usually hear such awe in her voice.

'I know, you don't see dresses like this in Primark, do you?' I say, half to myself, as I gaze at them like a child in a sweet shop. 'What do you think she does with each collection after the shows?' I wonder out loud.

Before I can wonder too long, one of the younger stylists bustles over with an air of self-importance. 'Please don't touch any of Mara's pieces, they are particularly delicate this season,' she says, stretching her arms out and forming a barrier between us and the clothes as though we were mauling them in some way.

'It's all right, we were just looking at how beautiful they are,' Natalie says, hackles up but remaining calm, professional and respectful. She's such a lady.

'They are very beautiful,' stressy stylist replies, topping Natalie. 'Too beautiful to get marked or dirty.'

'Yes, I was just saying to my colleague here that I thought they were beautiful items when Mara showed me samples a few months ago, when we won the pitch for all the hair and beauty work. Right, I'd better not keep my team waiting. I'll leave you to your steaming. As you say, they really are too beautiful to mark or dirty.' Natalie delivers this with such poise and authority that I can see the whites of the stylist's knuckles as she grips her steamer handle. Natalie. Is. Fierce. I love it when I see that in her and fear ever being on the end of that (again).

The trestle tables are heaving under the weight of palettes, trays, bottles of foundation, moisturiser, primer, brow gel, lip liners, lipsticks, lip glosses, mascaras, subtle fake lashes, concealers, highlighters and blushers. Tucked in amongst all this are food packages of bagels, yoghurts, fruit and muffins that Stuart has run around fetching for everyone. I don't know where it's all coming from but he's doing an amazing job. The models are happy and chatty, some of them with three people working around them; the assistants have found their groove passing products at just the right time, touching up with powder and keeping the kit in order; the juniors are coming to an end with the priming while Natalie, Skye, Kareem and I are fully in the zone, applying individual lashes, dewy highlights and creamy shadows to bring out their glow and turn our models, simply, into absolute goddesses.

Every time I stand back and look at them I feel like my breath has been taken away. They are exactly how I wanted them to look – simple, healthy, glowing – and in my eyes, the epitome of beauty. They look like one of those delicious Italian Renaissance paintings, but with women with skin tones of every hue. I wish that the beauty industry would see these women the way I do – maybe they will after this show.

As each model finishes with us and the hair team are happy (there are shaved heads, Afros, curly locks, sleek bobs, glossy black waves, brunettes, redheads, blondes, silver-greys – right now the team are giving some of the models soft waves with gentle tendrils framing the face and more shine spray than I think I can bear to inhale), they are sent off to be dressed and styled, ready to line up for the runway.

I thought arriving at 5 a.m. to get ready for the models at 6.30 a.m. was too early. It wasn't – that ninety minutes of set-up and briefing went by quickly. I thought four hours of models in chairs and dressing was going to be comfortable timing but with twenty-four models, we've had to work at absolute lightning speed and I can feel the sweat running down the back of my knees – thank God I'm not walking the runway!

As I finish on my last model and send her off to be checked by Natalie, I look over to them all dressed and gathered by the door. If I thought they looked beautiful with hair and make-up done but still in their joggers and comfies, you can bet your bottom dollar I think they look sensational now.

Each outfit is a triumph. Unlike most plus-size fashion, which errs on the side of caution, with loose blouses and frumpy paisley sack tunics, Mara Isso has taken what God gave these women and run with it. Rather than using the clothes to hide them and disguise their 'larger' bodies, she has created each piece to celebrate the curves and contours, showcase their beautiful skin and highlight everything they are.

Each dress is a mixture of pastels, metallics and a few hints of bright cobalt blue. The soft and hard hues contrast, combine with the gold, silver and copper threads and work perfectly with our dewy make-up. The shades all sing against the range of skin tones and colours. These women look like they're lit from within. I can't help but grin, I am so proud to be working on a campaign where women of all shapes, sizes and colours are being celebrated. I'm proud that my daughter won't only attach 'tall and slim and white' to her ideal of beauty but will see all these women and all this diversity as part of that, too. Rather embarrassingly, I feel a huge wave of emotion may be about to break. The balls of my feet are hurting, I haven't stopped to eat or even sip from my blessed keep-cup. I know my friends, Lyla and possibly even Edward will have arrived by now and will be starting to be seated, ready to see the models I've lavished so much creative energy on, and suddenly, I'm crying.

Not wanting to be seen as weak or silly, I turn back to rifle through my kit case for a tissue, when Skye hands me one from hers.

'I get it. It's a beautiful thing to see such confidence in so many women who don't fit the traditional standards of modern beauty,' she says, looking over to them all, too. 'OK, so I lifted that line from the final pitch document,' she confesses, and actually cracks a sheepish smile. 'But I see it – I really see it, now.'

Wow. Wow that she 'gets it' and wow that she means it. This is huge.

'Skye . . . I . . . I didn't think you'd feel that way,' I say in utter disbelief.

'Why? Because I'm tall and slim? Don't put me in a box, please, Robin. This whole gig has been a wake-up call for me. I care just as much as you do.'

And that's me told.

THE AIR IS FRAUGHT with ecstatic tension. Everyone on the row in front of us looks like they too should be on the runway. As I realise everything they are wearing is basically hot off the runway itself, I feel very underdressed in my Next black skinny jeans and TK Maxx loose black jersey top. I was so engrossed in my job, I didn't think to style myself, and so I spend a moment or two trying to brush off make-up stains. I contemplate licking my index finger and wiping it on a few of the more stubborn marks but recognise that we're not at home now, so I sit with as much make-up-stained dignity as I can muster and see if there are any celebs I recognise.

Across the way I can see Gillian and Finola with all four children waving frantically like they do in school plays and assemblies, even though you know they've been briefed not to. I give a very demure half-wave back, so nobody thinks I'm encouraging this. It seems to do the trick. Lyla throws me an exaggerated thumbs-up and I send one back, less demurely this time. She deserves a full one.

Just as the lights are starting to dim and the already-loud music is turned up even louder, I scan the back row for Edward. I know he hasn't been over for a few weeks so he's due a visit, and this is the guy who said he wanted something to happen with me so I know he'll be here somewhere. Won't he? I look back and forth across the row but he isn't there. There are a couple of people just taking their seats, a tall guy and a pregnant-looking woman, but no Edward. I swallow the pang of disappointment. Hang on, the lights are going down even more and now I really can't see a thing bar the runway but is that . . . Lacey?

Throughout the entire triumph of a show my mind is racing. Why would Lacey come to this? How would she have got hold of an invite? Why hasn't Edward come? Why am I so bothered that he didn't, since I don't want a relationship, anyway? Do I? Don't I? But Lacey. Lacey is here.

The entire time the press are flashing their cameras,

our models are flaunting and strutting and drawing gasps and cheers, bloggers and vloggers are tweeting and Insta-storying as fast as their rose-gold-ringed fingers let them, and journalists are firing emails off as quick as lightning about 'Normal Bodies Being In Vogue' (still a problematic headline, I think, but it's a step in the right direction). By the time Mara Isso comes onstage to take a bow of thanks, the entire audience are on their feet, and though I don't know it in that moment, the show will go down in fashion history as the first of its kind. Utterly groundbreaking. Next to me, Natalie offers me a tissue, expecting me to be in floods of tears – but I'm as surprised as she is to find I'm grinning, proper ear-to-ear grinning.

'A RESOUNDING SUCCESS, MY dear! Best in show!' cheers Finola as she comes over to me twenty minutes later in the Mara Isso hospitality suite. She's still flushed from the excitement. Or is that a bit of blusher I spy?

'Mummy, they were princesses! Queens! Fairy mermaid princess queens!' Lyla sings as she grapples for a cuddle from me and then instantly releases me again to take Roo's hand and hurtle over to the catering table for snacks.

'Well done, Robin,' Gillian says softly with a warm

smile, 'they all looked so pretty, I wish I could do my make-up like that every day,' she laughs gently. Clara and Corinthia stand next to her, each holding onto one of her hands, a bit unsure in their new surroundings.

'What did you think, girls?' I say to both the children, though mainly aiming it at Corinthia.

'I loved it!' enthused Clara. 'I'm going to get a muffin,' she also enthuses, running off to join Lyla and Roo. I'm under no illusions, the snack table is just as exciting as the runway show in the eyes of an eight-year-old.

'Corinthia, what did you think?' I ask gently, kneeling down to her level and regretting that move because I'm so exhausted I know it will be tough to get back up again.

'I feel funny about it,' she says, looking at the floor.

'Why, sweetie?' I feel sad for her, looking so meek; away from her tyrant of a mother, she really is quite small.

'Because they were fat but they were so beautiful,' she almost whispers, looking at me with big, confused eyes.

'Can I tell you something important, Corinthia?' I say, taking her hands in mine and feeling like it's just me and her in the whole room. I'm feeling such love for this confused little girl who can't help the things her mother imprints upon her.

'Yes.' Corinthia nods, wide-eyed, sensing the importance

of the moment. Or maybe she just wants to follow Clara to the snacks.

'Being beautiful doesn't just mean slim,' I say as softly but firmly as possible, which is very hard to do.

'But my mum lost weight and is skinny and beautiful,' she says seriously.

As much as I can't bear Val, I know I need to do Corinthia this service.

'Your mummy *is* gorgeous. She's a very beautiful woman. She's very slim, too. But it's not that, that makes her so beautiful. It's her happy smile.' I'm not sure I've ever actually seen Val do a happy smile, but I continue anyway. 'And her kind actions and her loving heart. They're the things that make her beautiful. A person who is very, very, very big is beautiful and a person who is very, very, very small is beautiful. A person who is tall or short or curly-haired or straight-haired or even no-haired is beautiful!' I say in my best cheery teacher tone.

'I'm beautiful?' Corinthia says, almost a question.

'Yes, you are very beautiful. You can also be kind or clever or brave or strong. There are so many things you can be, it's not all just about beauty. And the best bit is, none of these things needs you to be big or small or tall or short.'

'So the ladies in the show . . . they were big . . . and . . . beautiful!' Corinthia says almost with a cheer.

'Yes!' I say, jubilant that she's grasped it.

'I'm going to tell my mum that we're ALL beautiful!'

'Yes, all right then!' I say, slightly gutted that I won't see Val's face when she hears the big news. For the second time today I feel like I might cry with pride. I blink the tears away as I see the beaming smile on Corinthia's face.

Gillian and Finola, who have watched this exchange, shimmy her along to join the other children who are sitting at a coffee table with muffins and drinks (in disposable cups – don't tell Skye) and we all laugh and collectively sigh. There's so much emotion in the room that I don't think anyone really knows what to say.

Before we can begin, though, I feel a tap on my shoulder and turn round – only to be looking into the familiar face of Karl, Lacey's husband.

'Oh my God, I knew it was you two I saw!' I say in shock, as I see Lacey standing there, too. In my head I'd practised all the things I was going to say to Lacey the next time I saw her – I was going to be all wise and Buddha-like – and that definitely was not it.

Karl looks as dashing as always in his smart jeans and weekend shoes, a crisp white shirt collar peeping over the top of his slate-grey cashmere jumper.

'I think my wife has something she'd like to say to you,' he says, holding Lacey's hand, which looks so small in his.

Lacey looks equally as stylish as Karl. She's in a soft grey smock dress with sheer black tights and soft, knee-high boots. Despite the loose fit of the dress, I can see her neat bump pushing through the fabric and feel a double pang of joy for her and sorrow for me.

'Robin, I'm sorry for how I was and for what I said.'

I can see the pain in her perfectly kohl-lined eyes and my heart crumbles with how much I've missed my friend.

'Oh, Lacey, I shouldn't have gone off the deep end at you,' I say, stepping towards her and putting my arms round her.

'I'm sorry,' we both whisper at the same time.

They say things come in threes, well, so does crying at London Fashion Week because here I am, a blubbering mess. It's as though so many weeks and months of my life have led up to this day and here it is, a total, utter and complete success.

Part Five

WILDE BY NAME, WILD BY NATURE

THIRTY-TWO

OCTOBER

After all the hubbub and thrill of London Fashion Week, being at home feels like a novelty again. I can't believe we've been in this house ten months now. I warmed to it instantly but I'm finally starting to feel like it's a full and proper home, rather than just a nice house I like a lot. Nothing is rickety and broken like Granny's old terrace; everything is new and fresh, I suppose a bit like me.

When we first moved in, I didn't think I'd be able to fill it. Granny's house was full to the brim of all the things Lyla and I had accumulated over the years. Then I watched a documentary on Netflix about minimalism and spent three days completely purging it all. *Such a good plan,* I thought, *I won't have to move as much,* as I told everyone. Well, that was all true but then when we moved into this much more spacious house, it felt very sparse. Although money is better this year, it's not 'go cray-cray in West Elm' better, but it's definitely at a 'treat yourself in Homesense here and there' point, and that's exactly what I've been doing.

After her making such an effort at the fashion show, I invited Lacey round for a girls' night of wine and cheese, or more accurately, a night of just the fizzy grape juice and hard cheeses she's allowed. I considered cracking out the rosé for myself but being the nice friend I am, I've downed a glass before her arrival and will stick to the non-alcoholic stuff while she's here. I also won't mention the wedge of brie I shovelled in before her car pulled up on the drive, either. We don't both need to suffer.

'Ooo-ooo, I bring decaff Coke, low-fat pitta crisps and hummus,' Lacey calls down the hall, as she lets herself in.

'Ooo-ooo, luckily I've got proper snacks then!' I chime back, opening a packet of chocolate fingers and having a flashback to the Christmas Kath said, 'My God, I absolutely love a good finger', much to the horror of Mum in her two-piece who would not dream of eating more than three Cadbury's Roses and an M&S mince pie to celebrate the birth of Jesus Christ. Thinking of Mum, I must email her soon. She and Dad have spent the year cruising. Apparently, Dad's Premium Bonds came in and so they are finally doing all the cruises they've ever wanted to do. I never knew they always wanted to do six in a single year, but this is the woman my mother is now. I bet she's only doing it to show off to the ladies at the Rotary Club. Still, the best kind of relationship with my generally absent parents is the email kind. I have Kath if I want any genuine mothering, and Mum if I want to be told I should never have left Simon and I'll never amount to much.

Lacey comes in and I notice her bump without instinctively putting a hand to where my own should have been. In this short time since LFW it's really 'popped', as they say. I think that's such a disturbing notion. You grow a child within you and then your own body just 'pops' out. I remember being pregnant with Lyla and a woman at Simon's office constantly passing comment on my 'popped' tummy, making me want to scream, 'Can you stop talking about me like I'm a bag of microwave popcorn, for fuck's sake.' I decide not to verbalise my bump thoughts to Lacey. I note that she hasn't stretched a tight maternity top over it but is wearing pale blue skinny jeans (even at nearly six months pregnant she looks good in skinnies) and over them, a loose A-line white cotton top with delicate scalloped edging and spaghetti straps that really sets off her faux tan. Her face is glowing, her hair looks thick and long and she seems to exude joy from every pore. Rather than feel rage and envy, for the first time I absorb a bit of her joy and feel it as well. Good for her. Good for her lovely baby in there, too.

'Now, Karl thinks I'm eating nutritious and balanced foods at every opportunity but if you've got a pint of full-fat milk and half a box of Coco Pops, I'll love you forever,' she says, plonking herself down at the table and disregarding the pitta crisps.

'That's the spirit, lies and deceit,' I say, pulling the giant sliding cupboard door open to reach the cereal.

'Lies, deceit and sugary carbs, please,' she responds with a laugh.

I pour her the biggest bowl of chocolatey goodness with ice-cold milk (while slyly eating a bit of brie from the fridge when she can't see – I mean, pregnancy is a miracle and all that, but does it compare to the joy of soft, creamy cheese? I ask myself) and place it in front of her as I take a seat, with the box of fingers.

'So, how have you been?' I venture. A safe question.

'Oh yeah, really good, just the normal stuff: Dovington's,

sorting bits out at home, all the usual things,' she says nonchalantly.

'Normal, that must be nice,' I say, without any venom at all.

'Oh, Robs. You've had a weird time recently, haven't you?' Lacey says kindly.

'Yeah. Weird, shit, good, nice, stressful. Is it possible to have had every single emotion all in a matter of months?' I say, stuffing in three fingers at once and resisting the urge to make a dodgy joke.

'I think it is. You've been through the wringer, and I wasn't there. I'm so sorry.'

'I know, I know, let's not do all this again, let's leave it behind us and move on. I wasn't exactly a saint, either. Anyway, we don't have enough chocolate fingers to rehash it all.'

'OK, a clean slate it is. Pastures new. So, Edward. What's the deal there?'

'Edward is definitely not a new pasture, Lacey,' I say with a firm look and another chocolate finger.

'True enough, but I need to know. I thought maybe he'd be at LFW – Natalie mentioned you'd invited a mystery man when Karl and I asked her if we could come along – but he wasn't there, and when I messaged to ask where—'

'You messaged him? How? Why?' I feel horror rising up through my body. After he didn't come to the event I'd decided I needed to cool it down and not get in touch with him about it. Why should I have expected him to cross the Atlantic at the drop of a hat, when I'd already made it abundantly clear I wasn't looking for us to be anything more than casual? When I realised how much I had hoped he'd be there, it reminded me of Theo and how I'd felt when I'd wanted him but hadn't had him. Feeling panicked that I was allowing myself to be hurt again, I'd vowed not to mention the show to Edward. And now here we are, Lacey dragging it all back up again.

'It was only on Facebook, he's on your Friends list. He was totally relaxed about it – said something about being busy at work and to say hey to you next time I saw you. I didn't message him in a weird way, just an "are you in London" way.'

'That IS a bit of a weird way,' I huff, failing to hide my annoyance that she's got involved. It's the grown-up equivalent of when she went over to Ben Ingleson in Year Ten and said, 'Well, are you asking Robin to the Valentine's Party or not?' But I remind myself that although it might be a bit awkward, it's meant (as always, when it comes to Lacey) with love. 'Look, thank you for trying but you don't need to. It's all in hand.'

'It doesn't seem very "in hand",' Lacey says with her usual frankness, finishing the last of the Coco Pops.

'Well, it is. We had a fling in New York, it carried on over here, things looked like they could get serious for a while, then things . . . didn't. He said he wanted more, I said I couldn't go there again with anyone. He got upset, I'm perhaps regretting it, he doesn't answer my messages much anymore and that's it. So you see, it's completely fine and not a shit-show at all,' I gabble, getting up to pour a proper glass of wine. Just because she's knocked up doesn't mean I need to stay on the wagon all evening, I've suddenly decided.

'OK, so completely in hand and exactly how you want to leave it with someone then.'

'Yep. Perfect.'

'Well, I'll say no more.'

'Probably for the best.'

'You know, Tinder's always an option,' Lacey says, tapping her phone and smiling mischievously at me.

'Lacey Hunter, I would rather eat those cardboard pitta chips for the rest of my life than go back on Tinder. Now, before you start catfishing on my behalf, do you want a makeover? I've bought a whole new set of skin products that, if possible, will make you even more glowing than you are now, and I promise this is in no way a distraction technique to get you to stop talking about Edward.'

And with one final slurp of chocolate milk from the bowl (classy lady), she heaves herself up and off to my front room, where I spend the next hour fiddling with her face, listening to her tales of the NCT groups she's joined (they sound even more PSM-y than my PSMs) and telling her about how Skye might actually not be so hideous and might – crazy world, I know – be a friend.

By 10 p.m. I've eaten my way through more snacks than is healthy (sympathy-eating for Lacey, who is eating for two, though), tried out all my new kit and made Lacey sad she can't go *out*-out with her full face on, swatched fourteen new shades of shimmer eyeshadow up my arm, drunk half a bottle of wine (oops) and feel fully bonded with my best friend again.

Going to bed that night, I feel very rich. Not with money and gold bars (be real for a moment, who actually has gold bars?), but with friendship and company and satisfaction with life. We're back on track, I'm back on track, hello new lease of life, it's wonderful to have you.

THIRTY-THREE

Half-term arrives and our first proper 'family' holiday beckons. I'm fully in the swing of autumn now, wrapping Lyla and myself up in matching purple scarves, taking Instagram photos of our feet in our matching Joules ankle boots standing on top of crisp fallen leaves and making Lyla take eight hundred photos of me holding a (reusable!) Starbucks cup while I pretend to look happily into the distance. My own mother would never have asked me to do this. She'd have been too busy organising the community centre bonfire night while wearing her sensible M&S trousers and a buttoned-up cardigan, to care about filters and framing. I must give her a call soon and see what the plan is for Christmas. Last year, she and Dad went to a golf hotel with 'some of the Rotary gang' so I escaped the whole affair, but this year I expect she'll want to come up and finally see the new house, spend some time with Lyla, berate me for being single and tell me I need to get a 'real' job. So festive.

Back in the summer when I was in a very low place and Kath was holding the fort, I agreed it would be nice to 'get away from it all' with her and Lyla – and after all the support she's given me this year, she more than deserves a treat too. It turns out this means a cottage in the Lake District for two nights and, to make it 'even more special', Colin is coming along too. It's a two-bedroom cottage with lake views so I'll share with Lyla and, of course, Colin will share with Kath, or as he put it, 'bunk in'. God help us all.

By the Monday morning of half-term (after a successful first six weeks at school with no tennis racket incidents and Chloe living each day in peace), I've filled the boot with every conceivable home comfort including the cheese toastie sandwich-maker, two backup laptop chargers (heaven forbid I can't binge-watch Netflix while we're there), my favourite White Company candle (you know how cottages can be musty) and an entire backpack of Palace Pets for Lyla. The site says 'luxury cottage hire', but almost echoing Lyla's sentiments as I put her to bed last night, 'I'm not really a fan of camping or cottaging.' I had to try not to laugh to avoid explaining what 'cottaging' actually means – I think I got away with it. Kath is going in Colin's car because she wants to 'keep him company' on the drive (luckily, Mollie the dog is staying with one of Kath's neighbours) and really, I'm relieved we're not all driving up together. Lyla still hasn't fully come round to the idea of Colin being in our lives, and at home she has started to refer to him as 'the slimy worm'. I shouldn't really have laughed the first few times she said it because that only seems to have egged her on and now she says it so often I'm worried it will slip out in front of him.

On the drive, we have a long chat about minding our manners, respecting Kath and Colin's privacy and allowing Kath to enjoy herself. Lyla seems on board but the proof will be in the pudding, and with a few careful glances in the rear-view mirror I can see I've lost her interest. I stick on Little Mix to lighten the mood. Hurrah for girl bands with catchy songs that make you feel like it's OK if your exes are scumbags. I sing passionately, thinking of Theo for the first time in months and feeling liberated that he's not in my life anymore. Even if he was devastatingly good-looking and took me to a lot of really nice places, I'm better off without him. I'm quite content not to be wined and dined and guided round museums and whisked off in private cars. I don't care.

'Mummy, you're shouting,' Lyla interrupts my empowering thoughts of freedom.

'I'm singing, sweetheart.'

'It sounded like shouting.'

'Well, I was singing and thinking of the biggest, slimiest, stinkiest worm I've ever known,' I say, exaggerating each word and knowing I'll regret allowing this kind of language by the time we arrive at the Lakes. Oh well.

THE COTTAGE IS BEAUTIFUL, exactly what you'd hope for in a couple of days away. Warm Aga in the kitchen, soft tartan sofas in the lounge, exposed beams in the bedrooms and a quaint little garden with trees full of fruit, it's like something out of a storybook.

Kath and Colin have already arrived and come to the door to meet us from the car. I have to admit, they do look sweet together. Colin steps out to help me with my bags ('Cor blimey, have you packed the kitchen sink?') and Kath stands in her holiday attire (brown sensible walking boots, deep crimson socks pulled up to her knees, a mustard circle skirt with a white apron over the top – which means something's already in the oven – and a deep purple polo-neck top tucked into the skirt. Complete this with a chunky green glass bead necklace and two messy plaits, and you've got the picture). Kath stretches her arms out ready to welcome Lyla, who hurls herself at her.

'Oh Auntie Kath, you smell like kitchens!' she says optimistically.

'We've got a sticky toffee Bundt cake in the oven, and the local pub is bringing four plated-up roast dinners in an hour,' she says casually as though everyone just whips up incredible puddings and arranges hot dinners as soon as they arrive on holiday.

'Oh my, what a great start to the trip!' I say enthusiastically, carrying even more bags into the cottage. 'I've brought prosecco, Baileys and sparkling elderflower.' All the essentials.

Before long we're all in our comfies. Well, Lyla and I are in onesies, Kath has donned a pair of paisley trousers she hand-sewed and while Colin is still in his beige slacks and navy crew-neck jumper, he has at least joined in by donning a pair of slippers. We sit round the table by the Aga, enjoying the finest offerings from the pub.

'I thought tomorrow we'd try out some of the local walks,' Colin suggests. 'There are some short three-milers we might be able to tackle.'

'Three miles!' I say, before I can hold it in.

'Yes! Nothing at all, you'll barely feel it. We used to come here all the time and spend the whole day trekking, seeing it all, breathing it in,' he says, shutting his eyes and taking a deep breath for effect.

I wonder who 'we' is.

'Ha, well, we'll certainly give it a go, won't we, Bluebird?' I say, looking at Lyla, who looks utterly horrified at the thought, but is clearly remembering our chat in the car about manners.

'Yes,' she manages.

'And then afterwards,' Kath offers, sensing how hard that little yes was, 'we can wander into town and look round all the shops. Colin and I saw lots of tiny toy shops and I think there's even an old-fashioned sweet shop, if we're lucky!'

Good old Kath, she reads Lyla so well.

'Yes! I've got pocket money from Daddy and Storie to spend.'

'Great! We'll set off by eight to get a good go of it, shall we,' Colin chimes enthusiastically, clearly happy the walk is on.

Eight o'clock! Is the man some kind of sadist?

'Oh, love, why don't you let me cook us all a proper breakfast and then we can set off once we're working on full engines?' Kath soothes, coming to the rescue again. She should have a job in NATO or the UN with these tactics. She'd be ace.

I WAKE UP BEFORE sunrise to the feel of Lyla's small hands stroking my face. I lie with my eyes closed, enjoying the moment, thinking about all the times I leant over her cot as a baby and ran my fingers over her short fine hair, round the top of her tiny velvety ears, across her soft cheeks and over the most delicate rosebud lips. I used to look at her and think about her future, where she'd go, who she'd be, who I'd be. I liked my quiet daydreams more than my reality in those days. Reality meant day upon day of monotonous routine, household chores and minimal support from Simon. Things are so different now. I might not have the dream boyfriend, or the stomach of Julia Roberts in the *Pretty Woman* piano scene, but I have choices and freedom and joy.

'Good morning, smiley Mummy,' Lyla whispers.

'I'm not awake yet,' I whisper back.

'Then why is your face smiling?' she says.

'Because I was thinking such happy things about my Lyla Blue,' I say, flinging my arms out, wrapping them around her and bringing her in for a huge squishy cuddle.

'Mummmyyy, you're so squeezy!' she giggles, trying to wriggle free.

'That's because I'm so full of love I need to squeeze it all out onto my favourite person,' I carry on.

'But your breath smells like dead rats and bin juice!' she screams.

Ah, such sweet words from said favourite person.

'Ohhh, doooesss iiittt,' I say, breathing all over her face and laughing while she breaks free, climbs out of bed, climbs back on and starts jumping all over me.

Once you have an eight-year-old jumping on your thighs, it's time to get up, so I concede the early start (6.45 a.m.), nip to the loo (and brush my dead rat, bin juice-smelling teeth), have the quickest of showers (it might be a luxury cottage but that doesn't include hot water on demand) and get dressed. Lyla had a hot bath last night so there's no need to subject her to the cold shower routine, and I lay out an outfit for her to put on while I play Netflix on my laptop (luxurious enough for Wi-Fi, though, thank God) until we hear Kath and Colin stirring and head downstairs.

Kath is clattering around with frying pans and Colin is singing something about sunrises and birds tweeting. Kath has a dangerously rosy glow, is wearing a floor-length, floral satin dressing gown and definitely no bra under it. I can only hope it's done up securely, otherwise I'm either going to have to avert my eyes or she's going to do herself an injury over the hob.

'Good morning, you two!' Kath almost bellows as we walk in. Wow.

'Morning! Did you sleep well?' I ask politely, guiding Lyla to the table and heading to the fridge for some orange juice.

'Um, yes, I slept very well,' Kath says, not looking at me.

'She slept very, very well,' Colin says, sauntering over to her by the Aga and kissing her on the side of her face.

I try very hard not to let my brain go anywhere with this display of middle-aged love and look over at Lyla, who isn't trying as hard and instead is pulling the same face as she makes when she's seen dog mess on the pavement.

'So, looks like good dry weather for our walk then!' I offer, as Kath starts serving up fried eggs on huge white buttered rolls.

Fortunately, my conversational diversion does the trick and before long we're all seated in front of delicious breakfasts, robes securely tied and chatting about which routes through the Lake District offer the best views.

* * *

For someone who classifies an afternoon at soft play as a 'workout' (and I'm talking about sitting with a latte until the children are thoroughly worn out and/or have initiated World War Three in the ball pool and you need to make a speedy exit before someone's mum comes and has passive-aggressive words with you), I'm surprised by how nice a hike in the great outdoors actually is.

We don't have any phone signal but I do take a lot of photos and film Lyla a little bit. Colin seems very knowledgeable about the area and is actually quite interesting when he's not being ever so slightly creepy about Kath's nether regions. I'm relieved to see Lyla is listening intently as he tells us about ancient glaciers and how ribbon lakes are formed. Also, seeing as he runs a fruit, veg and flower warehouse he knows an awful lot about the autumn flowers, and Kath hangs on his every word. It's quite sweet to see her letting someone else take the lead and enjoying it, rather than always being the person in our family who takes the lead, planning and fixing everything. Maybe she's been waiting a long time to be led. I've always assumed that the goal is to be a strong, independent woman, but is it just as independent to allow yourself to enjoy someone else being the strong one from time to time?

Lyla, having found a huge 'magic walking stick', is way

up ahead, Kath and Colin saunter a little way in front of me and I just put one foot in front of the other, being soothed by the quiet sounds of gravel under my feet and knowing there's nothing else I need to do other than walk. So simple. Walk forward. Life gets so easily complicated by everyday tasks, work goals, social media comparisons and the pressure to be the very best at everything, but ultimately all we need to do is this, walk forward.

Lost in my thoughts, I don't notice time or distance and before long, we are at the top of a hill with beautiful views of the lakes and villages dotted below.

'Breathe it in, Lyla,' says Colin, 'this air is pure.'

'Our air is pure too, Colin, we've got a plug-in,' she says nonchalantly, sitting down on a bench and laying the stick at her side.

'This is nice, isn't it?' Kath says, sitting beside her but looking at me. 'All of us together, on top of the world.'

'Ha! Well, Kath, this isn't really the top, this is actually a very low-lying hill, one of the more junior of the walks we could be attempting—'

'Yes,' I interrupt. 'It's lovely. We should do this sort of thing more often.'

Maybe the 'pure' air really has gone to my head. Maybe Storie is on to something. Perhaps simple living in nature really is the answer. Perhaps I'll go home and create a minimalist lifestyle. I'll Project 333 my wardrobe, build a compost bin, stop buying anything with packaging and drink only organic, locally sourced wines. Yes! This is it. This is my awakening, my epiphany, my eureka moment!

'Mummy, I need a poo and then I want to go to the toy shop,' shouts Lyla with zero shame. My epiphany crashes down and I realise we're either going to have to find a bush or peg it back to the village for a loo and then spend fifteen quid on a load of plastic tat she won't give a crap about forty-five minutes after we've opened it. We'll take the pestered-for item home, I'll leave it out for a while until it gets dusty or sticky (I don't know what the mystery stickiness is that somehow adheres itself to ALL children's toys) and then I'll shove it in the garage with all the other dusty, sticky crap. Essentially, the least-minimalist, least-eco thing ever. At least I tried. For a solid twelve seconds, I was that woman.

Once we're in the village and toilet-related crises have been averted, we mooch around quite happily. Colin and Kath meander off to the local pub to thank them for the wonderful meals last night and book some more, while Lyla and I explore the little shops and boutiques.

The lovely little village has one long high street running through the middle and a few tiny side streets spreading off that. The high street is lined with some boutique clothes shops selling couture for the over-fifties, a bakery, quaint hairdressers, ye olde toy shops flaunting their wooden wares in the grand old bay windows, sweet shops that no child or adult can resist, two or three weather-worn pubs and, sticking out like sore thumbs, a bank, a Co-op and an estate agent, to bring you back to reality with a bump.

Off the smaller side streets are more little shops, tea rooms, a big old church and lots of paths and alleys that lead you to streams, hills, paths, waterways and basically, the Great Outdoors. After wandering about for a while, we pop into a tea room for hot chocolate and warm scones. I'll never tell Kath but these might be the best scones I've ever sampled in my life. Maybe it's the fresh air and exercise or maybe it's the zen epiphany I had, but they are delicious.

Before too long, Kath and Colin have strolled in holding hands, laden with bags, and sit down for a cup of tea and more scones. Scone calories don't count when you're on holiday. I mean, scone calories don't count when you're anywhere, but on holiday they're almost negative. Eat all the scones, I say.

'Oh, love, I've bought all sorts of bits for the house,' Kath says, gesturing enthusiastically to her many bags full of treasures. 'A shawl for Moira, and Colin's picked up loads of second-hand steam train books, haven't you?'

'Yep! You can find all sorts up here.'

'Once Colin even found the *Kama Sutra,* didn't you, Col?' Kath laughs.

'What's the *Kama*—' Lyla begins.

'Oh, wow! Lots to be found then! Do you come up here often, Colin?' I say much louder and firmer than I ever normally would, just to avoid the *Kama Sutra* question from my bat-eared child. Funny how she always seems to hear the things I don't want her to, but never hears the first fifty times I ask her to do anything useful.

'Yes. Well, not for a few years. I used to come here with my family,' Colin says, looking down at the tea that's just arrived, ready to be poured.

'Do you have a big family?' I venture. Really I want to know the details of his immediate family but that seems a bit personal to ask, somehow.

'No. Just me and the boys. I had a wife, Shirley, but . . . not anymore.'

'Is she dead, like Derek?' Lyla says innocently and painfully bluntly.

'No, no. She's very much alive. She lives far away from me now, in Dorset, near our grown-up sons. Mike is twenty-four and Gareth is twenty-six. All getting on with their lives. All very happy. We used to come up here a lot when they were little,' he says, pulling himself back from clearly quite a painful place.

'Why don't they come on holiday with you anymore?' Lyla continues, clearly unfamiliar with the concept that people might not want to holiday with their parents forever. I feel a bit sorry for him being interrogated like this, so step in to rescue.

'I bet Mike and Gareth are busy going on lots of their own lovely holidays now and want to visit new places, since they've been to the Lakes lots of times before,' I offer in a jolly voice, ladling clotted cream onto my fourth scone. They're really very small. Mini-scones, if you will.

Kath smiles at me appreciatively and Colin says, 'I expect that's it! Very busy boys nowadays!' and pulls out a book about steam trains which I pretend to be fascinated by, because I suddenly see Colin without all his mansplaining and innuendo, and instead as a lonely older man who misses his sons and really likes trains. Bless him.

THE NEXT MORNING LYLA and I sleep till about 8.30 a.m. and are woken up to the delicious smell of bacon being cooked. Kath knocks gently at the door and says, 'I've made bacon sandwiches, if you're up.'

'I'm always up for bacon sandwiches, Kath!' I say, sliding my feet into my slippers, pulling on my dressing gown and encouraging Lyla to do the same.

The kitchen smells even more amazing than the faint waft on the landing. Fresh orange juice has been poured, thick slices of bread have been buttered and Colin has picked some flowers from the garden to make a little arrangement in a spare glass as a table centrepiece. It's all very civilised and I feel a bit scruffy in my PJs and dressing gown.

'We're going to head off straight away today, see if we can get a few good climbs in before lunch, but we thought you'd want to do your own thing,' Colin says to me, taking a bite out of his sandwich.

'Oh, only if you don't mind,' I say politely, filled with absolute glee not to have to physically exert myself that much. Even though yesterday was lovely and I did have that epiphany, I'm not ready for a repeat performance. You only need one epiphany a week, really.

'Colin wants to show me some of his favourite places,' Kath adds, gazing at him with the smile of a lovesick teenager.

'Well, we wouldn't want to get in the way of that. Perhaps we'll have another look round the town, Lyla?' I suggest.

'Yep. Let's go shopping again and have more cake!' she says, clearly happy with the plan.

'Cake day!' I say, smiling at her.

BY ABOUT ELEVEN WE head out down the short lane to the town.

We spend a happy hour wandering through the toy shops, playing with all the goodies on display and haggling with each other over pocket money. I really do try and keep a tight rein on these things and limit the amount of treats Lyla gets, but that mad holiday mentality takes over again and we end up walking out with a bag of tiny things that I know will have lost their novelty value (and half their components) by Christmas. Still, she's happy, we enjoyed forty-five minutes in the shop and can you put a price on precious memories together? Yes, you can, it's £22.45 – but that's not important right now.

By about one o'clock, despite our amazing breakfast, we're ready for food and so we pop into the bakery to pick up a snack. Why don't The White Company make candles called 'Warm Bakery in the Lakes'? I stand inhaling like a madwoman with sinus problems for a few minutes while Lyla presses both hands up against the glass to take it all in. This place is like Greggs on steroids.

It takes a solid fifteen minutes of drooling, polite chit-chat with Debra (who runs the bakery and is the most friendly woman in the world, apparently) and a lot of toing and froing before we leave with a huge, hot vegetable pasty, a cheese scone with butter, an apple custard doughnut, a chocolate crispy cake with a plastic ring embedded in the top and two Ribenas. We wander out of the bakery with our sugar-laden goodies and head down a tiny side street which leads to a wooden playground with plenty of benches.

'I like this picnic more than Storie's picnics,' Lyla announces with a mouth full of warm vegetable pasty.

'Oh,' I say casually, trying not to encourage her to bad-mouth her dad's weird girlfriend.

'Storie only eats organic food. We're not allowed cakes or chocolates or processed foods,' she says, still eating happily.

'Well, organic food is very good for you and we shouldn't always have treat food like this,' I say, trying really hard not to roll my eyes and say, 'Maybe Storie needs to get a life.'

'Sometimes, though, when Storie is at her Expressive Earth dance class, Daddy takes me to Tesco and we get Krispy Kreme doughnuts and eat them in the car before we pick her up!' Lyla scrunches her nose, draws her hand to her mouth and giggles mischievously at her and Simon's antics. I'm almost impressed that he has the gall to defy Storie, and I laugh along.

'Cheeky old Daddy, eh?' I manage, finishing my bit of pasty and taking a swig of the strawberry Ribena that Storie would most definitely disapprove of. I tear open the paper bag with my apple custard doughnut inside. 'Sometimes, Lyla, sometimes you have to take a breath and remind yourself not to worry about all the little things in life, treat yourself to a something nice and enjoy it. It's good to try your best at everything and make good choices, but occasionally you're allowed to stuff your face with a doughnut and have a giggle.'

'I know Mummy, YOLO,' Lyla adds sagely. She's so wise and also so . . . street.

THIRTY-FOUR

NOT LONG AFTER THE Best Autumn Picnic Ever 2018, we head back down the little alley to the main high street for one last loop round before popping into the butcher's, the baker's and the candle-stick maker's. Well, not actually those shops, but we do venture into the butcher's, the greengrocer's, back into the bakery for a loaf of warm tiger bread and then guiltily into the Co-op (I can't bear to use chain shops in a tiny, rinky-dink town like this unless I really have to) for a few other essentials. I've decided I'm going to flex my cooking muscles and prepare a beautiful meal for all four of us and have it waiting for when the elderly lovebirds return. Lyla is fully on board if it means she can sit at the table and watch Netflix while I do it all. She's a savvy negotiator.

The grey skies above stop threatening and the heavens open.

To Lyla's great joy we splash our way back up the hill to the cottage (her, glad she wore her wellies and making the most of every single muddy puddle; me cursing myself for wearing my gorgeous embroidered ankle boots and trying to avoid every single muddy puddle) and throw ourselves through the front door, dumping all the bags on the kitchen table, delighted to be back at base.

Lyla jumps about, peeling her soaking coat off. 'That was the BEST!' she sings.

THAT EVENING IS LIKE something out of a film. A couple of hours after us, Kath and Colin come in, wet and flushed from the rain but in high spirits from all their hiking achievements and singing my praises for the welcoming smells of roast beef with rosemary, dumplings, gravy and whipped-up-from-scratch Yorkshire puddings.

I pour us all a gin and tonic (well, Lyla has an orange and tonic) and we raise a toast to the last night of 'cottaging', as Lyla keeps calling it. As we tuck into a feast fit for a king, Colin tells me how he doesn't cook much so it's a real treat to be surrounded by women who want to fatten him up. For a little while he drops his guard and, once more, instead of being the creepy guy who touches Aunt Kath's bottom a lot, I see him as a man who has been lonely for a long while and is relishing the company of someone as magical as Kath.

Perhaps it's the third G&T or the fresh country air, but I feel myself warming to Colin and his stories of the great walks he's been on up here in previous years. For a split second, I think Lyla might be warming to him, too.

'Colin, can I tell you something?' she says after we've finished eating and I'm getting ready to serve up home-made Eton Mess with seasonal fruits (yeah, look at me bloody go).

'Yes, Lyla, you certainly can!' Colin says, clearly enthused that she has decided to engage specifically with him in conversation.

'I'm glad I'm sitting opposite you,' she says with a deadpan face.

For a moment we are all stunned, a smile spreads across his face and he attempts to reply, but before he does, Lyla has more to say.

'Because I didn't want to sit next to you.'

Ah. Poor Colin looks rather dejected. OK, maybe she isn't warming to him. It was very nearly like a film, anyway.

As always, Kath saves the day with Lyla's seating plan revelations and sweeps it all under the rug, saying something about how glad she is that she's sitting with two of her favourite people, Colin and Lyla. That, combined with the arrival of huge bowls of pudding, really takes the edge off Colin's burn. Poor guy. With my new-found appreciation for him, I realise it's high time I find a way of getting through to Lyla.

The rain continues pattering against the windows all evening and as I put Lyla to bed in our shared bedroom, I talk to her about being kinder to Colin as he is trying to be kind to all of us. I decide to try the 'having a grown-up word with her' tactic first, and at least that way I know I still have the 'be nice or I'll confiscate your Shopkins' approach in reserve. Once we have had a story, a cuddle and listed all the good things we've enjoyed that day, I creep back downstairs to the lounge, plonk myself on the tartan sofa with my G&T and watch Colin light the log fire, wondering where men learn these skills. Are they just born with the ability to make fires or are they taken off for secret Fire Skills lessons in secondary school while the girls are all segregated and sent off to have the Period Talk with Mrs Tampon? It will always be a mystery to me.

It might still be down to the rather generous G&Ts I

have poured, but our last evening at the cottage really is lovely. Kath talks about some of her travels around the Middle East with Derek. Colin listens intently, adding in where he can with bits about his travels as a young man with some of his friends in the 1960s. There's no awkwardness about both of them having a past or mentioning previous partners. I suppose when you get to that age it's expected that you have already led a full life up until then. They both seem to respect the exes as part of previous chapters and just enjoy the conversation and sharing. It's something I vow to try to do in the future, if I ever manage to let anyone else in. I drift off into a gin-fuelled daydream and think about how I'd quite like Edward to be here, how balanced that would make things feel. Even though I know Lacey was wrong, and we've sorted it all out, sometimes in my head I can't quite forget her line about Lyla needing a family unit. I know our family unit isn't conventional. But it's strong. And I'm proud of it.

'Ooof, I'm sinking into this sofa!' I declare, wafting my empty glass about above my head as if to prove my point. 'I think it's time I left you to the gin and the fire and headed to bed myself. I'm leaving early, so I ought to get an early night.' This isn't why I want an early night, of course, I just want to stop myself going down the

Edward thought trail and drift off into dreamland with my sweet Lyla by my side instead, the only companion I really need.

'Night-night, love, thank you so much for a lovely meal. You're a star,' Kath says as I lean over to give her a hug.

'Ah, you're worth it all,' I say. 'And obviously you as well, Colin,' I add, hurriedly. I don't want him to think I'm endorsing Lyla's attitude.

Colin smiles gratefully and I climb the stairs. As I brush my teeth, pull on my brushed-cotton PJs and squish into bed next to Lyla's warm sleepy body, I admit to myself that he's growing on me. Now I just need to convince my daughter.

'MUMMY. MUMMY, WAKE UP, there's a burglar,' Lyla whispers frantically in my ear, rousing me from the warmest, deepest sleep.

'What? Where? Jesus fuck!' I panic, before switching into 'Mummy Mode'.

'Mummy! Bad words! Listen!' she says, scrabbling even closer to me under the duvet.

We lie silently in the darkness for a second, but I can't hear anything.

'Lyla, maybe it's the wind, this is a very old hou—'

And then I hear it. A rhythmic banging of furniture,

the odd grunt here and there, pierced only by the sound of faint, muffled squeals of what I think are delight, but I don't want to analyse them too much.

'Mummy, that's the sound! Someone's burgling us!' Lyla says, frightened.

How in God's name do I say to my terrified eight-year-old, 'Don't worry, darling, that's just Colin getting his end away with lovely Auntie Kath! They're having a whale of a time shagging each other senseless all over the bedroom. You just go back to sleep and try not to think about it'?

'It's not, it's definitely not, don't worry,' I reassure her, still racking my half-asleep brain for something else to say to her.

'What is it, then?' she says, as the slightly speeded-up thudding continues.

'It's, um, it's—'

'Oh, Colin, yes! Yesss!' We hear Kath from across the landing.

'Is it Auntie Kath and Colin?' Lyla asks, wide-eyed with shock.

'Errm, maybe,' I say, stalling.

'What are they *doing*?' she says, terror instantly swapped for curiosity. Before I can say another word, she's scrambling out of bed and going to the door to find out.

'No, no, don't get up, stay here, they're playing! They're playing a game and Kath's saying "yes" because she's happy she's won the game and—'

'Auntie Kath, are you playing a game?' Lyla shouts out before I can stop her. This is potentially the most awkward experience of my entire life.

The thudding, grunting and squealing stop, of course, and there is what can only be described as a 'panicked' silence. I certainly wouldn't want to be Kath right now. I can hear movement from inside their room and I instinctively sit up in bed to ready myself for whatever might happen, wishing I was wearing a bra and that you couldn't see my nips through my PJ top.

After what feels like an eternity, Kath opens the door wearing a short black satin dressing gown. This is the least 'Kath' item of clothing I have ever seen her wear.

'Oh, hello, lovey! Are you all right?' Kath says a little breathlessly to Lyla, who is still standing in the doorway of our bedroom.

At last my brain kicks in. 'Lyla was just getting up to use the loo and heard a bit of a kerfuffle and was worried you'd tripped over,' I lie as I walk over to Lyla and hold her hand, desperately willing her not to defy me and call me out on my lie.

'Oh, yes! I, erm, bashed my knee and made a bit of a

noise, thank you for caring, lovey, very nice of you. I'll just go back in and sort it out and then go to bed and see you in the morning. All right? All right,' she gabbles, walking backwards into the room.

'Mummy that was so, so weird,' Lyla says, looking up at me in disbelief.

'Yeah. Really, really,' I agree, still standing by the bedroom door, holding Lyla's hand and staring numbly at Kath's closed door. 'You get back into bed, I'm just going to nip to the bathroom and I'll be back in a mo.'

I take the four steps to the bathroom, have a quick tinkle, splash a bit of cold water on the back of my neck to try to refresh myself (and the situation) and wish with every bone in my body that I hadn't clocked the half-used, still with the lid off, tube of Vagisan by the sink.

WE LEAVE EARLY THE next morning with no discussion about the night before, and happily the Vagisan was no longer in the bathroom when I had a quick shower at 7 a.m. Rather than facing too much chat with Colin the Stud, I decline a cooked breakfast, deciding to pick up a Starbucks on the drive home.

'Such a lovely weekend getting to know you all better!' Colin says, getting up from his place at the table and his poached eggs on fresh tiger bread (you're welcome), to hug us goodbye.

I try to be polite, agree and hug back, fully expecting every muscle in my body to cringe as I remember last night. But as he goes in for the embrace, I remind myself that he is making Kath happy, and sure enough, the thought works. I smile and hug him properly. Lyla, however, leaves her arms by her side and simply allows him to hug her, saying only, 'Yeah,' when he says what a nice time he's had with her.

'Bye-bye, Auntie Kath,' I add, edging over to her side of the kitchen, past the sideboard and the Aga.

'Bye-bye, lovey, sorry for waking you last night with bashing my knee, I—'

'No, no, these things happen, don't worry at all, I just hope your knee feels better soon!'

'All right, yes, well, you be on your way and I'll see you in a few days when I'm home! Love you lots.' She waves and we yell back, 'Love you too!' as we scurry off, back to the real world.

THIRTY-FIVE

NOVEMBER

As November rolls in, the nights become darker and the days become greyer. I try to carry on with an upbeat attitude and I can confidently say I'm not feeling The Emptiness, but I am feeling something else. Or rather a lack of something. Life after nearly two years of some pretty full-on highs and lows has started to feel a little bit humdrum. We all seem to strive towards building the perfect routine, getting on top of things, keeping life simple; but then you do it, figure it out, and suddenly you find yourself in your reasonably tidy house, with your child's school bag packed and ready by the door for the next morning, your work inbox clear and you, alone, on the sofa, glass of wine in hand, binge-watching *Mad Men* for the third time, wondering if you too could pull off a pencil skirt that tight. I'm not sure this is *exactly* what I've been striving towards . . .

I've been thinking about Edward quite a bit. Maybe it's the darker evenings and seeing couples in bobble hats holding hands and looking cosy, or maybe it's just that, actually, he was a good guy and I blew it because I'd been scarred by the bad guy. Fucking Theo. I hope he's happy doing whatever he's doing. This, clearly, is a lie. I hope he's unhappy. Not in a serious depression or severe physical illness way, but at least a few mild ailments. Maybe head lice or a light skin condition. Perhaps a bout of shingles. On his face. Anyway, peace and love, peace and love.

I should be thinking about my future, not my past. So, channelling my inner sassy pencil-skirt-wearing redhead from *Mad Men,* I ping Edward a message for the first time in a while.

Heya! Just watching Mad Men *and thought of you in New York. Wondered how things were going and if you're this side of the ocean any time soon? R xx*

I hit send before I can analyse it and then, obviously, analyse it. Worst message ever. Who says 'heya' these days? I sound so desperate. I may as well have put 'TB' at the end, for 'text back', like we used to do at school.

I wish I lived in New York. I could skip about in $400 high heels like Carrie from *Sex and the City*, and then come home to my trendy studio apartment and write about all the men who have been throwing themselves at me. That's exactly how it would be. As it stands, these days Auntie Kath has a more exciting love life than me.

What I need is a night out. The problem is, I also need people who can come on a night out with me. Gillian and I were supposed to 'pop out for a couple' last week, which I had high hopes for, but at the last minute she cancelled because Clara had a temperature. I'd asked Finola, too, but she said something about 'loading the horses' the next morning and I didn't question further.

Lacey and Piper used to be a good bet for a night out, but with one sister on the other side of the world living her art-curation dreams and the other one at home probably knitting gender-neutral booties, neither of them is much help right now. Natalie, too, has been known to let her hair down a bit, but since her overwork-induced marriage wobble last year, she's spending a lot more time with Martin.

In a desperate bid for some excitement, yesterday I even asked Skye what she was doing on Friday night. Lyla is with her secret-doughnut-scoffing dad all weekend, and I'd wager that Skye knows all the places to be in Cambridge. Unsurprisingly, though, she has plans with

Neil. They're going to Bath to watch him compete in a body-building contest and then having a night out with 'the lads from the show'. Skye has to help Neil 'oil up', and that's not something I want to know more about. I will say, though, she looked genuinely touched when I asked her if she fancied an end-of-week drink. You'd think I'd told her I was going to offer her one of my kidneys or something – I saw a glimmer of real emotion for at least forty seconds. Good.

I give in and text the likely bootie-knitter.

I'm SO bored. Are you up to much? Send.

Karl and I are practising our hypnobirthing breathing. Reply.

Ooohhh that sounds fuuunnnnn. Do you fancy doing something Friday night? Something chill? Maybe pop into a pub for a nibble? I omit the part about me drinking a bottle of wine by myself and perhaps drunk-dialling Edward once I'm home.

Love to, but I can't. Having a new supplier start with Dovington's on Saturday so doing a stock take. Come to that though, if you want some company?

So we've gone from a fun night out of fizz and flirting to sitting in a closed florist's on a Friday night helping my pregnant friend tidy up and rejig the shop. Not ideal, but better than another solo sofa night.

Can I bring wine? I ping back.

Yep, as long as you bring me the imitation stuff too!

See you at 7 with a bottle of Shloer! I reply.

Not exactly what I was looking for, but a plan is a plan.

Yes, excitement is on the horizon! After essentially being tricked into free labour for Lacey (it turns out she decided at the last minute to completely reorganise the entire shop and it was non-pregnant muggins here who did all the lifting and dragging for her), we sit in the back room with non-wine, real wine (ha, take that, Preggo – you may get to put your feet up, but I get all the wine), a bag of Babybels (cheese and wine, very classy) and a tube of ready-salted Pringles, and I have a good, full moan. I talk about how boring things feel at work now we've experienced the high of LFW and it's back to regular jobs again, how I've organised everything in the house and there feels like nothing else to do at home. I tell her how we don't see Kath as often because Lyla is so unsettled by Colin, and about how all the PSMs are too busy with their sick kids and horses to hang out. I even confess how I've messed it up with Edward. He seems uninterested these days (he did reply to my last message, but simply to say that he was well, that he also loves *Mad Men* and that he's not over again till Christmas. There were no leading questions or conversation starters, so it fizzled out there. I replied with just an OK-hand emoji because I'm easy-breezy (I tell myself). Lacey listens as I try to explain how I feel like I'm just plodding through motherhood, not doing anything amazing or 'wow'. It's funny how for so long my goal has been to be this settled and sorted, and now that I basically am, I'm bored. I need a 'thing'. There's something very cathartic about a good whinge to a good friend.

'What you need is something to look forward to!' declares Lacey, wafting her bottle around dramatically (why use a glass when it's all for you, anyway?).

'Yesh!' I slur.

'You've got three weeks till the big three-oh. Let's have a party!' she says, like this is the best idea anyone has ever had.

'Nooo! Oh no, no, no,' I protest, instantly visualising all the ways it could be a disaster.

'Robin Wilde, you are turning thirty years old on December the tenth and you need a party. I will do the whole thing. I want to do this for you. You deserve it. It will be magnificent. You will be magnificent. I will be magnificent.'

'Why don't you say "magnificent" some more?'

'Magnificent,' she says with a twinkle in her eye.

'OK. Magnificent,' I agree, weakly.

THIRTY-SIX

LACEY'S PARTY PLANNING ISN'T the solution to everything, however. Despite numerous pep talks and heart-to-heart chats, Lyla is really struggling with Colin being in our lives.

I had thought a little time would do the trick, or that our mini-adventure to the Lakes would help (though I still shudder at the knee-bashing incident), but unlike me, Lyla just cannot bring herself to let Derek go and warm to Kath's new relationship.

Derek was a wonderful man. He really was Kath's other half, and even though he passed away before Lyla came into the world, he has been so often talked of and so highly elevated that he's become almost godlike to Lyla.

Of course he had his faults, and I'm sure he and Kath had their off days, but once someone's gone, you don't talk about those bits, do you? You never hear someone saying, 'Oh, such-and-such had a beautiful soul . . . never bloody unloaded the dishwasher, though, did they?'

And we don't just talk about Derek – so much of his essence, his photos and possessions still adorn Kath's house, it's almost as though, to Lyla, he's still here. A friendly, comfortable part of our lives, and her innocent childhood loyalty can't cope with Colin edging in. That, and she hates sharing her beloved Kath, of course.

Breaking point came three days ago, when we visited Kath for only the second time in a month. Lyla is used to going round there a lot more than that, but Kath has been saying she's a 'bit busy' when I've asked if she can babysit, and likewise, Lyla hasn't been itching to go 'if Colin's there too'. So it's been a bit of a stalemate, and I thought if I went too, and on a day when Colin was at the warehouse, we'd make less of a hash of it.

We went through to her front room and sat in our usual places: Lyla and I on the chintzy floral two-seater sofa opposite the fireplace and Kath in a high-back crushed-velvet cerise chair. Just as I was about to dive into conversation about Lacey planning a thirtieth birthday party for me, Lyla jumped up, marched over to the tiled hearth, crammed with photos, trinkets, old pine cones and candles, and in one big movement, kicked over a silver-framed picture of Kath and Colin. Glass smashed everywhere, Kath and I jumped up and Lyla screamed at the top of her little lungs, 'Where's Derek?'

'What are you thinking?' I shouted back, shocked, as Kath started picking up shards of broken glass without saying a word.

'This is Derek's place, not HIS!' Lyla shouted back.

'Lyla Blue Wilde, what is the matter with you? You say sorry right now!' I said through clenched teeth, trying to regain control.

'No! Where is Derek?' she carried on, her shouting subsiding now, and her voice wobbling.

'You know where he is. He's in Heaven with Granny Wilde and Coco the cat. Why are you being like this?' I asked, exasperated and upset.

'Not actual Derek, I mean his picture,' she said, with big fat tears now rolling down her hot, red cheeks.

'Lyla, I moved Derek's picture into the dining room so that in here I could have my nice photograph of me and Colin on the top of the hill in the Lakes. I haven't forgotten Derek, but I want to be reminded of the happy times I'm having right now, not all the happy times I had many years ago. Smashing my pictures won't stop me having those happy times but it will make me feel very cross inside, and your mummy doesn't like seeing you behave like this, either,' Kath said calmly but firmly. Kath is rarely firm, so the change in tone was very effective on my petulant eight-year-old.

'But Derek has always been just there,' she said meekly, still crying.

'I know he has. Now, though, he's in the dining room. It's not a big deal, it's nice to change things around in your house sometimes. You have to keep things fresh, otherwise if everything stayed the same, life would be very dull, wouldn't it?' Kath said more softly now, putting the shards of glass on the coffee table and bending down to take both of Lyla's hands.

'I don't like things to change around,' Lyla mumbled. 'I like them to always stay the same. Just me and you and Mummy and nobody else.'

'Bluebird,' I say, picking her up and sitting with her on my lap, even though she's far too old to sit there comfortably, 'you and me and Auntie Kath will always be a team, we'll always love each other and will always be a girl gang, but it's nice to let other people join us and have fun. Derek has died and is waiting in Heaven for Kath. Until then, Kath is allowed to enjoy her time with Colin, OK? You need to stop behaving like this. You're a big girl, you're eight, this behaviour is unacceptable. I love you, Kath loves you, but this is absolutely not OK.'

After the hulk smash incident, I knew we had to do something. She'd gone as far as apologising and giving Kath a hug, but we'd been through that before and I know how Lyla works – sometimes rather than just talking, she needs to actually see something before she's truly on board with it. And this time, I've got a plan.

On a cold late-November afternoon we pop into Dovington's and pick up a small holly wreath with berries and gold glittery polystyrene bells hot-glued to it (Lyla's choice, not mine), then drive out to the edge of town where the cemetery is. I've been here a handful of times and, each time, never want to return in a hurry. Cemeteries are odd places – everything is calm and relaxed but nothing is happy. It's not like a country park, where you feel your spirits lift and the weight of the world slip away, yet you're surrounded by the same peace and quiet, the same smells and twittering birds.

I park the car at the edge of one of the little roads that weave through the plots and open Lyla's door for her. She climbs out with the wreath in her hand.

'Right, where is he, then?' I say gently to fill the silence as we survey the headstones in various stages of age and decay.

Lyla, unlike her usual self, clings to my hand and doesn't respond. I've never taken her to a cemetery before and, unsurprisingly, she isn't feeling at ease. But I know we need to find a way through this together.

We walk a couple of hundred metres until I start to slow, knowing his plot is reasonably near the lamp post we passed a second ago.

'Look, here he is,' I say quietly, coming to a stop and feeling Lyla moving even closer to me. We stand in silence for a few moments before I hear very gentle footsteps on the grass and turn round to find Kath walking towards us, a poinsettia plant in her hands. Lyla looks over to her but doesn't say anything.

'Hello,' I say, giving her a big cuddle with my free arm, Lyla refusing to let go of my other.

'Hello, lovies,' Kath says, hugging back and then leaning down to give Lyla a squeeze, too.

She kneels on the grass despite the November damp and cold, carefully places the little red-leaved plant down by the headstone and looks at Lyla.

'This is one of my most special places, Lyla. I come here when I want to think about Derek in peace. Underneath the ground we are on now, Derek's body is resting. I made sure he's wearing his very best suit, the one we married in, and I tucked photos of me in as well, and a pair of lacy white gloves I wore on a ship we went on once we knew he was going to get poorly and leave us,' Kath says, so gently and quietly I too have to bend to hear.

'Is Derek wet and cold in the ground?' Lyla asks, practically.

'Derek's body is in the ground, lovey. A person is two things. A body and a soul. Your body is like a machine. It is the thing that allows you to run and play and eat and laugh and talk and touch. Inside your body, though, is your soul. Your soul is the most perfect, unique, fantastic thing about you. It holds all of your love, your memories, your kindness, it's who you are. Without your soul, you're just the machine – but with it, you're a person. Derek was a beautiful person. His soul was made for my soul. We matched in every way and every day he made me happy. He made me laugh harder than anyone in the world could, he took care of me more sweetly and more kindly than anyone I've ever known, he made me feel brave and adventurous and like I was the most cherished thing he'd ever had. When Derek died, before you were born, we buried his body in the ground because he didn't need it anymore and because that's what he wanted, so we could always have a place to come and talk to him and think of him. But Derek's soul is not here. You can't bury a soul. A soul lives on in Heaven.'

'Where is Heaven, though?' she asks.

'Heaven, until we know for sure – when we've gone there too – is wherever you want it to be. I think Heaven is all around me, in every little thing that brings me joy, because that's exactly what Derek brought me: pure, complete joy. So, every time I feel it – sometimes in a big way and sometimes in a little way – I think of Derek. I think of him smiling and nodding, reminding me that he's here, wanting me to have a good day and to enjoy each moment of life as much as he did. Derek didn't live a sad life, Lyla, he lived a life full to the brim with fun. He would be so sad if he thought I wasn't carrying on doing that. So you must remember, whatever I'm doing, I'm always thinking of Derek with love, and when it's my time to go as well, and my body is buried, my soul will find his soul. It will be so wonderful it will be like fireworks of joy. Can you imagine that?'

Lyla looks like she's thinking really hard.

'Mmm-hmm.' She nods. 'So, when a person dies, their soul is all around you all the time, like air?'

'Sort of,' Kath says, standing up, making that little noise that people with bad knees or backs make as they manoeuvre themselves upright. 'Sometimes, when I see the sky just as the sun is setting and the clouds have gone golden and pink, I feel myself smiling for no reason other than how lovely it looks and I think, *That's joy; that's Derek reminding me of himself.* Sometimes you might be quite engrossed in something and feel a warmth in your heart and think of the person you have lost. I think that's them saying hello and reminding you that they are always with you, surrounding you with love and care, and watching you live your life until it's time for you to join them.'

I think of the baby I lost and wonder if their soul is around me, surrounding me with the love and care I never got the chance to give them, and feel a tear trickle down my cheek. Kath notices, shuts her eyes for a moment longer than a blink and takes my hand.

'You see, the people we have lost are not lost. They're just waiting. We don't need to spend each day feeling sad and downtrodden about them dying. We are supposed to spend each day living the happiest lives we can, so that when we eventually join them, we can say, "I lived my life to its very fullest, just like you wanted," and then sit down with them in some amazing, heavenly cake shop and tell them all the marvellous adventures we had while they were waiting!'

'Yeah!' says Lyla triumphantly. 'And you're making new adventures with Colin, aren't you?'

'I am, lovey, yes.'

'But you will always love Derek?' Lyla asks, still looking for a hint of reassurance.

'Absolutely!' Kath says firmly.

'And me?' she questions.

'Of course,' Kath reassures her.

'And Mummy?'

'Both of you. More than ever.' This time the serious tone is gone and a more jubilant one replaces it.

And with that very emotional but very clear breakthrough, we wander back up the winding road to where both cars are parked, hug for a long time until Lyla says, 'Guys! Mummy! Kath! You're squashing me,' and we head home for an afternoon of classics – spag bol and crappy YouTube vlogs. Bliss.

KATH WAS RIGHT. DEREK would want her to continue living life filled to the brim with happiness, and that's what I'm going to do, too. I like Edward being in my life. Maybe I'm not ready to throw myself into a full relationship, but he brought me joy and I recognise that now.

I bite the bullet and FaceTime him. I don't send a warning text or dither about. I just brush my hair a bit with my fingers, wipe the smudged mascara from under my eyes and press 'call'. Hashtag brave.

I stare back blankly at a video image of myself, waiting for him to pick up. It's quite late here, so a decent time for him there, so I'm hopeful he can answer.

'Heeeyyy.' Edward's face and voice boom into life.

'Hey you! Just thought I'd check in and say, well, "hey", haha,' I respond awkwardly. Maybe I should have rehearsed this just a little bit.

'Oh, right. Cool. Hey, haha,' Edward says back even more awkwardly. God, this is going from bad to worse.

'So, how are things?'

'Yeah, awesome, things are awesome. We're expanding the business so my job is expanding, too, which is cool. Buying up more stores, searching out new stockists, it's awesome.'

'Awesome!' So, I think we've covered that – it's definitely all *awesome*.

'How's things your end? Any more fashion shows in the pipeline?'

'No, not for now. We're back with our local jobs right now, and next summer we'll have the film franchise gig. Remember we won it from New York last year? Well, they begin shooting again next year, but in the UK, so that'll keep us busy, I think . . .' I trail off. Since when did we only talk about work stuff?

'Oh, neat,' he says in his British accent but with his distinctively American vocab, and that smile. I do like that smile.

'So, I wondered if you're back in England anytime soon? I'd love to hang out,' I venture.

'Well, not for a while, but I'll let you know when I am.'

'You'll be back for Christmas, though, you said. To see your mum and dad?' I say hopefully.

'Yeah, I don't know . . . I haven't thought that far ahead yet,' he says vaguely.

I give up. He clearly doesn't really want to go anywhere with this and I'm starting to sound a bit desperate. This isn't my best life, this is living my life like a saddo on FaceTime at nine o'clock on a Sunday night, trying to get a guy back into me who was into me but who I pushed away. Fuck this, I'm going to bed.

'OK, well, let me know if you are and if you want to hang because I think it'd be fun, but no worries if you don't!' I say in my classic faux-cheerful voice usually reserved for Lyla.

'Will do!'

And we say our goodbyes before ringing off.

I'm not sure that's what Derek would've called living life to the full.

THIRTY-SEVEN

DECEMBER

The week leading up to my thirtieth, Lacey is buzzing with excitement about my party. I've told her not to work too hard or go all out since she's seven months pregnant now, and, deep down, I'm a bit worried I don't have enough friends or pizzazz to be worth an actual party. A couple of drinks in a nice bar maybe, but a party just for me seems uncomfortably exuberant and I'm not sure it sits well.

Lacey assures me that she's enjoying it, it'll be small and classy and nothing over the top. She's sworn to me there won't be strippers, fishbowls or hideous forced fun party games with balloons between knees, but this assurance has fallen on deaf ears. It was Lacey who organised my twenty-first and those three things basically sum up what the party was, with the addition of my vomit on Simon's shoes at 2 a.m. and him being so cross he didn't speak to me all the next day. Such sweet, tender memories.

Anyway, with no details to go on except 'meet me at Dovington's at 7.30 p.m. and we'll go from there', and the fact that Kath has offered to have Lyla for the night, I'm completely in the dark.

My birthday falls on a Sunday, but with the party on the Saturday evening, I can spend the day luxuriating. Kath collects Lyla at 11 a.m. for a fun-filled day of making lavender flower crowns, apparently, and I, quite shockingly, head to the gym. I'm going to be so healthy in my thirties. I'll treat my body like a temple and work on core strength for body and mind. I'll probably even turn vegan and maybe I really will go minimalist.

The gym's quite busy, though, and I make the executive decision to just do a 'power fifteen minutes' on the bike and call it a day. It's never a good idea to overexert yourself at the first hurdle, everyone knows that. The sauna and steam room are a lot less busy and, in my expert opinion, I'm working out my mind in here. I'm calm and collected and reflective, and I'm basically just sweating out all the fat stores. Very valuable time spent. I promise myself I'll come back next week.

Back home, I feel energised and serene. I am a goddess. A twenty-nine-year-old goddess with a lovely home, a beautiful daughter and a solid four friends. I have my shit firmly together. It's only 2 p.m., so I'm going to have some spaghetti hoops on toast and watch TV for a bit, like all successful twenty-nine-year-old goddesses do.

RIGHT, I HAVE A wardrobe spilling out with clothes but apparently nothing at all 'dressy'. I know this, really; I've always known this, but I did think I had *some* nice pieces. Apparently not. Apparently everything is either denim, jersey or summery. Lacey's told me to 'dress up', so I'm assuming we're going somewhere special.

Why have I never invested in a selection of winter cocktail dresses? I'm going to put this on my list of things to do in my thirties (as well as work out, consider veganism and be a minimalist. A minimalist with an emergency selection of winter cocktail dresses).

For a moment I consider the silky shell dress I wore to Lyla's birthday, dressing it up with tights, heels and a blazer, but it looks ridiculous. It looks like 'Mum's having a go', and that's not the vibe I'm going for. I push each hanger back and forth until I notice an old crumpled plastic bag at the back of the wardrobe, and lift it out. Inside is the skirt and top combo I wore to that fateful night at the OXO Tower with Theo. I'd forgotten how beautiful this skirt is – it's made of layers of black lace and tulle and in between the layers are tiny stars embroidered in gold thread, which are barely visible until the light catches them and then they look like the night sky – and how incredible I felt in it. Well, how incredible I felt on arrival. By the time I was leaving, with hot wax up the backs of my calves (don't ask) and my heart in pieces, I didn't feel so incredible.

I try it on and look in the mirror. It's so flattering. It's not the skirt and top's fault that Theo didn't want me. It's not my fault either, I don't think. I was never going to be what he wanted, who he wanted. The skirt doesn't deserve to live a crumpled life at the bottom of the wardrobe, the skirt deserves to enjoy its life and feel beautiful, whether a man validates it or not. That's that decided, then.

My favourite part of any getting ready process, unsurprisingly, is the make-up. I spend so much time planning, organising and applying other people's that I rarely spend time on my own face. Today is all for me, though, and I sit at the dressing table for a happy hour with vlogs playing on my phone as I apply a good base, make my skin luminous, tend carefully to my brows and accentuate the almond shape of my brown eyes with the most beautiful shimmering shadows, perfectly blended. It's only your thirtieth once, so I take a further twenty minutes applying individual lashes to give myself a full, fluttering effect, and by the time I've swept on a deep crimson lipstick, I feel gorgeous. Actually gorgeous.

Being the thoroughly modern woman I am, I make the most of this opportunity to take approximately six hundred selfies, as it would be a crime to let this look go to waste. I text the best one to Lacey.

*So excited!!!! *champagne emoji**

*Me too!! *party popper emoji** she pings back.

Would it be easier for me to just grab a cab to yours or meet you in town? I ask. Dovington's seems like such a weird place to meet before a night out.

No, just head straight to the shop, I've left your present in the back room – oops! she replies straight away.

*Ah, bless you, I don't expect gifts! Just a night out is enough for me. A bit of excitement! Might even go wild and have a cheeky flirt with the finest bachelors Cambridge has to offer, haha. *kiss emoji**

Wilde by name, wild by nature! she sends back.

Since I'm ready early, I give Kath a call to check Lyla's OK and isn't causing any Derek/Colin-related havoc. I can hear music in the background and Kath assures me Lyla's had a lovely time making flower crowns for everyone and dancing about to 'all this modern music'. I can only assume by 'everyone' she means the middle-aged mad lot from Cupcakes and Crochet Club, who will sit tomorrow afternoon in the church hall with their balls of wool and their perms beautifully adorned with lavender wreaths. God love Kath.

THIRTY-EIGHT

With the final touches of highlighter and lip gloss applied, I look out of the window to check for the taxi. It's running late, and I notice that snow has very gently started to fall and is lightly settling on the street below. I'd usually groan about traffic delays and schools being closed, but just in that moment, standing in my restyled skirt and feeling so special, it looks like magic. It feels like the sky is acknowledging my birthday too, showering me with frosty white confetti as a celebration.

Typically, since I was dressed and ready an hour early, the taxi arrives twenty minutes late, and so by the time I pull up to Dovington's, I'm slightly frazzled and have sent several apologetic texts to Lacey (who says everything's fine and she'll just wait out front). I'm out of the car, £7 lighter and with no 'sorry for the delay' from Mr Ambivalent Cabbie.

'Robin! You're here!' comes Lacey's familiar voice. She looks an absolute vision standing outside the shop in a deep berry-coloured jersey maxi-dress that falls beautifully over her bump and makes her hair look like actual gold. I look up from shovelling my change into my clutch bag and before I can reply, it hits me.

Dovington's isn't Dovington's. Well, it is, but it's not like it usually is. It's not an out-of-hours florist's with a few promotional posters in the window. It's breathtaking. The posters are gone, the huge three-foot vases of bouquets that sit in the window are gone and the shelves and cabinets that are usually groaning under the weight of succulents, gifts and more flower arrangements have been pushed back to the walls. I can see that lighting the much-bigger-looking-than-usual room are strings and strings of warm white fairy lights. They go backward and forward across the ceiling as well as cascading down the walls, making the whole shop look magical. Hanging from the ceiling between the fairy lights are paper pompoms, much smaller than the ones we made for Mother's Day, in berry, gold, moss and purple. All around the edges of the room

I can see displays of winter bouquets with eucalyptus, deep red roses, twig sprays with glitter and, of course, since Kath has surely had a hand in this, lavender.

'Lacey, I don't know what to say – this must have taken you days!' I stammer, still standing on the street.

'Nope, everyone helped!' She beams, placing a hand lovingly on her bump.

'You shouldn't have gone to all this trouble – not in your condition. You're supposed to be resting,' I say, welling up and walking over to her and grasping her hands.

'I told you, I wasn't alone. Kath, Colin, Mum, Dad, Karl and your posh mum friends all came to help! Even that Skye from your office messaged saying she'd be happy to give us all makeovers before you arrived, if we wanted them,' she says, fluttering her lashes and showing off a hint of holographic glitter in the corners of her eyes.

'Oh my God, I don't know what to say, I really don't know,' I laugh, while trying not to cry.

'Don't say anything then, let's go inside – it's freezing!' She loops her arm through mine, walks to the door, pushes it open and as the warm air hits us, a surge of people come forward from the back of the shop shouting, 'Surprise!'

'Oh my God!' I half shout, half cry, bringing my hands up to my face.

'You didn't think I'd do things by half, did you?' Lacey says, being the first to hug me.

The shop is suddenly bustling with people, all smiling and hugging me, wishing me Happy Birthday and saying 'you look beautiful' and lots of other lovely things. There's Gillian and Finola with their husbands; there's Karl, Tina and Michael (Lacey's mum and dad), Natalie and Martin, Skye and muscle man Neil (who looks slightly sulky, but I can let that slide), and there, in the middle of them all, Terri from Dovington's and *Piper*!

'Piper!' I squeal, practically skipping over to hug her. 'You're not in New York!'

'Nope, I had loads of holiday accrued anyway for Christmas at home, so I figured coming a few days early wouldn't hurt!'

'Ah, I'm so glad you're here. I've missed you!'

'Me too! Let's go out over Christmas. I want to get wrecked on this side of the pond.'

'Absolutely!' I say, feeling a particular wave of excitement washing over me, something I've missed for a long time.

I'm so giddy with people and music, and the glass of champagne that's magically appeared in my hand, it takes me a moment to register the 'Mummmyyy,' Lyla shouts out as she pushes her way through the throng to get to me.

'Bluebird! I didn't know you were going to be here,' I say, scooping her up and thinking how perfect she is. She's wearing a soft moss-green dress with lilac lace scalloped edging round the cuffs and hem with a matching lilac lacy collar. Round the waist is a lace belt garnished with little pearls. 'Where did this dress come from?' I ask, amazed at how gorgeous it is.

'Auntie Kath made it for me! We set up your party today. I made floral crowns in the back room with Kath and Colin put up all the lights. It's been a huge secret, Mummy.'

'Did anyone ever tell you you're the best, Lyla Blue?' I say, squeezing her even tighter than before.

'I know! Do you want a crown? They're eucalyptus, lavender and berry and then I sprayed them all with a sprinkle of glitter to make it look like frost!' she says, jumping up and down on the spot in anticipation, eager to show me now that I've released her from the squishiest hug ever.

'I can't think of anything I'd like more. Go and get them,' I say, watching her run off into the crowd and seeing Kath walking towards me, with Colin in tow.

'You've done all this. It's amazing!' I say, hugging them both.

'You deserve it, lovey. It's been such a year,' Kath says in my ear.

'Many happy returns of the day!' Colin toasts his glass with mine just as Lyla comes running back with about ten of the beautiful crowns, all looped onto her arms.

'Wow! So many,' I say, taking one off and balancing it carefully on my head.

'Yep, there's enough for all the ladies! I thought the men could have one too, but Colin said to save them for the ladies because they're the real princesses tonight.'

'Ah, that was very nice of him,' I say, noting how she isn't glaring at him or letting us know how much she despises him.

Once Lyla has shown me all the components of her handiwork about four times over, I leave her holding Kath's hand and make my way further back into the shop to find Finola, Edgar, Gillian and Paul standing with full glasses near a wall of photos.

Before I can take in what the photos are of (or perhaps I'm avoiding it because I have a sneaking suspicion it's a memory wall of hideous snaps Lacey has taken and stashed away over the years), I do a double-take at Finola.

'Finola, you look ravishing!' I say, reaching out to take her elbow and air-kissing both cheeks.

'Well, darling, I decided to take a leaf out of your glamorous book and make a bit of an effort,' she says, matter-of-factly.

'Christ! I wouldn't say I'm very often glamorous!' I laugh.

'Anything that's not horse muck or Vaseline is glamour to me, dear. I made a good fist of trying this glamour thing at home, but maybe fisting isn't my thing,' she says innocently. I know what she means, but I wish she wouldn't say 'fisting' so vigorously, and I try not to chuckle. 'Then your chum Lacey messaged me and said that nice blonde whippet from your work was offering to do us with her make-up kit and she fixed me right up, didn't she, Edgar?'

'She did, dear. You look very fine,' Edgar says with no emotion at all, but it seems to make Finola blush. I smile at how lovely she looks and at how nice Skye has been to her. She's all right, under all the pretentiousness (Skye, I mean, we all know Finola's a good egg).

'Now, let's just take a minute to appreciate this wall, shall we?' Gillian interrupts, with a mischievous glint in her eye.

'Oh lordy, I dread to think what we've got on here,' I say, stepping over to take a proper look.

We stand a bit closer, looking at each photo by the (thankfully) dim glow of the fairy lights, and I find myself simultaneously laughing and cringing. There are all the classics, like me and Lacey on the school field during a heatwave with our shirts rolled into crop tops; a photo of me dressed as Sporty Spice, Lacey as Baby Spice and three of our old classmates as the others; a few Lacey's mum must have taken when were eight or nine and wore old puffed-sleeved bridesmaid dresses in the garden to 'put on a show' for the grown-ups. Then as we move along you can see us growing up a bit. The toxic green fishbowl of my twenty-first birthday with all of us sucking on giant straws; a hideous out-of-focus shot of me kissing Simon in a club at uni (not sure why Lacey's left that up, maybe to remind me of the good times?); me holding Lyla in the hospital the day after she was born; Lacey, Piper and me on the first day I moved into Granny's old house, surrounded by boxes but holding up mugs of wine, and then lots of nice, more recent photos of me that I've uploaded to Instagram, often including Lyla.

'Doesn't look like a bad life, Robs,' Karl says, as he walks past and sees me enjoying the wall.

'It certainly doesn't. You're lucky to have a lady like Lacey. I can't believe she's done all this!' I say to him, almost in tears again.

'You haven't seen anything yet,' he says with a wink, and walks off to find his beloved pregnant wife.

'Oh gawd, he doesn't mean a stripper, does he?' I ask Gillian out of the side of my mouth. 'She promised no strippers.'

'As disappointing as that is, I don't think he meant a

stripper. Have you been over here and seen your cake and memory jar, though?' she says, leading me to the back of the shop where the till usually rests on a huge antique table.

We meander past Tina and Michael, who are talking animatedly to Natalie and Martin about their travels, and come to a stop at the table.

'Shit me! This is so beautiful,' I gasp.

'Your auntie made it and Lacey decorated it,' Gillian says, reaching out a hand to touch the side of the cake very gently.

At first look, it is just a simple round sponge with some flowers round the base, but the closer you inspect, the more tiny details there are. The sponge itself is very lightly glazed so you can still see the soft, pillowy texture, but when you move and see it in different lights, the whole thing has an iridescent sheen to it. Round the base are the same flowers as the ones in the crowns and dotted all over the room, eucalyptus, dark red roses, lavender and a touch of baby's breath, but placed carefully in between those are pearl-, opal- and diamond-looking gems, all catching the light and shimmering back at us. On top of it is a hand-cut, gold-leafed number thirty, sticking up about four inches and twinkling with its gemstone counterparts. It looks too beautiful to eat.

'They should sell these! This is more beautiful than

any wedding cake I've ever seen,' I say, feeling the bubbles of the drink go to my head a little bit. Who keeps topping this up?

'And, Lacey's organised you a memory jar! How lovely is that?' Gillian says.

'Ooh, a jar for me to fill with my memories?' I say, really feeling the fizz setting in.

'No, you ninny, we all write our favourite memories of you in there on one of these pieces of paper,' she laughs, picking up a little square of deep purple paper that is lying next to another Mason jar full of gold gel pens. 'It's a keepsake for you to share with Lyla or to enjoy in years to come.'

'If it's to share with family, I'm not sure I could write down all of my favourite Robin Wilde memories,' a deep voice says from behind me.

Surely not? Why would he be here? In Dovington's. In England?

I turn.

'Edward?' I say, then just stupidly stare at him with my mouth open like a ventriloquist's doll.

'Hi,' he says softly, reaching out both hands and taking both of mine, pulling me in for a little hug. I'm vaguely aware that a few people have turned round, sensing the event, but I don't care.

'Hi,' I say back, into his neck, still dumbstruck. One of us is going to have to say more than this.

'I brought you a present,' Edward says, stepping back, pulling open his blazer and lifting out a gift.

Without speaking, I take it from him slowly, unwrap the black shiny paper tied up with gold ribbon (either Edward is a master wrapper or this is the craft of a department store worker) and pull out the most luxurious notebook I've ever had. This is no £1.49 jobby from WHSmith, like the ones that I've mostly used to write all my thoughts and ideas in, and the one I found in my shell box of memories and trinkets last year. No, this is a proper grown-up notebook. How lovely that he remembered me talking about this. The jacket is the softest, butteriest leather in a deep navy, and on the spine, embossed in gold lettering, is 'Robin Wilde'. I run my finger across my name and look up at Edward.

He looks as choked-up as I am.

'I messaged you so many times,' I manage.

'I know. I didn't know what to say. I wanted to say so much but I didn't want to get hurt.'

'I'm sorry I hurt you.'

'I'm wild about you, Robin. I think about you all the time. I know it's been a weird year, and I know there have been hard . . . things . . . but I think there's something worth it here. I mean, I hope there is. Otherwise I'm just standing in a mad florist's with your mad friend Lacey, who somehow found my work number and harassed me till I gave in and—'

'I'm in.'

'What?'

'I don't need convincing. I'm not scared. I want to see what happens.'

Wow, this is romantic. The fairy lights, the notebook, the man, several of my closest friends pretending they're not listening but obviously they're almost giving themselves hernias, they're straining so hard to hear us.

'Mummy! Who is this strange man?' Lyla bounds up, shattering any sense of movie-like romance, and I panic. She's never met Edward. Is this the wrong way to introduce him? We've only just got over the pink snake MatchMe app incident of 2016 – I don't want to psychologically damage her any further.

'This is Mummy's friend Edward,' Lacey interjects, walking over and giving Edward a hug. They've obviously already been introduced. She looks at me uncertainly. 'Look, I had to do something, you were so mopey; I'm pregnant, my hormones are crazy, OK?'

'I love you, Lacey and, for once, I love your hormones.'

Lyla, who has been watching the whole exchange, adds,

'I think you want Edward to be your boyfriend. You talk about Edward to Lacey on the phone ALL the time. You love him. You want to marry him,' she laughs, and skips off. Hmmm, maybe it wasn't all that psychologically damaging after all.

'You talk about me all the time to Lacey, do you?' Edward says with a wry smile.

'No! Literally never. Like once. Maybe. In a fleeting moment,' I start gabbling, with a big smile across my face.

'My dear, is this the famous stud from the Americas?' comes Finola's voice, really not helping me prove my point at all.

'No! Well, yes! I never said he was a stud!' I stammer, taking a big glug of my drink and turning red.

'Robin Wilde, you think I'm a stud. You want me to be your boyfriend. It's your thirtieth birthday. Lacey's shown me all the teenage pictures. I've met your Auntie Kath. Why don't you just give up and kiss me?' Edward says, moving closer.

And, actually like the movies, Edward puts one hand on my lower back, one on my shoulder, swoops me down and kisses me, just as all my friends cheer and clap. *I've peaked,* I think. *I've fucking well peaked.*

Part Six

HERE COME THE GIRLS!

THIRTY-NINE

A NEW YEAR . . .

'CHRISTMAS WAS LOVELY,' I begin writing on the first page of the magnificent navy leather notebook Edward gave me for my birthday just over a month ago. 'Christmas was lovely' feels so meh, though. It doesn't fully bring to life how it all felt, but to write all that in my notebook would be too much.

Rather than committing the heinous stationery crime that is ripping a page out of a new book, heaven forfend, I underline 'lovely' twice. That helps. Underneath it, I add, 'Perfect, actually', and underline that, too. I foresee a lot of underlining in this new notebook.

It's mid-January. I'm sitting up in bed, lit by the glow of my bedside lamp at 6.30 a.m., waiting for Lyla to wake up in about an hour, and then we'll start the school run routine. I don't usually wake up this early but today I did and felt compelled to start writing in my notebook, almost like a diary, just as I used to do so often. Last year I didn't write a journal at all. Not because I was sad or bleak or totally consumed by The Emptiness all year, but because I was just too busy. I'd felt like I didn't need my old notepad habit, but this morning I knew it was time to start writing again. I know I will want to read these things back one day, and I'll be glad I kept a record. Even if it's just here and there, pockets of time, I'll be glad.

After my birthday, so many significant life-things happened that I want to write them all down so that I can relax, knowing the memories are safely stored, here in this little book.

First, Edward. Edward happened.

Remember when I was a bit miffed at Lacey for sending him a message on Facebook after London Fashion Week? Well, it turns out I have a lot to thank her for because they began chatting, and as much as I don't like the idea of Lacey (or anyone, for that matter) interfering in my love life, I'm so glad she did. In a risky move, she took it upon herself to tell Edward all about Theo. She told him how I'd been so lonely for so long, how I had let someone into my heart and then had been completely let down and felt utterly rejected. She helped Edward understand that my pushing him away was never a reflection of his shortcomings, but really a reflection of mine. Despite my year-long protests, she saw through my 'I'm not that bothered about him' facade and told him how much he meant to me. All this on Facebook chat, potentially the modern-day ink and quill love letter.

When Edward turned up to my party it wasn't just for a fleeting visit. He had a month-long stay booked. He's researching some new business opportunities in London and already had leave planned to see his mum and dad over Christmas, so pushed it all together.

We've never had the opportunity to spend more than a few days together at a time, and although I was apprehensive that the magic would wear off, it didn't.

We spent long, lazy days in bed together making up for all the lost time over the autumn; we spent afternoons in country pubs talking about our childhoods, our previous relationships, our work goals and, more poignantly, our family goals. We talked about the miscarriage. We talked about how it had affected me, but also, how it affected him. I had never really thought it would have such a deep impact on him, because he didn't go through the physicality of it, but that just wasn't the case. He felt it. He felt a great loss, a great robbing of the future, and, just like me, he grieved too. I wish we had grieved together. I wish I had known he was feeling this way, but to his credit, he held it together to support me. As I write my notes in the beautiful navy book, I pause my pen. That baby would be here by now. It would be a couple of weeks old and I'd be in that newborn, sleep-deprived, hazy bubble. How different my life would be.

During his stay, Edward also spent some time with Lyla. After seeing us kiss at the party and apparently picking up so much about him over the year (who knew children were so astute and had such bat ears? Me now, apparently), it seemed pointless trying to fob him off as 'Mummy's friend' and treating her like she's less intelligent than she is.

'Lyla, this is Edward,' I told her when he popped over for brunch the weekend after my party. He'd had a chocolate Santa in one hand and a bunch of glitter-dipped daisies in the other.

'Are those flowers for Mummy and the Santa for me?' she asked, even before saying hello, clearly trying to establish the lie of the land.

'No, actually they're both for you. Nice to meet you properly, Lyla,' Edward said sweetly, stepping into the hallway and handing her his offerings.

Lyla was thrilled. Never before had she been treated to something so grown up as her own bunch of flowers, especially not glitter-dipped ones. I smiled at the scene, feeling happy for Lyla and so touched that Edward had made such a well-thought-out gesture.

We walked through to the kitchen where I'd laid out a hot pot of tea, warm croissants, jams and butter (which I'd decanted into a little dish because although I'm really at ease with him, I'm still semi-playing the game. If butter in a dish is a game. What am I doing? I'm over-thinking butter).

'So, Edward,' Lyla started as she hoisted herself up onto a bar stool and dug into a croissant, 'are you my mum's new boyfriend?'

I instantly felt the blood rush to my neck and face, and wished the ground would swallow me up. It was painfully awkward.

'Argh! Hahaha! Kids eh?!' I gabbled at Edward, trying to pass it off as a joke but feeling super-flustered.

'It's OK,' he said calmly, putting a hand on my lower back to reassure me and looking at Lyla with a smile. 'You know what, Lyla, I would really, really like to be.'

Lyla hunched her shoulders and giggled into her croissant at Edward's brazen act of bravery. The tension dissipated all at once.

'Oh, would you?' I laughed. 'Well, we'll have to see about that,' I said, giving him a little kiss on the lips, much to Lyla's horror.

'Ewww, Mummy!'

With that, he and Lyla were fully introduced and everyone knew the score. I never officially said 'yes' to being Edward's girlfriend, but I think we all knew. Just to be sure, I bought him a Christmas card with 'boyfriend' on because when you're just a smidge too emotionally scarred to utter the words yourself, there's always mass consumerism to help you out.

Lyla gave him a card for Christmas, too. In Lyla language, it was the highest compliment. On the outside were penguins dancing round a frozen lake (just a normal one that she'd got out of the multipack I bought her to give out to friends), but on the inside she had written:

Dear Edwood,
you are not a slimy wurm.
Merry Christmas!
Love,
Lyla
****

A whole row of kisses is standard fare from her, but I was delighted to see the real indication of festive cheer, the declaration that Edward is not a 'slimy wurm'. I explained this huge act of goodwill, and Edward was most pleased. He returned the favour by clamping his arms tightly to his side and wiggling around saying, 'Oh, help me, I thought I was a worm, but I'm not a worm! I'm wiggling like a worm, but I'm not a worm!' while Lyla ran round him laughing heartily and trying to 'unstick' his arms with spells. I watched and smiled and felt so thankful to have found a man like Edward, who indeed, unlike all my others, is not a slimy worm.

As well as the card to Edward, Lyla surprised me with another . . .

We had decided that I would host the family Christmas this year. Mum and Dad spared me another trip to Cornwall as they'd only just docked, back from their Scandinavian cruise and 'needed a few days to reset'. I'm not sure how much 'resetting' you need to do after a two-week, all-inclusive relaxing holiday on a boat, but I wasn't going to argue because the thought of driving all the way down and enduring my mother for three days was quite the burden.

Since the new house has a much bigger kitchen than Kath's, and open-plan dining, we decided we'd do it here and cook together. Edward, naturally, was spending Christmas Day with his family, but planned on coming back up on Boxing Day for some festivities here. Lyla was set to be with me and then her dad would pick her up at seven on Christmas night. It was a good set-up, and I was so excited about spending the day in my PJs, eating Kath's incredible food, watching Lyla unwrap her presents and making my way through the selection box Kath would inevitably buy me, even though I'm thirty now.

A week after my birthday, while I was in the downstairs loo, cleaning all my work make-up brushes in the little sink, Lyla plodded down with a letter.

'Mummy, I've been thinking about what you said,' she said bluntly, as though I knew exactly which thing she was talking about.

Racking my brains, I asked her what she meant.

'About Colin.'

Still lost, I waited for her to explain.

'About letting Colin into our lives and making Kath happy. She was so happy at your birthday party, and Colin was really kind all day. He did all the setting up and said my flower crowns were the best he's ever seen,' she said earnestly.

'OK,' I said, 'so what's in the letter?'

'I'll read it to you.'

'OK.' I was intrigued.

Dear Colin,

you are not my best friend but I like you a bit. Roo is my real best friend and Kath is my family best friend.

Even though Kath loves Derek, she does like you and you are kind to her. you helped make Mummy's party be special and Kath cried happy tears when she walked in.

we are having Christmas dinner at our house and we would like to invite you too. you can sit next to Kath but I'm sitting closest on the other side of her.

Lots of love,

Lyla

'I'm going to fold it up and put it in a Christmas card for him and you can post it,' she told me.

I had to catch my breath. I knew how much of a step that was for Lyla (and really hoped Colin would see it, too, despite the rather blunt honesty).

'Lyla, that's so sweet of you to invite him, we can send it later.'

Using my best judgement, I decided to take the letter and stash it in a drawer, pretending that it had been posted. Later on that night, I sent a text to Colin inviting him to Christmas dinner – making clear the invitation came from Lyla as well.

His reply was swift. *Well now, that is very nice of you indeed to invite me but I think it would be appreciated by Kathy if she could spend some time with you on her own. We have lots of time ahead for big events, but I'd like Lyla to have all of her aunt on this special day, and I shall be travelling down to spend some time with my sons. All the best, Colin x*

I felt a huge wave of respect for Colin. He may have already had plans with his boys, but the fact that he recognised Lyla's need for some solo Kath time meant a lot. He's a good egg, that one. Mentally I took him off my 'any bottle of wine that's on offer' Christmas list and added him to the 'nice jumper from John Lewis' list. An upgrade!

So Christmas was spent as a happy trio, and it was bliss. The run-up was filled with the usual fare: school concerts (complete with dance routine, of course), a heavy workload thanks to clients trying to squeeze in commercial shoots before the Christmas break, lots of people booking an hour of services for special parties and a few of our community centre jobs, and, of course, late-night Christmas shopping. This has always been a tradition of mine and Lacey's, but since she's just a human ball waddling about huffing and puffing now, she brought her iPad over and we both lounged on my sofas with heated party food and did it all online. I don't think I'll ever do it any other way, again. And I even got my promised girly night out on the town with Piper, while Lacey babysat – with her fully packed Hospital Bag reassuringly by her side 'just in case'.

FORTY

JANUARY, SURPRISINGLY, HAS BEEN a good month. I said my goodbyes to Edward but didn't feel a great sadness as he was booked to be working in the UK all of February on the new business expansion, so really it was just a three-week break and he'd be back again. Usually January is a pretty dull month, but it turned out Gloria had a plan to beat this.

'Ladies, forget Dry January. Let's go out! I need to let my hair down after three weeks of solo-parenting my two beasts, dearly though I love them,' she added for good measure.

'I'm always up for a night out!' I said eagerly. Maybe a bit too eagerly. 'Gillian, Finola, can I tempt you two?'

'You certainly can, my dear! Edgar bought me the most beautiful Charlotte Tilbury palette for Christmas and I'm desperate to give it a whirl,' Finola said straight away.

Gillian and I feigned falling over backwards in shock.

'I don't know what I love more, Finola, the fact that you are going to glam yourself up again or the fact that Edgar bought you something better than garden centre vouchers!' Gillian said in thrilled tones. 'I'd like to come out just to celebrate this!'

'Hurrah, then! A night out for the four of us.' Gloria cheered eagerly, just as her phone pinged in her hand.

She tried to move it away but my speedy eyes caught the name: *RavelleySir.* Dear God. For a split second we locked eyes and exchanged the slightest of knowing smiles. She's in. We have a new mum in our gang, and I'm more than happy about it!

WITH LACEY'S FEBRUARY DUE date looming, I can't help but think of the baby I didn't have. Since all my chats with Edward, I feel a great sense of healing, but I don't think it's something I'll ever be fully 'over'. Gillian has been such a support and has shared more of her coping strategies. She, Paul and Clara still do special things for her angel babies, like planting roses or work on special art projects together. It means a lot to know she understands my journey.

I haven't told Lyla about the baby. I might do one day, but for now it's just me and Edward, Kath, Gillian, Lacey and a few people from work who needed to know. I'm happy with it like that. I haven't even told Mum: I know it would lead to a thousand other conversations that I can't be bothered with (interestingly, though, not conversations that I can't face).

This last year was so unlike the one before. The previous year was all about dragging myself out of The Emptiness and finding a way to live happily without the things I didn't have. The year just gone was allowing myself to find a way to let them in. To let Edward in, to let myself lead on big projects, to help Lyla navigate letting Colin in and, most joyfully yet painfully, to let in the thought of Lacey's gorgeous new baby.

'The year just gone was full. Full of love (eventually!) and creativity and people and soon, a new baby. Here's to the new year and all that it will bring!' I write in my notebook, underlining 'all' with gusto.

THE NEXT DAY I drop Lyla at Kath's to work on the latest batch of lavender lotions, pick up a little posy of the fragrant lilac-coloured flowers and then head out in the car.

Twenty minutes later I'm pulling up to the cemetery we visited a few months ago with Lyla.

It feels more peaceful today than it did last time. Perhaps I'm somehow more peaceful.

I walk the few hundred yards from the car to Derek's grave and note that the wreath we laid is still there, but the glitter has been washed off the polystyrene balls by the rain. I place my posy of lavender down next to it and stand up, tilting my head to the sky.

I'm aware of my breathing, in and out. I'm aware of the weak sun on my face and the damp of the grass soaking through the seams of my ballet pumps. I try to focus just on these three things as I let my body stand very still, very calm.

It's been such a big year, without me ever having meant it to be. I keep my eyes shut and say a silent prayer for the baby I never knew I wanted to love so much. I'm not particularly religious, but I like to think that he or she is up there, sitting on Derek's lap, waiting for me, like he is.

'Derek,' I whisper to his headstone, 'keep my baby safe for me. I can't wait to meet it and cuddle it and kiss its little hands. Until then, I've got to live properly for Lyla, so I'm leaving this one with you. I'll take care of Kath, and then when she's up there with you, she'll have a cuddle too.'

I'm whispering to a piece of black marble but my heart feels such a weight removed, such a tension soothed. I whisper my goodbyes, wipe the tears from my eyes and head back to the car.

Bye-bye, baby, see you one day soon.

FORTY-ONE

LACEY IS NOW TEN days overdue and ten days beyond the end of her tether.

'I've tried everything to get the bloody thing out, but it's not moving!' she huffs as I walk into the back room of Dovington's to see her sitting amid a technicolor heap of Valentine's decor debris.

'Shall I assume by "bloody thing", you mean the baby you have lovingly grown for nine months?' I say, smiling and sitting down at the table, reaching for an open packet of custard creams and helping myself to one.

'Yes, the bloody thing I've grown for nine months and is now outstaying its welcome inside me. I can't walk comfortably, I can't sleep comfortably – my skin feels like it's going to burst open.' She huffs some more.

'I'm assuming you've tried all the tricks? Pineapple? Curries? Sex?' I offer in support.

'Robin, I've tried them all over and over again. I'm tempted to try eating a pineapple curry while Karl shags me senseless if it will bring on labour.'

'Wow, that's a vision. Thanks for that,' I say with a half-laugh. 'The best thing to do is take your mind off it, and that's what I'm here for. Your trusty friend is here to lighten your load and tell you about my life, and then you can tell me all the answers and all will be right with the world!' I carry on, in my peppiest of pep-talk tones.

'Oh my God, no!' Lacey says, horrified.

'What do you mean, "Oh my God, no"? You usually love sorting my life out! I'm not beyond saving, am I? Has this baby addled your brain?' I say, mocking her slightly but also thinking, *My life's not* that *bad, is it?*

'No, I mean, oh my God, you're better than sex and curry!' she says, beaming.

'Erm, OK. So my life *is* interesting to listen to?' I ask, completely clueless.

Lacey stands up. 'I think my waters have gone!'

'What? You're supposed to have gentle contractions and surges for hours before that happens. You're meant to have signs of labour and be practising your breathing. You should be leaning over a birthing ball with a midwife when this happens, shouldn't you? It's not meant to be like this, like in the films. It's all happening so fast. I don't know what to do!' I say so quickly I almost can't hear the words properly.

'Robin. Robin! Get a hold of yourself! Research says that ten per cent of women will start their labour with the breaking of waters.' Only Lacey could greet the start of childbirth with a handy selection of statistics. 'I've been having little squeezes all morning but I thought they were Braxton Hicks. It's OK, I'm calm. I'm ready for this, I've been waiting so, so long for this day. Just pass me my bag, I need to phone Karl. Also pass me that tea towel, I need something dry!' Lacey is in control. She's in her element. Her tranquillity is catching. I feel calm has been restored.

I pass her the phone and watch her ring her husband.

'Karl,' she says, her eyes shining with excitement, and maybe just a little trepidation. 'It's happening.'

LYLA AND I PACE down the hospital corridor, almost dizzy with excitement. I have a bunch of flowers in one hand and Lyla's hand in the other. She has a balloon, which is bobbing about vigorously as we walk, and I can feel such a fizz of excitement in my chest I keep having to take huge great gasps of air to contain myself.

As we turn onto the ward, I see her.

Lacey is propped up in bed in the corner by the window. The other three beds are unoccupied, so it's just us. And there it is in her arms, the most lovely little bundle of blankets and teeny squished baby face I have seen since my own teeny squish was born.

'Laceeey,' I whisper as we approach the bed.

'Meet Willow,' she says, moving the blanket away from her brand-new daughter's face a little bit. 'Willow Faith Hunter.'

I can't talk for crying. I just lean over and smile and cry and look at Lacey, who is doing the same.

'I can't believe it,' I manage.

'Mummy, she was pregnant for ages,' Lyla pipes up, ever the voice of reason.

Lacey and I laugh as I pick Lyla up and pop her on the end of the bed, and pull up the guest chair to the side.

'Oh God, she's absolutely gorgeous,' I say, gazing at the tiny face.

'She's my everything. She's just everything. Willow Faith – and Faith is for Granny Dovington, isn't that lovely? Do you want a little cuddle?' she says, tearing her eyes away from her new daughter just for a moment to ask.

'I'd absolutely love to,' I say, choking up again. I knew I'd be happy, but I never thought I'd be this happy. I think because we all waited for so long, because our friendship has had its knocks this past year and, of course, because this baby is everything that mine never could be. It's a lot. It really is a lot.

I stand over Lacey to gently pick Willow up out of her arms. I'm as careful as possible not to nudge Lacey post-birth and to be as tender as I can be with this beautiful new life.

I sit back down, holding precious Willow in my arms and marvelling at her, taking in every curve of her pink face. I take a deep breath in and beam at Lacey.

'What do you think then, Robsy?' Lacey asks.

'Lacey,' I say, pausing for effect, 'I'm wild about the girl.'

And with that, Lyla laughs as though I've just said the funniest thing she's ever heard; Lacey laughs – and then cries because she's 'pulled the stitches' – and Karl walks into the room laden with sandwiches, crisps and drinks to celebrate Willow with a joyous, messy, emotional bed picnic. She is surrounded by love, food and balloons, and I know she's going to be the miracle we'd all wished for.

Welcome to the world.

The End

ACKNOWLEDGEMENTS

Well, here we are, another book and another chance to say my most heartfelt thank yous to so many people who have made this book happen.

Last year I recall writing it at my dining table in a big old sweatshirt with a bag of Wotsits to hand. This year things have ramped up a bit and I'm sitting on my bed, in a faded Mickey Mouse tee with half a Toblerone to hand – not bad going, eh?

Wilde About The Girl is fantastic, even if I do say so myself. Like when you have one baby, you don't think you will ever love your second as much, but actually, your heart doesn't split in half, it doubles, and that's what's happened here. I now have space for two wonderful stories and I'm bursting with joy for them both.

Much like with *Wilde Like Me*, I could not have produced this book myself and so I would like to thank a selection of people who are so very valued.

Firstly, as always, I would like to shout from the rooftop

my thanks to my team at Gleam Futures who have helped co-ordinate all of my many work projects so that I have had the time and creative space to pour love into *Wilde About The Girl*. Special thanks to Dom, Maddie, Charlotte and Abi. Air hugs all round!

Just like last year, Bonnier Zaffre have absolutely aced it. Whilst I sit in my soft office (aka, on my bed), tip-tapping away on my laptop, dreaming up Robin's life, there are a team of diligent book bods, book bodding away, ensuring the book makes it from my laptop to your fair hands. This is no small task. It takes months and months of planning and meetings and logistics and effort to ensure the book looks the way it does, sits in the places it does and reaches the people it does. I don't take Bonnier Zaffre's efforts lightly. They are, quite frankly, excellently good eggs.

My thanks go to, and brace yourself because things are about to go all Oscars on you now, Eleanor Dryden, my Editor Extraordinaire, who we'll discuss more later, Sarah Bauer (who not only worked hard on the book but also posed in front of a giant Pixar Sully statue with me whilst holding my book out so I could promote it on Instagram – if that's not commitment, what is?) and Tara Loder.

I'd like to thank Sahina Bibi (I knew I liked her from

the moment she made the most inappropriate joke at my house at our first meeting – love a gal with humour like that!), Alex Allden (who spent so much time with me umming and erring over the exact Pantone of the book cover: 'It's quite a pinky-coral isn't it? Or is it a reddy-pink coral? Not a reddy-red coral though?'), Francesca Russell (who said it was OK to have two glasses of wine pre-book signing and thus, it was the most lively and jovial book signing to date!), Clare Kelly, Imogen Sebba, Stephen Dumughn, Felice McKeown, Nico Poilblanc, Angie Willocks, Victoria Hart, Vincent Kelleher, Gen Narey, Sandra Ferguson, Jenny Page, Becca Allen, James Horobin, Kate Parkin, Mark Smith, Perminder Mann and Laura Makela. Without the tireless efforts of these most brilliant people, this book would still just be files on a laptop somewhere in Northampton. I VERY much look forward to raising a glass or three with them at our book launch and potentially over-sharing how much I love them all.

Whilst it has definitely been a huge team effort, the person I would most like to thank, so much so that I have dedicated this book to her, is Eleanor Dryden (Editor Extraordinaire), or, 'Eli'. It would make sense that I would love Robin and her friends and family very deeply because they are my creations. I think, though, Eli loves them more. Eli constantly champions everything Robin stands for. Eli encourages, supports, teaches and mentors in the very best ways. I have never, for even a day, felt like Eli didn't have mine – and most importantly Robin's – back. Eli has, again, gone above and beyond in her role as Editor. She's schlepped up to my house, pushed deadlines to the very limit for me (I went and had a bloomin' baby right in the middle of this whole process!) and handled every single thing that's been thrown her way. I enjoyed writing *Wilde Like Me* but I LOVED writing *Wilde About The Girl.* Having Eli as my teammate has made this journey feel so joyful and so full of fizz and excitement. I love that Eli hasn't tried to dull down the most heart-breaking themes in this book or tried to fluff up the most wonderful ones. Eli has allowed me to make this book raw and genuine and exactly how I want to it be, and I'm so grateful. It is worth noting, too, that without Eli, this book would just be a bunch of themes, mini stories and blurbs, and without Eli's finesse and skill, it wouldn't be woven so beautifully together in the gorgeous way that it is now. Eli, too, is a good egg. She is actually my favourite egg.

Talking of eggs, (ew this is a weird transition – see why I need Eli now?!), I went and had a baby during the writing of this book! Despite this being my second, I somehow completely forgot how much time babies take up and so would like to raise a glass to my wonderful boyfriend, Liam, who has stepped up and taken such wonderful care of our daughter, Pearl, whilst I focussed on the book. We are firm believers in equal parenting, but Liam has done far more than his share so that I can write this book. Thank you, Liam. I love you.

I read back the acknowledgements of *Wilde Like Me* and in those I thanked my sweet daughter Darcy for having faith in her Mummy. I was surprised that she had grasped what I did when I saw that she had written, 'My Mummy is clever because she wrote a book!', on a piece of school work. This year, of course, she is fully in the loop after seeing all the copies of *Wilde Like Me* in shops and at home. This year, with the arrival of her little sister, it's definitely been a more challenging task, but Darcy has been my tiny cheerleader, constantly being excited for 'the next winner Wilde book!', and, as always, having such faith in me. Darcy, when you can read this, thank you. You and your sister are such motivators!

I could happily sit here and thank more and more people, it's a very satisfying thing to do! However, the Toblerone is gone (shhh, let's blame it on the baby) and it's time to wrap up this year's Oscar moment.

Thank you so much team, you're the freakin' best. Xx

Dear Reader,

If you've found your way to this letter then chances are you've bought, read and finished my book. Unless you stole it and then skipped straight to this page to spite me, but that seems a bit 'extra' right? 'Extra' is what the youth say for 'keen'. Other words I have noted of late are 'muggy', 'prangy' and 'sick'. Perhaps I'll try and slip them into book three!

Anyway, I digress. Assuming you haven't stolen the book and behaved in an 'extra' way, I'll go with option one, and if that is the case, I would like to thank you.

Buying a book is quite a commitment. Did you know this? You're not just parting with a few pounds and pennies (or whatever currency you have used), you're vowing to yourself that you're going to spend time reading and understanding something. The hope is that you will enjoy it, feel entertained by it or be moved in some way by it, but it's always a risk. Thank you for taking that risk.

As you'll know, Robin Wilde takes a few risks here and there. Protecting Marnie and standing up to Val in *Wilde Like Me* and now opening her heart to Edward and taking on so much at MADE IT in *Wilde About The Girl*. I want you to know that Robin isn't any braver, stronger or riskier than you are. Robin is an ordinary woman with the potential to do anything, just like you and me.

Robin shows us that even the meekest of people can fight for what they believe in, even from our most damaged moments we can find healing and even from our lowest points we can pull ourselves up. Remember that Robin is just like you and me and if she can do it, so can we. There is nothing you cannot do, if you put your mind to it.

Thank you so much for believing in Robin and sticking by her for another book. Trust me, she appreciates it. It's been a big year for her and those around her. I have loved watching all the characters progress, but I think a particular favourite has to be Kath. I couldn't help but cheer for her several times, and, of course, cringe for her too – you know the bit.

This book has gone so much deeper than the first and tackled some really huge issues. I'd like to thank you for reading those and letting Robin and her 'gang' explore them.

I want you to know that I appreciate your support so much. Thank you for making your Book Commitment, thank you for reading a deeper, (hopefully) more evolved book, but most importantly, thank you for loving Robin again. I love you for it. If I could give each of you an air hug (not a huge fan of physical contact, haha), I would. I loves ya!

Big kisses,

Louise xxx

JOIN MY READERS' CLUB

Thank you so much for reading my novel!

If you enjoyed *Wilde About The Girl*, why not join my Readers' Club* where I will tell you – before I tell anyone else – about my writing life and all the latest news about my novels.

Visit www.LouisePentlandNovel.com to sign up!

* Just so you know, your data is private and confidential and it will never be passed on to a third party. I'll only ever be in touch now and again about book news, and if you want to unsubscribe, you can do that at any time.